DEVIATIONS:
DISCIPLINE

CHRIS OWEN
JODI PAYNE

Deviations: Discipline
Copyright © 2007, 2016 and 2019 Chris Owen and Jodi Payne

Garrett Leigh at blackjazzdesign.com
Cover content is for illustrative purposes only and any person depicted on the cover is a model.

First Edition, published 2007 by Torquere Press

Second Edition, published October 2016 Pretty Muses Publishing

Third Edition, published December 2019 by Tygerseye Publishing, LLC.

ISBN: 978-1-951011-22-2

1

"**Y**our young man called me again," Mrs. Miller said with a broad smile as she walked into Tobias' office at the farm house. "Is he as polite to you as he is to me?"

Tobias looked up from his desk and tried not to smirk. One did not smirk at Mrs. Miller; at eighty-three years of age, his housekeeper was still a formidable force. "Usually, yes," he conceded. "He does, of course, have his moments."

Her smile grew. "I bet he does. So, is his cooking as good as my sweetie pie's?"

Tobias put down his pen and closed the file he was working on. "It is," he said. "Noah is a wonderful cook, thank you. His friend Allison has taught him technique, and he tells me that you've given him wonderful advice, not to mention a pile of recipes." He smiled as she sat down in the easy chair. "He tries very hard." He couldn't resist mentioning the point; she'd invited it, comparing Noah to Phantom, Tobias' former lover and forever Mrs. Miller's "sweetie-pie." Of course, she'd claimed Noah as her "darling," so it was a pretty even playing field, all told.

She nodded and sat back with a sigh. "You're very lucky, Doctor," she said, keeping to her habit of using Tobias' title. She swore she'd worked just as hard on his veterinary degree as he had, and she would use the title over his name in celebration. Tobias didn't mind. "Having someone learn to cook just to please you is a great gift."

"I know," he said simply. He'd occasionally wondered just how much Mrs. Miller knew about his relationships; in his more honest moments, he allowed that she likely knew the important parts, if not the actual details. That she seemed not to mind the nature of his tastes didn't make it any easier to contemplate.

She could hardly be oblivious, he knew. There were the stables behind the house that he never permitted anyone to enter and the lovers who cleaned and cooked and did chores; it was hardly subtle.

She looked around the office and sighed contentedly. "It's good to be home, you know."

Tobias smiled. "I have often found that my two favorite parts of travel were the day of arrival there and the day of arrival home. Tell me you enjoyed the trip, though. You're breaking my heart," he teased.

"It was--"

"Astounding," a voice said from the door and Tobias turned to smile at Robert, Mrs. Miller's son.

"Very," Mrs. Miller agreed. She looked up and nodded her head. "Astounding is exactly right."

Tobias gestured to a chair, inviting Robert to join them. He had no issue at all with Robert simply walking into the house; the two men had known each other almost all of Tobias' life, and the house was practically a second home to Robert since Mrs. Miller had moved in after Mr. Miller had passed away. But for some reason, Robert had always hesitated to go into the office without Tobias' leave. The kitchen and living room were fair game, though.

"So you had a good time?" Tobias asked as Robert settled in the chair. "I'm glad."

"It was a great trip," Robert said. "A great gift. Thank you, Tobias."

Tobias inclined his head. "It was the least I could do; I wasn't about to send her to Italy alone -- she'd have adopted the country and caused an international incident without you there to keep her in line," he teased.

Mrs. Miller snorted, but Robert laughed. "Too true. As it was we had to send her to bed a few times -- do you have any idea how much walking she wanted to do?"

Grinning, Tobias nodded. "I thought you'd lost a few pounds."

Robert laughed. "Right. You're looking fitter, too. Is Noah slipping you low fat milk in your coffee?"

"Just getting lots of exercise," Tobias said with a wink.

"That's it," Mrs. Miller said, standing up. She was clearly trying not to laugh and working on looking disgusted. "No respect for an old lady; you two should be ashamed of yourselves."

Tobias and Robert grinned at each other. "You should have seen Mom and a certain man who was in the same hotel."

Tobias raised an eyebrow. "Do tell."

"You'll do no such thing, Robert," Mrs. Miller said, pointing to her son. "Now, if you will excuse me, I have things to do for Noah in the kitchen; he was asking about desserts. Lord knows why; you don't deserve any." With that, she turned on her heel and left the room.

Robert was still grinning. "She had a great time, Tobias; it was really the best gift you could have given her."

"She deserved it," Tobias said easily. "It was the least I could do, really. She's taken care of me for so long, I wanted to do something nice for her -- for you all."

Robert waved it off. "Family. Been far too long to pretend otherwise. You and I might not be as close as brothers, but that's pretty much just down to me being ten years older."

"Twelve," Tobias said with a wink. "Or are you getting younger as I get older?"

"Smart ass," Robert said standing up. "And let's just keep pretending that sending Mom to Italy for three weeks didn't let you and Noah have some extended peace here."

"Yes, let's pretend that," Tobias said, grinning.

"I like him," Robert said suddenly. "Well, I like what I know, anyway. Mom was worried about you being alone after Phantom, you know."

"Everyone was," Tobias said, also standing. He followed Robert out and added, "Bunch of worrywarts."

Robert nodded and headed to the kitchen. "You know it."

"I do indeed."

"Just have to live with it, I guess."

"I know that, too. Wouldn't have it any other way, really."

Robert laughed and nodded, and Tobias found himself smiling. All was right in his world.

2

Tobias cursed as he came across yet another torn up intersection. Traffic was a mess all through the downtown core, and his frustration level was rising with every one-way street he had to navigate. He was going in a circle, he just knew it, and Lincoln Avenue was always just out of reach.

The trouble, he decided, wasn't so much the damn construction as the sheer idiocy of the drivers who simply wouldn't get out of his way and let him get home. "It's not even close to rush hour," he muttered, talking out loud in uncharacteristic frustration and trying to ease around yet another truck offloading dirt or equipment or something. He hit the gas and then the brakes as a woman in a PT Cruiser cut him off and gave him the finger.

"And you would think," he added, "that with all this crap going on... I could at least lose this fucking erection." An incredibly persistent one at that, one that had been with him to varying degrees since he'd woken up from a morning dream about Noah and new leather wrist cuffs that had complex and intriguing chains dangling from them. He'd been hard off and on since then, and his body was definitely settling on full hardness at the moment.

He took another breath and looked around at the traffic as he shifted uncomfortably in his seat, his irritation growing. "But no. Not today. Today, I'm cursed with an iron dick, a schedule that's opened up, a submissive at work, and endless traffic. God *damn* it!" He slammed his hand down on the steering wheel and a miracle happened: the road in front of his car emptied.

So he hit the gas and took off, heading for home. The sudden siren and flashing lights in his rearview mirror made him glance down at the speedometer in dismay. "Ah, shit." With a sigh he pulled over and undid his seatbelt.

A chest in uniform appeared at the driver's side window. A knuckle tapped on the glass, and Tobias rolled down the window, stifling another sigh. The cop had one hand on his gun. As if Tobias could make a bid for freedom in *this* traffic.

"License and registration, please," a voice requested in an official tone, and Tobias dutifully reached for the glove compartment. "Wait a minute." The cop rested an arm on the door and ducked to see better into the car. "Do you have any idea how fast you were going, sir?"

"Jesus Christ," Tobias groaned, his head falling back on the seat. "Yes. Too fast. Would you like to know why, Noah?"

"That's 'Officer Dolan,' sir, and, yes. Yes, I would." Noah grinned widely.

Tobias rolled his eyes. "Well, you see, Officer Dolan, I have a smart-mouthed lover whom I can't get out of my head." He pointed to his lap. "I was in rather a rush to call him. Or at least think about him in private."

"Tsk. That's no excuse to break the law." Noah was having fun with this, damn him. Tobias frowned as he heard a car door slam.

"Everything all right, Dolan?" came a woman's voice.

"Oh, uh..." Noah gave Tobias a wicked grin. "Actually, you know, I think this guy might be drunk, Carol. He's definitely disorderly." Noah stepped back from the car.

"Right. Out of the car, sir," Carol ordered.

Tobias stared at Noah. "You are in so much trouble," he hissed. He opened the door slowly and got out of the car, unfolding himself carefully and willing his erection to go away. Sadly, it seemed to like the excitement of seeing Noah at work and the promise of all the spankings his boy was building up. He wished for a longer coat.

"Hands on the roof of the car, legs spread," she continued with the orders. "License and registration?"

Tobias looked at his hands and sighed. "My registration is in the glove compartment. My license is in my wallet, which is in my back pocket. Shall I get it for you, or shall I place my hands on the roof as you requested?"

"On the roof. Dolan?"

"I got it." Noah tugged Tobias' wallet out of his pocket and pulled out his license, then ducked into the car and got his registration. He handed both to Carol, leaving the wallet on the roof.

"I'll run these, you got him?"

"I've got my eye on him," Noah said with a grin, and Carol disappeared into the car. "I really just wanted an excuse to touch you," Noah breathed in Tobias' ear as he patted him down.

"Do you have any concept of what your weekend has just become?" Tobias demanded.

"Some," Noah answered with a nod. "But I know you have a sense of humor, and this isn't your time after all. It's mine."

"I don't..." Tobias stopped dead, unable to actually utter

the words "don't humiliate you," because... well. "Noah," he tried again. "This isn't funny. I just wanted to get home. I'll pay the damn fine, all right?"

Noah laughed. "Oh, please. I'm not going to fine you, sir."

"Noah!" Carol snorted at him as she got out of the car. "You little shit. He's your lover!" She hurried over and landed a solid punch in Noah's arm.

"Ow! He is," Noah admitted, stepping away from Tobias. "Dr. Tobias Vincent, meet my partner, Carol Thompson. Carol, Tobias."

Tobias let go of the roof of his car and offered his hand. "Officer Thompson. It's a pleasure." He even managed to make it sound mostly sincere, he thought.

Carol shook her head. "It's a pleasure to meet you, too. Noah's told me a lot about you. You're a vet?"

Tobias nodded and turned his body as discreetly as he could. It seemed that even small talk wasn't going to kill this hard-on. "Yes. Large animal, so I'm usually out of the city. Today was clinics, though, so I got to actually face the monster that is city construction."

"Ugh, it's a mess, isn't it?" She looked at Noah. "I can't believe you."

"It was a joke!" Noah protested.

"Best way out of here is to take this to Fifth and head west a few blocks," Carol told Tobias, ignoring Noah.

"Thank you," he said, trying not to sound like an utter bore. He really had to get out of there, and soon. He glanced at his watch and then at Noah. "Are you off at four?"

"Yes, sir." Noah glanced sidelong at Tobias. He obviously knew what was coming. "Four o'clock."

"Oh, good." Tobias allowed himself a broad smile. "I'll expect you at my apartment right after, then. Don't bother to change, I think I like this look. We'll have a chat about authority." He turned to Carol, his smile growing. "He's a naughty boy, don't you think?" he asked brightly.

Carol grinned knowingly and winked. "He certainly needs a handler," she replied, laughing. "Nice meeting you, Dr. Vincent. Noah, I'll be in the car." She turned and headed off.

Noah was blushing. "See you at four, sir," he offered almost pitifully.

"Mm-hmm. And I suggest you plan your pleading now, pet. It'll be an interesting evening." Still smiling, Tobias slipped his license back in his wallet. "Your ass is so mine." He pulled open the car door and used it to shield himself as he adjusted his erection. "Go back to work, officer."

"Will do. And, uh, good luck with *that*, Dr. Vincent." Noah grinned and touched his fingers to the brim of his hat before heading back to his squad car.

Tobias snorted. He didn't need luck. He needed a paddle, lube, and a certain officer. In uniform. Over his knee.

With a moan, he started the car and prayed he'd get home soon.

———

Tobias was pacing back and forth in the hallway when Noah got there. As soon as the buzzer went off, he flung the door open and said, "Living room. Now."

Noah headed for the living room. Quickly, he pulled his sidearm from its holster. Everything else he left in place. He set his gun on a side table and then he went right to his knees.

Tobias circled him like he was prey, which was pretty accurate. "So, where shall we begin, pet?" he purred.

"With me apologizing for my joke this afternoon, sir," Noah said quickly. "Honestly, I was just having fun. Carol keeps saying she wants to meet you, so I thought..."

"So you thought that a sobriety test would be an appropriate way to introduce us?" Tobias asked acidly, trying his hardest not to laugh. Noah had been right, he did possess a sense of humor, and, an hour removed from the situation, it was funny; there was no need to let Noah know that, however.

"I... it's not that I thought it would be appropriate, sir, I thought it would be..." Noah stammered and then stopped himself, apparently deciding better of making excuses. He sighed. "No, sir. It was a bad idea. I'm sorry, sir."

"It wasn't your best idea ever, no," Tobias agreed, walking around him again. "But you had some fun with it, didn't you?"

"Yes, sir." Tobias saw Noah try to hide a slight smile. "I did think it was funny at the time. And I got to run my hands over my Master in the middle of my work day, which was quite a pleasure. Oh, Carol said you were very handsome, by the way." Noah bit his lip, effectively stopping the flow of words.

"I'd thank her, but I doubt she asked you to pass that along." Tobias stopped in front of Noah, knowing full well that he was getting an eyeful. "And did you think it amusing to display me like that?" he asked softly.

"I didn't think about it that way, sir. I was thinking more about... just detaining you for a bit. But, yes," Noah sighed. "I did think it was funny at the time. Again, I'm sorry."

Tobias decided to relent a little on his pissed off routine. "Did you like touching me?" he asked, just as softly.

"Yes, sir. I always do."

"Did you have any idea of what you were doing to me?

Touching me in public, with your uniform on?" Tobias began to rub himself through his trousers right in front of Noah's eyes. "Did you realize that I was speeding because I was so hard from wanting you, I ached?"

Noah's breath caught as he was about to speak. He seemed delightfully distracted by the way Tobias was fondling himself and licked his lips and cleared his throat before continuing. "No, I didn't realize the full extent of your... discomfort, sir. I'd forgotten how much you liked my uniform." Noah seemed to struggle to get the words out.

"I was like this before I even saw you, boy." Tobias undid his button and eased the zipper down. "I would have come if you weren't being such an utter shit."

"I only meant it as a joke, sir. Truly, I'm sorry!" Noah sounded almost desperately contrite. "Please let me make it up to you? I'll take stripes, I know I deserve them... only, don't be angry with me, I only meant it in fun."

"You'll take what I give you," Tobias said, pulling his cock out and stroking it. "A nice spanking, I think, for being a naughty boy. But right now I think I'd rather have a uniformed officer of the law sucking me off."

"My pleasure, sir," Noah answered, his grin returning. He reached forward and took Tobias' cock firmly in his fingers, pushing Tobias' hand out of the way. He moved closer on his knees and smoothed his tongue over the head. "It is my duty, after all, to serve the occupants of the city," he told Tobias. How he managed to say it with a straight face, Tobias would never know. He didn't have much chance to contemplate it, however, as serve Noah did, swallowing Tobias' aching shaft into his throat.

Tobias didn't bother holding back a moan; he'd been waiting far too long. Noah's mouth was wet and hot, his throat welcoming. "God, yes," Tobias whispered, his hips rocking slightly. "So good, pet. Suck me."

Noah reached up and removed his hat, setting it beside him on the floor. He took hold of Tobias' hips and sucked eagerly, his gun belt squeaking as he moved. He made enthusiastic sounds, and his tongue was doing wonderfully creative things to Tobias' shaft.

Tobias let himself look down at his submissive, on his knees in his uniform, lips swelling. His prick throbbed and he watched Noah lap a drop of fluid from the head. "Not going to last long, I'm afraid," he said with real regret.

Noah slid his fingers down Tobias' cock and circled the base of his shaft tightly with finger and thumb, effectively ringing him. Then he opened his mouth wider and took Tobias deep into his throat, followed by several shallow strokes before swallowing him deep again.

"Oh, God!" Tobias gasped and thrust, not really able to stop himself. He watched his cock slide between Noah's lips, felt the head slip into Noah's throat, and shuddered. "Yes," he hissed.

Noah repeated the pattern -- deep, then shallow, shallow, then deep -- only this time, he let go of the hold he had on Tobias' cock and continued until Tobias shuddered.

"Sweetheart," Tobias whispered. His balls throbbed and he let go, shoving himself into Noah's mouth as he came in long pulses. "Oh, God, pet." He shook, his legs unsteady, as Noah sucked him and licked him clean. "I need to sit," he admitted, dizzy with the release.

Noah got to his feet. It was almost embarrassing the way he helped Tobias to the sofa and sat him down.

"Jesus, it's hot in here," Noah said, licking his lips again. He tugged off his clip-on tie and opened up the top couple of buttons on his shirt, revealing his silver collar. "Feel better, sir?" He grinned, kneeling again at Tobias' feet.

"You have no idea," Tobias groaned, his eyes closing. "Then again, I suppose you do." He smiled, remember how many times he'd had Noah begging to come, not to mention the week he'd forbidden Noah to orgasm at all. He lifted his head and studied Noah's collar. "I still love seeing that, you know. It just doesn't get old."

"I like looking at it, too, sir. Every morning when I'm shaving it reflects light in the mirror. It's really beautiful."

Tobias smiled and worked on his breathing for a moment. "God, I needed that," he said with a grin. "You know, pet, if you liked it I'm sure we can work something like earlier into a scene. Fantasy play in the stables, perhaps."

"You want to be searched and patted down by a horny cop, sir?" Noah laughed softly. "Sounds like fun. I'll just need to make sure to get an extra uniform."

"Do that," Tobias said crisply. "But for now, you can march yourself down the hall and find a nice hard paddle, boy."

Tobias smiled to himself as Noah rushed off, hoping he was more concerned about the spanking than the fact that he'd just agreed to be dominant in a scene. Or, rather, he wondered if Noah even realized that he had. Either way, he wasn't up for the long talk they were likely to have about it.

No, what he wanted was to wallop the little tease's ass and make him remember not to fuck with his Master, no matter the time of day. He was grinning broadly as Noah came back with the paddle.

Noah brought his favorite, of course, with the metal studs. It suited Tobias just fine; it would leave Noah red and sore for a while. Noah knelt again and handed over the paddle. "How would you like me, sir?"

Tobias fingered the metal studs and pretended to think it over for a moment. "I think we'll stay simple, pet. Lower your trousers, and lie over my lap. And you don't get to come, so don't bother asking. I had to wait two hours to get your mouth on me, so you can hold it for a bit."

Noah stood and removed his thick, heavy gun belt and set it on the sofa beside Tobias. He opened the metal clasp at the top of his fly and lowered the zipper slowly, then slid his pants and his briefs down around his thighs.

Tobias got a good look at Noah's erection as it was freed from his briefs. "Tell me, pet. Is that from sucking me, or in anticipation of the spanking?" Tobias asked with a smile. "It's rather nice, you know. Too bad you can't wear your cock ring during the day, though."

"It's first from blowing you, because you are so hot when you come, sir. You make the best sounds." Noah grinned and knelt, maneuvering himself over Tobias' thighs. "And then because I know I deserve the paddle and I am looking forward to being forgiven. Unfortunately, the ring is at my apartment, sir."

Tobias ran a hand over Noah's ass. "You'll have to do without," he said happily. "And it thrills me know that closure makes you hard, pet. Really." He was teasing and let Noah know it by his tone. "Ready?" he asked. Not waiting for a reply, he slapped Noah's ass hard with the paddle, one hand on Noah's back to steady him.

Noah flinched and his cock pressed into Tobias' thigh. "Thank you, sir," he said in a tight voice.

"You're very welcome, boy," Tobias growled as he brought his arm down again. He rained blows down, alternating between heavy and light, covering Noah's ass and raising a healthy glow. He could feel Noah's cock between his thighs, hear every moan and panted breath Noah took. He knew his boy now, knew what each sound meant, and that knowledge made him hard again.

Noah clung to Tobias' thighs and kept himself in check as Tobias had instructed. Tobias was very aware of the moment when Noah transitioned from the sub who was also a cop that had just gotten off his shift into *Tobias'* sub, cozy and safe in his subspace. Sessions like this always took Noah there easily; anything with just enough discomfort to change his breathing, force his concentration and push him deep.

Really, they were both at their best when Noah was in his space.

"That's it," Tobias said softly, his strokes getting lighter as he slowed and backed off. "There's my boy. Well done, pet." He smoothed a hand over the heated skin of Noah's ass. "Kneel and reflect for a while, Noah. Shed the rest of the day. And then you'll get your release."

Noah slid off Tobias' thighs and directly to his knees. Tobias grinned, noting that he chose to stay up on his knees rather than sit back on his heels. Noah clasped his hands at the small of his back, lowered his head, and closed his eyes, going silent and still.

Getting up, Tobias moved about the room as silently as he could. He picked up a few things and tidied up a little, watching as Noah made the final transitions that allowed him to let his other life go. Tobias had admired Noah's apparent ability to snap from subspace into the role of supportive lover, but he never lost respect for this, the shedding of Noah's other life to become the obedient submissive.

Finally, when Noah was calm and had been reflecting

for about half an hour, Tobias cleared his throat. "As much as I like looking at you in your uniform -- and, better, with the pants shoved down and your cock on display for me, I think I prefer you naked, pet."

Noah nodded silently and stood to undress. Piece by piece, the last remaining reminders of his day job left him. When he was done, he neatly folded his uniform and returned to his knees, this time sitting back on his heels and dropping his hands into his lap.

Tobias smiled. "Good boy. I promised you release, didn't I?" He settled in his chair and sighed happily. "I think I deserve a treat as well, after being shown off to your partner. I'd like to watch you, pet. You may begin when ready. There's lube on the table, and if you'd like a toy you may fetch one. Feel free to move."

Noah shifted a bit and then stood, disappearing into Tobias' bedroom and returning with a sleek black dildo. He fetched the lube, as well, and set both on the couch. Then he wrapped his fingers around his cock and stepped forward, walking slowly toward Tobias as he worked his shaft with one hand. "Thank you, sir," he said, stopping in front of him.

"No, no. Thank you," Tobias said with a grin. "It's a lovely cock, boy."

Noah inclined his head. "It's my pleasure, sir."

And it did seem to be, his prick filling even further until it strained away from his body stiffly. Noah licked his lips and looked down at his hand, circling the head of his cock with his thumb and swallowing hard. "I love thinking about you when I do this," he said, backing up a few steps. He sat on the floor with his back leaning on the couch. "It's so much better with you right there to look at."

Noah was taking it slow, lingering over his own body. He

flicked at one of his nipples and then tugged on the ring there, the one that Tobias had meant to be temporary for Bradford's New Year's party. Noah had surprised him and kept it; Tobias had been thrilled. Noah moaned softly and slouched a bit more. "So good."

He continued to pump himself and run his other hand over his body until he was panting gently, until the first hint of wetness leaked from the head of his cock, and then he reached for the dildo and lube. Still tugging at his prick, he opened his mouth and bathed the dildo, then threw his head back and swallowed it into his throat.

Tobias swallowed as well. The sight of Noah doing that never left him unaffected, and he dropped a hand to his own lap, not quite brushing his balls, but close.

Noah spent the next few moments slicking the dildo slowly, suggestively. Finally, he moaned, pulled it out his mouth, and lubed it quickly before shifting so he was on his hands and knees. He reached around behind himself, teasing with it at first, sliding it over his hole and pressing it in just enough to stretch. His sounds were lovely, and his brow furrowed in concentration.

"Oh, yes..." he breathed just before he arched his back and pressed the dildo deep inside of him. "Sir."

Tobias moved his own hand, pressing it against his renewed erection. "Talk to me," he said silkily. "How does it feel? Is it big enough? Hard enough? Are you stretched around it?" His hand pressed again, and he teased at his zipper.

"It's big," Noah replied with a growl as he worked the dildo in and out of his body. "It's a nice burn, feels good. Seems a bit..." He swallowed hard. "Yes, it gets wider toward the base so... so it keeps--" His words were cut off by a hiss. "So good, when I... there! Ah!" He rode the dildo, rocking back to meet it as his fingers forced it deeper. "Oh, fuck, yes!"

He rode it hard and fast for a bit, his breath coming in short, tight pants until suddenly he forced himself to stop. He hung, frozen mid-thrust for a moment, then shifted to a sitting position with the dildo pressed deep inside him until the wide flat base sat flush against his ass and was held there by his own body weight. "Got a bit too close..." he panted. "Want to give you more than that, sir." He tucked his fingers around his balls and fondled them, rolling them gently in his hand while he caught his breath.

"I appreciate it," Tobias managed, rather breathless himself. He slid his zipper down, finally letting himself have more room. His prick twitched as he freed it, and he rubbed his palm down the length. "See what you've done to me, pet?" he asked, stroking himself and letting his legs part.

Noah smiled. "I love your cock, sir. So much better than this toy." He wiggled a bit and moaned as the dildo shifted inside him. "You taste so good." Noah's fingers moved back to his own erection, and he started to pull at it while he continued to roll and massage his balls with his other hand. "So hot, sir. I can't take you in my mouth without getting hard."

Tobias stroked himself slowly, watching Noah's face. He could almost feel Noah's blood surge, almost hear his heartbeat. His gaze flicked to Noah's cock, to his ass. "I'm going to fuck you," he growled.

"Yes, yes, want you." Noah's hand sped on his cock and he rolled his hips, working the dildo in his ass. "Please, sir, fuck me." His eyes were squeezed closed and his voice was strained.

"Not until I watch you come, boy," Tobias said, his voice low and serious. "Now."

Noah shot instantly, throwing his head back and shouting his response to the ceiling. His cock jerked in his fingers, and he stroked himself gingerly until he was spent, finally lifting his head and inspecting the job he'd done of soaking his stomach and chest. "Oh, my. Thank you, sir."

"Don't thank me yet," Tobias said, standing up. He walked to Noah in two easy strides, then shoved him back down onto his hands and knees. The dildo was disposed of with a twist and a pull, and then Tobias slammed himself home, plunging into Noah's heat.

Noah grunted. He was loose and relaxed, his body damp with sweat, and he was still breathless from his own release. He pressed back wantonly to meet Tobias' thrusts, utterly shameless. "Sir!"

Tobias didn't say anything; he merely grabbed Noah's hips and pulled him back onto his prick, stabbing into him again and again. Noah's body clung to him, the scent of sweat and spunk and cop all around him, making him growl and rumble in his chest. "Mine," he roared as he began to come. "My boy." He filled Noah to the hilt, balls deep in him as he spilled.

"Yes, sir, yours, sir." Noah shivered as Tobias came, clenching around him.

Satiated, exhausted, Tobias finally stilled, then slid out of Noah's body. "Shower, pet. And then you can make me dinner." He smiled and ran a hand down Noah's back. "All is well, sweetheart. Well done."

3

I t was just pizza, but, man, did it smell good. Veggies galore. Noah peeked into the oven to see if it was done yet. Just a few more minutes, he decided and closed the oven. He checked his watch right as the doorbell rang.

Damn, Phan was punctual.

He dumped his apron on the counter and smoothed his clothes, stopping by the hall mirror to check his hair before answering the door. "You know, I could set my watch by you. You have been a sub way too long." Noah smiled and stepped back to let Phan in.

"No such thing," Phan assured him as he stepped into the hall. He passed over a bottle of Coke and gave Noah a quick hug. "Can't be too subby or too pretty. God, that smells great." Phan certainly had the market cornered on pretty. He was tiny and lithe, his coppery hair sticking up in tufts and random, wild curls.

"Doesn't it?" Noah asked, setting the soda down so he could take Phan's coat. "I think I've outdone myself." He hung the coat in the tiny hall closet and, taking Phan by the hand, he picked up the soda again and headed for the kitchen. "Here I am trying to keep you healthy, and you're feeding my weakness for sugary colas. Tsk." He put the Coke on the counter and pushed Phan into a chair.

Phan giggled at him. It wasn't a laugh, it wasn't a chuckle; it was most certainly a giggle. A naughty one, and one Noah suspected Phan actually practiced. "I've decided it's my job to feed your weaknesses. Make sure you have fun." He giggled again and winked. "What's on the pizza? Extra cheese?"

"Extra everything, except meat," Noah answered, pulling the pizza out of the oven. "Are you saying I look like someone that doesn't know how to have fun?" Noah asked, grinning, as he brought the pizza to the table and set it on a couple of trivets. He reached into a drawer and pulled out the pizza cutter.

"Oh, I know you can have fun," Phan said with a grin and a leer. "What I'm not so sure of is your ability to break a rule or two."

"I don't break rules, I'm a cop and sub, remember?" He pulled two glasses from a cabinet and filled them with ice.

"See, that's what I mean," Phan persisted as he opened the Coke bottle. "You're good, very good. And good boys get rewards. Naughty boys get a spanking. Once in a while, it can be fun to break a couple of rules and just... play. Not the serious rules of course, but giving the Dom a chance to be a Master and aggressive can be a thing." He blinked and grinned as he poured the Coke. "If you see my meaning."

"Oh... break the rules with a purpose. Yes, I see." Noah cut the pizza and gave Phan his most mischievous grin, though he kept his tone casual. "You mean," Noah pretended to ponder, "like threaten to arrest him for speeding while he's headed home with a hard-on?"

Phan laughed. "You don't think small, do you? That's

exactly the sort of thing I mean -- but, God, if you do that I'm leaving the country. I don't think he'd find that as funny as you and me."

"Don't rush to update your passport. I did it yesterday," Noah told Phan, serving him a slice. He couldn't quit grinning.

"No shit!" Phan yelled, his eyes wide. "You didn't. You did. Oh, my God. What happened?"

Noah laughed. "My God, was he pissed off. Amused, too, I think, but pissed off."

Phan was staring at him, his eyes still wide open and his jaw hanging. "Seriously? You stopped him and he was hard? And then what?"

"I swear I was just going to flirt a little, jerk his chain, and let him go, but when I saw he was hard, something... I don't know; the practical joker came out. I told Carol, my partner, that I suspected that he was drunk, and she made him get out of the car." Noah was snickering. "Oh, man," he sighed. "So then I frisked him and said some suggestive shit in his ear. He was so mad."

Phan blinked several times. "How hard did he spank you?" he asked finally. "And when are you allowed to come again?"

"Well, first he made me blow him on my knees, and, frankly, given how long he'd been sporting that erection, I'm surprised he could stay standing that long," Noah said and took a bite of his pizza. "And then," he continued, mouth full, "he smacked the hell out of my ass and let me think about it for a while." He swallowed, remembering the evening. "And then..." He grinned and stopped talking to take another bite of his pizza.

"Then?" Phan hadn't even glanced at his food.

"Oh, did I mention I was still in uniform?"

Phan groaned. "You're killing me. Bastard." He wiggled in his chair but didn't reach for his food. "And then?"

"Well, then he told me I could undress, which I did. Don't like your dinner?" Noah winked.

"Shut up," Phan said mildly, finally picking up his slice of pizza. "Talk."

Phan was so easy. This was entirely too much fun. "Okay, so then he told me he wanted to watch. I found a dildo in his bedroom and brought myself off for him, you know, talking the whole time like he likes."

Nodding, Phan chewed. "Dirty talk. Uh-huh, huge button. And you do know I'll have to kill you if you keep stopping, right?"

Poor boy. Noah figured he might as well give him the punch line. "Okay, okay. So he directed me a little, but not too much, and then he took me hard on my hands and knees right there on the living room floor. I thought he was going to blow something, he was so pent up. Jesus."

Phan stared at him. "And he let you get off? Wow. He must have really liked that blow job. Mind you, your mouth? Can't say I blame him -- and the uniform would be a huge treat for him." He grinned and shoved the rest of the pizza in his mouth. "Me, too," he mumbled as he chewed.

"He says he wants to play with me in uniform," Noah said. He winked at Phan, acknowledging his mumbled suggestion.

"Of course he does." Phan downed half his glass of Coke and burped discreetly. "And you're okay with fucking him now? Cool."

"What?" Noah snorted. "I didn't say that," he protested.

Phan raised an eyebrow. "Oh. I... huh. Noah? Wanna tell me what was said? Because I don't see Sir wanting to do fantasy play where he's all aggro on a cop. I could be wrong, though." But he didn't sound like he thought he was.

"He just said if I wanted to play in uniform he'd be up for it... I made a joke about him wanting to be patted down by a horny cop--" Noah stopped talking. "Oh." He gasped softly, the implication of those words becoming clearer in his mind.

Phan nodded sympathetically. "Uh-huh. Sorry, sweet thing. You pretty much told him you'd top."

He had, hadn't he? And not just top, but fantasy top, almost Dom even. Or actually. Oh, fuck. "Oh, fuck," he said out loud this time. "Why would he want that? You think he really wants that?"

Phan looked around, behind himself. "It's me. Didn't we already have this conversation? Yes, that's what he wants." Phan tilted his head. "I'm giving the cuddles this time, aren't I? Right then. Couch time. Come on." He stood up and took Noah's hand, almost dragging him into the living room.

"Yes, we already had this conversation," Noah reluctantly had to admit. "I don't need cuddles, I need a reality check." Noah sulked along behind Phan. "And I'm cuddling you. I've been looking forward to it all day."

"Really?" He got a shy smile. "Me, too. Okay, you cuddle me and I'll give you a reality check. Wanna lie down or sit up this time? I fell asleep last time we were lying down, remember."

"That answers your question." Noah sat and held out his arms.

Phan curled into Noah, wiggling and squirming until they were both comfortable and warm against each other. Noah knew that part of the cuddling -- the largest part -- was that it made Phan feel safe. He was able to talk better, be more honest, if he felt cared for. And it was an easy enough thing to do, once Noah understood what Phan was after.

"So," Phan said. "You haven't managed to get any more comfortable with the idea of... being with him that way. Any idea why?"

"I'm submissive, Phan." The answer was so perfectly clear to him that Phan's question seemed almost ridiculous. Subs don't top. Subs are fucked, used, loved, whatever; they're not in the driver's seat of a scene.

"So?" Phan sighed. "He's a Dom. He likes anal sex -- getting laid by having a nice hard cock up his ass. You like it, why can't he?"

Noah sighed. "It's just... weird." That wasn't terribly eloquent but it was true. It was weird. Awkward. Unusual. "I know what he wants me to do, Phan, I just... I'm not sure I can do it." He hugged his arm tighter around Phan. "I mean if I'm in my space first, then maybe I can do whatever he wants, right? But then he'd have to ask me. And you said he wouldn't ask. But if he did, I guess I could pull it off. It's just hard to think about rationally." He was babbling now, he knew. "Damn it. Am I making any sense?"

Phan nodded. "Yeah," he said quietly. "Sounds like you're pretty sure you won't like it. What happened the last time you topped?"

"What do you mean what happened? It was forever ago, I barely remember it."

"So how come you're so sure you won't enjoy it? Look, kiddo -- we've got kinks. Our sexual identities don't fit into nice little boxes. Where on earth did you get so attached to the idea that subs don't ever top?" Phan looked up at him and brushed a hand along Noah's arm in a strangely comforting gesture. "If you really don't like it, he's not going to make you. Not this."

Noah sighed. "I know," he said softly. "I'd like to, though, if he'd enjoy it. There's nothing I wouldn't do to please him, really, it's just... it's not that I'm stuck thinking inside a box, Phan, it's just... it's complicated." Noah shook his head. 'It's complicated' were the last two words anyone should ever say to Phan, particularly if they wanted to stop talking about something. "Damn."

"Oh, *complicated*," Phan said expansively. "That changes everything. Just stick a sign on your dick that says 'Sorry, sir. It's complicated.' He'll just nod and let it go. Like I am right now. Because we know nothing from complicated. I'll shut up if you talk right the fuck now."

"You're a little shit, you know that?" Noah snorted, giving Phan a gentle shove and knowing that Phan knew he was just playing. "God." Noah rubbed his face and tried to figure out how to start. "Listen. This doesn't go beyond you and me, okay?" He knew he didn't have to say it, but something in him needed to.

Serious eyes met his. "Okay. But if I think Tobias needs to know, I'll tell you that's what I think. Talk." Phan snuggled down again, his hand still stroking over Noah's arm.

"Oh, he knows this part; it's about him," Noah said softly. "Christmas Eve, Tobias spent all night in my arms in tears. He talked about his parents, and about school and work, and you. He told me pretty much everything, you might as well know that." Phan's warmth was comforting, and he was always so easy to talk to. Nothing shocked him, nothing was too stupid or too juvenile; he just took everything at face value. It was a rare gift. "Anyway, he was desperate by the day after Christmas to win back his dominance. He was afraid that breaking down like that in front of me would... he was concerned it might..." Noah sighed. "Well, he was afraid he'd lost my respect, I guess.

That seeing him vulnerable would ruin things between us."

Phan shifted in his arms and nodded. "He... he'd be worried that you wouldn't take him seriously. Okay, so you're tying him bottoming to that sort of thing?"

"Right. I feel kind of the same way. That topping him -- especially in a scene where I need to push him around a little or restrain him -- I'm worried, not so much that he'll lose something in it, but that I will. That I'll start looking at him and wanting to fuck him, instead of wanting him to fuck me." He shook his head. "That probably makes no sense at all."

"No, it makes sense," Phan assured him. "Just lemme think a little. Just... hold on and cuddle, okay? I do my best thinking in a cuddle." He tilted his head up and smiled. "It's just sex, kiddo. There's always a solution."

"Just sex," Noah snorted, but he tugged Phan a tiny bit closer.

They sat for a few long minutes, Phan's warm body growing even warmer as he snuggled. "How about if it wasn't a scene?" Phan finally asked. "Tell me what you felt on Christmas Eve. If he'd needed it then, do you think you could have? And would you have enjoyed it?" Phan twisted right around in his arms, so they were chest to chest. "I don't think you're worried about topping, I think you're worried about being the dominant one. About being in charge and having to enforce it."

Noah's answer was easy. "I'd have done anything he needed that night. Anything at all." He looked at Phan. "And you're right, that's exactly what I'm worried about. How come you can say things so much better than I can?" He lifted a lock of Phan's hair out of his eyes and smoothed it back with his fingers.

"Too much thinking," Phan said softly. "It's all I do anymore."

Noah huffed at him. "Yeah. Must get old after a while, huh?" He leaned forward and kissed Phan on the forehead.

"Sometimes." Phan smiled and brushed his own lips across Noah's cheek. "But every time I get really down and fed up I seem to have a breakthrough of some sort. And honestly? It's better than the alternative."

Noah didn't have all the details, but he knew enough. Phan had been to hell and back since the intervention Bradford had staged with Tobias' help. Maybe more than once. He couldn't imagine what it was like, living and reliving and verbalizing everything, but something was working. Phan was different now. He wasn't the unpredictable fidgeter that Noah had first met for dinner that night months ago when he was still working through Tobias and Phantom's relationship. Phan was more settled, calm, maybe a little sad, but mostly he seemed optimistic.

He even looked a little different. There was visible depth behind his eyes now, like he'd been hiding it or protecting it before. Noah looked into them and smiled. "So, what did you deal with this week?"

Noah got a self-conscious snort, and Phan raised an eyebrow at Noah's quick change of subject. Phan let it go, however, and said, "We've left off the father issues for a bit, which is nice. That was getting kind of old. This week we've been talking about my mother, instead, and what she didn't do. You know, Dr. Brewer thinks it would be a bad idea for me to call my parents? She seems to think I'm still a little hostile to the idiots." He smiled brightly.

"Really? Whatever gave her that idea?" Noah laughed softly.

"I think it was the snarl. But at least I'm not having

nightmares after every session, and it's been almost a week since I've begged Bradford to flog me. The poor man is beginning to regret ever meeting me, I think." Phan sighed and buried his head in Noah's neck. "You're all too good to me," he whispered.

Noah stroked over his shoulder and back. "No, Phan. We're not too good to you, we're just as good as you deserve. Bradford will never regret meeting you; he cares about you too much. We all do." He'd said this probably ten times to Phan, at least -- certainly once every time Phan came over, and sometimes more than that. It couldn't hurt to keep reminding him that he was supported, that people cared. He was going through a lot of shit and dealing with memories of people who *didn't* care, after all.

"Far too patient?" Phan suggested after a long moment. His voice was still muffled, but he was apparently trying to be light; he'd had a good day, after all. A soft kiss was pressed into Noah's neck and Phan pulled away. "Thanks, Noah," he said, his eyes a little watery.

"You're welcome," he answered simply. And he was. "You hardly ate any pizza," Noah squinted at him. "Bradford will think I'm starving you."

"You just want me fat so you can be the pretty one," Phan teased. "Seriously, I ate. And I'll have another slice before I go." A hand slid over Noah's shoulder and Phan turned again, shifting once more into the cuddle they'd started with. "Damn, you're hot. Just sayin'. And no, we haven't got that far in therapy -- I've decided that it's perfectly okay to lust after my old Dom's new sub. So long as everyone knows, anyway. Speaking of, Brian says 'hi.'" He turned his head to peer up at Noah. "He thinks you're hot, too."

Ah, Phan babble. A true sign that the roughest parts of the evening had passed. At least no one had cried this time.

It was a success, really, even if there had been talk about fucking Tobias, which still wasn't really solved. The rest of that conversation needed to be had with Tobias, anyway.

"I've got a bit of a crush on my new Dom's old sub, too, so we'll call it even." Noah chuckled. "Speaking of Brian -- who, by the way, thinks everyone is hot -- I've been dying to ask. Is it crazy living with Bradford, or what? Seems like there's never a dull moment over there."

Phan laughed softly. "I think it was at its most crazy right after Tobias and Bradford decided to move me in. That was certainly when it was the most work for Bradford -- I think he put someone in charge at the club for a few nights, 'cause he didn't leave the house much. But now it's calmer." Phan looked up at him and smiled. "I get out and give him a break now."

"Yeah, you come mooch dinner off the rest of us now," Noah teased. "So it's been a whole week since you've had a rough scene with him? That's great."

Phan snorted. "I haven't had it rough since before New Year's. Said I haven't *begged* for it."

"Oh, so he doesn't give it to you even when you beg for it? Damn, that's like a sub's worst nightmare." Noah laughed, trying to keep things light. "He's good. I don't think I could hold out with you begging."

"Don't tell me that," Phan said with a grin. "I'll practice begging on you and get us both in trouble. Tobias would tan your ass, and I think Bradford would lock me in a closet and make me watch soft porn. Het porn." He shuddered and snuggled against Noah again.

"Het porn! Oh, God, it's a punishment worse than death. I should know, I'm subjected to it from time to time when I hang with the guys from work." Noah raised the pitch of his voice to sound something like a woman. "Oh, you're so big!

Watch, I'll fake an orgasm for you! Oooo!" He laughed. "It's just not sexy. At least guys can't fake it."

"Sure they can!" Phan grinned up at him again. "But it's way more fun to just do it. Poor baby, having to watch that nasty stuff. Tell you what, you can watch gay porn with me. But that could lead to me begging... and then we're right back at punishment." Phan sighed dramatically. "Hold me. Save me. Don't let Bradford lock me in a closet!"

Noah snorted and dug his fingers into Phan's ribs in a spot where he knew Phan was ticklish. Once he'd gotten the squeal he was looking for he relented, letting Phan wriggle away and enduring Phan's reproachful look. "Phan, I don't think anyone could put you back in the closet." Noah winked.

"Do you think I could fake it? I can be all manly. I can. I know what football is, and I can drink beer. Well, I don't, but I can fake that, too. I can tell stories about when I was a drunk, though, and all the guys I laid..." Phan shook his head. "I'm so gay," he said mournfully. "No woman will ever have me. I'll have to move in with you and be your... um. Dishwasher. Yeah. That's it."

"I think you're the gayest man I know." Noah laughed. "And you've already moved in with Bradford. I couldn't possibly take away his dishwasher." He stood up. "I want more Coke," he said, and headed for the kitchen. "Can I get you some?"

"Yeah, thanks," Phan called. "I can't stay with Bradford forever, you know. It's only until I'm better. Then I'll have to find a place again."

"Well, if mean old Bradford throws you out on the street, you know you're always welcome to my couch," Noah called from the kitchen. As if Bradford would ever throw Phan out.

Push him gently, perhaps, but Phan would never end up without a roof over his head.

He poured them each a drink and put a second piece of pizza on a plate for Phan. He frowned as he figured out how he was going to carry it all, and finally balanced the pizza on his forearm.

"Eat this," Noah said, and shoved the plate under Phan's nose. "Did I tell you Tobias is taking me to Paris in April?"

Phan nodded. "I'm green with envy," he said as he took a bite of the pizza. "I loved traveling with him. He... kinda relaxes a bit, but he gets more proper. If that makes sense. You going to renegotiate your contract there?"

"You know, I was thinking about that. It'll be up right about that time, so I suppose we will. I can't believe we're almost there already. It was a good contract to start with; I don't see myself asking for any changes." He looked at Phan. "I might sign on for a year this time, though, if he offers it. What do you think? Is that too long before a renegotiation?"

Phan shrugged and chewed. "You two are in love. I'd say a year, no problem. Why don't you ask for live-in?"

Noah blinked at Phan. Of course the idea had crossed his mind, at least a thousand times. "I would love that," he said honestly. "But I can't ask for that, he has to offer." He had to. There was no way Noah was going to ask and put Tobias in the position of having to either say no, or worse, reluctantly agree. The man liked his personal space, didn't he? If he offered, it would be one thing, but Noah wasn't about to ask.

"He will," Phan said, sounding sure of himself. "This is great pizza, kiddo. Hey, when you move into the condo maybe I can get dibs on this place. I like the fireplace."

Noah grinned. "Well, if I move into his place then you can sublet it. It's nice, if you don't mind the tiny bedroom and the tiny bath. Of course, the bedroom would be bigger if it didn't have a king-size bed in it. And the fireplace is definitely hot."

Phan grinned back. "Will you come back and cuddle me?" he asked, fluttering his eyelashes. "And, hey -- you won't need the bed; I can buy that from you. Um. After I get a job again." He shrugged. "Whatever. It'll all work out, Noah. Trust me."

"Yes, I'll come back and cuddle you. Or you can come over and we'll both cuddle you. How's that?" Noah sipped his Coke. "I know it will work out. For both of us, hmm? Everything has a solution, didn't you just tell me that? Or were you just talking about sex?"

Phan chewed the last of his pizza. "I was thinking about sex at the time," he said after he swallowed. "But I guess it's true of everything. Even when something hurts at first, it usually works out." He took a swallow of his Coke. "You mean it about you both cuddling me?" he asked, looking into his glass.

Noah shifted close to Phan again. "Of course I mean it," he said softly, putting his arm around Phan's shoulders. "We're friends now, right? Good friends. Tobias would love to have you around, I know he would. And you know I would. I look forward to your company on Tuesdays; it's kind of like my therapy. I get to... just talk. It's nice."

"It's nice," Phan echoed him, still staring into his glass. "Does... does he ask about me? I mean, he calls me and talks to me. But does he ask you about me? Us?"

Noah considered carefully how best to answer that question. Of course Tobias asked about him, but he was always asking for Noah's impressions of how Phan was, which was not necessarily what Phan needed to know. He decided to clarify something first. "Us? As in you and me?"

"Yeah, like... how we're getting along and stuff."

"Oh." Noah nodded. "Yes, he does ask, all the time. In fact, chances are good he'll call me late tonight after you go home. He wants to know how you are doing. It's not that he doesn't trust what you tell him, but I think he likes to hear me say you're doing well, and you look good and all of that stuff, too." Noah rubbed Phan's back and grinned. "And I wonder sometimes if he's worried about what trouble you and I might be getting into."

Phan made a face and finally looked at him. "He is. Not that he doesn't trust you, I don't mean that. But he knows me really well, and he knows how I can be. He worries that I'll seduce you, I know he does. That I'll manipulate you."

"You think he worries about that more than you do?" Noah asked frankly. "Don't you think maybe you're more concerned about what you want to do, or what you could do, than he is that I'd let it happen?"

"It's not about you letting it happen -- we all know you wouldn't. It's about me breaking trust. About... pushing you. Hurting him by..." Phan gestured with his hand, his movements becoming agitated. His eyes blinked too rapidly and his lips twitched in between his words. "It's about me reverting to form and trying to get out of my situation. Hiding from reality. He worries I'll use you to escape."

Noah took Phan's glass from his fingers and set it on the table. Then he slid off the couch and knelt in front of Phan, trying to get him to catch his eye. "Phan, look at me. It's okay. Look at me." He took both of Phan's hands in his.

Slowly, with apparent reluctance, Phan's gaze met Noah's. "Sorry," he whispered. "Didn't know I was going to panic like this."

"Don't apologize. This is what it's all about, right? This is why you're here. It's a safe place for you to relax and try not to worry about this stuff. Phan, if you were to do anything of the kind, we'd just deal with it. It wouldn't necessarily be a setback, you know? You're aware of that behavior; you're trying to work through it. No one expects you to be perfect every minute of every day. Everyone slips now and then. I do, Tobias does, we all have things that haunt us some, you know?"

Well that certainly was the truth, wasn't it?

"I am here to catch you if you fall."

Phan's eyes filled, and he blinked quickly until the tears went away. "Okay," he said. "But I'm not falling. Not right now." He sat up straighter. "Just kind of wobbling a bit, I guess. I should go."

"Go? Not like this, no." Noah moved back up onto the couch and tucked his arm around Phan's shoulders again.

"I kinda ruined the mood," Phan said with a sigh. "Sorry. I really do like this, Noah. And it means a lot to me that you put up with the twists and turns." He leaned in slowly, and Noah knew that it was only a matter of moments before Phan would be snuggling, and if he were really upset, he'd be clinging.

"Phan." Noah leaned back and got comfortable in case Phan ended up half in his lap. "You haven't ruined a thing. You tell me, do you want to talk or change the subject?"

One shoulder shrugged and Phan moved closer. "I just... well. Maybe I really should bring this up with Dr. Brewer, after all. It seems to be bothering me." He snorted softly. "A little, anyway. We didn't really deal with it all after, did we? I mean, the next weekend was when Bradford--" His voice faltered.

Noah stroked through Phan's hair, thinking about the weekend that Bradford had locked himself in with Phan, refusing to give Phan the pain he craved as penance for his happiness. He remembered how Tobias had hurried over to the club when Bradford summoned him as backup and how emotional it had been for everyone to help Phan open up.

It still felt odd sometimes to be the comforter, to be discussing someone else's issues instead of his own. Although, come to think of it, this particular issue had everything to do with him. Phan was right; they hadn't ever taken time out to discuss what might have changed between them after that hot scene together at Bradford's New Year's party.

"We didn't deal with it at all," he admitted regretfully. "In fact, we never really spoke about it, did we? Do you want to?"

Phan nodded. "I don't know what to say, though. I liked it. That sounds so inadequate."

"I liked it, too," Noah agreed. But Noah hadn't decided if he wanted it to happen again, or under what circumstances he'd be comfortable with it happening. "You're lovely, Phantom, it was easy to enjoy the privilege of tasting you like I did. But, you know, it was a scene. It was for Tobias, to please him, and we'd sort of agreed on doing it beforehand I think, you and I."

Phan sighed and nodded. "Yeah, I know," he said quietly. "I'm not saying I want it again, or I want more, or anything like that. I'm just saying it was intense. It was a good scene -- it was fun, and hot and it was--" He sighed again. "It was him. You know? It was you, and it was him, and it was just so big."

It was him.

Well, of course Noah ought to have prepared himself for Phan to say that. Noah really hadn't considered the extent to which that scene might have affected Phan. For Noah, especially as deep in his space as he was that night, it really was just a scene. But maybe Phan had felt more. Noah chewed his lip thoughtfully before answering.

"It was intense," he agreed, prompting Phan to say more. He just didn't know what to say himself.

"You two were so beautiful together," Phan went on, his voice soft. "It felt amazing, being a part of it. Being in tune with you, with him. Being able to push his buttons, to serve him." Phan turned his head and looked up at Noah. "I'm sorry." He looked terrified, his eyes wide again.

Noah looked into Phan's eyes and gently shook his head no. He didn't trust himself to speak just yet. Instead, he kissed Phan's forehead and pulled him closer.

After Tobias had left him that night, the night he went to relieve Bradford and work with Phan, Noah hadn't slept at all. All he'd been able to think about was what would happen when the barrier between Tobias and Phan fell. When the one thing that had come between them, that had broken both of their hearts, when that one thing -- Phan's need for pain -- was gone. At that point, he'd realized, there would be nothing to stand between them and their love for each other.

Except for Noah, himself.

He ran fingers through his hair and held Phan close. It wasn't Phan's fault that he still had feelings for Tobias. It wasn't his fault that he still wanted to serve. But it was very, very hard to hear.

"I'm sorry," Phan whispered again. "This is... I don't mean to hurt you. It was good. It was a scene, a taste. I know that. It was very special, Noah. Thank you for that."

"It's all right, Phan. I don't have any reason to be insecure. If I thought I did, I wouldn't have agreed to it in the first place. And it was good. And special." He sighed. "I worry too much."

"That's what I'm saying, you should worry. Tobias does. Bradford does." Phan moved even closer, curling up almost in Noah's lap. "I'm not a very nice person, Noah. Just so you know."

Noah frowned. "First of all, you've never been anything but nice to me, so I don't believe you, and second, you're not the same person you were a month ago. And next week you won't be the same person you are today. That's what this whole process is about. I'll take my chances." All the same, since no one had ever mentioned to him that Phan was 'not a nice person,' he filed it away to ask Tobias about later.

Phan didn't say anything for a few minutes, merely clung to Noah silently. "I think I should go," he said after a few moments. "I'm screwing things up and--" He stopped talking as the phone rang.

Noah looked at the phone and then at the clock on the table beside it. He knew who it was. "Stay," he told Phan, keeping him close as he reached for the receiver. "Hello, sir."

"Hello, sweetheart," Tobias said. Noah could hear his smile. "Did you have a nice evening?"

Phan's face tilted up, looking thoughtful for a moment before he sighed and buried his head in Noah's chest again.

"Phan's still here, sir," he said quickly. "We were just talking about you."

Phan groaned pitifully.

"I see." There was a short pause. "Are you all right, pet?" Tobias sounded calm, as always, but there was an undeniable tension in his voice.

"You know, we have a lot of leftover pizza if you're hungry." Noah said just as calmly, although he wasn't feeling terribly calm at the moment. He hoped that Tobias would catch on.

"Good answer. I'm on my way. Keep him there for me,

pet." There was a pause and Noah could hear Tobias calling for his car on the house phone. "Should I call Bradford? Dr. Brewer?"

"Why don't we see about that when you get here?" Noah hedged. "I know Phan will be glad to see you, too." He petted Phan's hair and ran fingers down his arm.

"I'll be there as soon as I can, sweetheart," Tobias said in his ear. "I'll let myself in."

"Oh, yeah, this is gonna be real fun," Phan mumbled as Noah hung up the phone. He shot Noah an accusing look. "Just wobbly. Not falling."

Noah sighed. "So much the better; we can all talk about it before you get to the point where you do. Are you angry with me? Was I wrong to invite him? You've been asking and talking about him all night."

Phan pulled away a little and then snuggled right back in. "I'm not mad," he said in a very small voice. "I'm scared."

"Tobias will fix that; it's hard to be afraid when he's around." Noah held Phan, and they remained pretty much silent and still until Noah heard a key in the door. Tobias didn't waste any time when he was worried.

"Hello, boys," Tobias said quietly as he came in. He was still undoing his overcoat as he bent down to kiss Noah's mouth and the top of Phan's head. "Phantom. Are you all right, or do you think I should call the doctor?"

Phan lifted his head and looked at Noah for a moment before curling up again. "I'm wobbly, but I don't need her."

Tobias sat in the easy chair and looked at them, one ankle across his other knee. "Noah? What do you think?"

"I don't think Phan needs her, sir," Noah told him. "He'll want to discuss things with her at some point, but right now I think we're enough. I'm glad you called."

Noah felt momentarily self-conscious about the way that

Phan was clinging to him, but Tobias didn't seem concerned about it, so he forced himself to let it go. "Phan's been telling me that I should worry about him 'reverting.' He says he thinks he's not a very nice person."

"Ah. Back to that." Tobias leaned back in the chair. "Talking about your mother lately, Phan?" he asked gently.

Phan nodded against Noah's chest. "Yes, sir. I shouldn't have come tonight, but I thought I'd passed the worst of it." He let go a little and looked up at Noah with bright eyes. "Sorry."

"Phan. Please stop apologizing," Noah said softly. "And you were talking about Sir and Master Bradford with me, and about New Year's Eve, not about your mother."

"But I talked about Mother in therapy," Phan explained, his tone patient. "And that always makes me wonky for days after. She used to tell me that there was only so much good in the world, and I was the little bit of a price she had to pay to be with my father."

Tobias winced, and Noah could see that Phan was serious, that his own mother had helped to form the demon he was fighting.

"Phan," Tobias said softly. "Do you want to talk about the scene on New Year's?"

Phan shook his head, his hands stroking over Noah's arms, making sure Noah was holding him. "No. But you're going to make me?"

"I'm going to encourage it," Tobias said. "Noah seems to think it's important, and as it involves all three of us, I agree. Noah?"

"I would also encourage it, but there's no point in making you talk about it, Phan. You won't get anything out of it that way." Noah tugged Phan into his chest to reassure him. "Why not just tell Sir what you told me?"

Phan turned again and sighed softly as he sat up. He hugged Noah, sitting next to him on the couch instead of on top of him, and took a breath that even Noah could see was shaky. "All right," Phan said, his hand still on Noah's arm.

Tobias cleared his throat softly. "You really aren't alone, Phan. If you need it, and if Noah doesn't mind, you can curl up with him."

"I don't mind," Noah said softly, watching Phan and then glancing over at Tobias. Tobias seemed a little agitated himself.

Phan crawled back into his lap. "You really don't mind?" he whispered. "I know it's probably weird, but you're warm and this is really hard and I'm just... is this okay?"

Noah had to remember for a moment that Phan wasn't a child, even though there were times, like this one, when he was given to wonder. "It's good," Noah told him. "You're warm, too. Go on and tell Sir what you told me."

Phan nodded and took another breath, like he was bracing himself. He closed his eyes for a second and began to talk, his eyes fixed on the floor, the words just spilling from him. "I told Noah that I liked the scene, that I liked being a part of it, of being connected to him and to you. That I liked serving you, liked moving with him for your pleasure. I liked... liked all of it."

"We knew that," Tobias said slowly. "All three of us liked it, it was a powerful scene. Intense."

Phan nodded and looked up. "That's it exactly. It was intense. I think, though, that we should have debriefed the next day or a couple of days later; it... it's gained weight for me. I mean, it shattered some walls for me, and that's good, but it gave me... I don't know. Noah and I have become friends after it, I can be like this with him. I can trust him. But it gave me a reminder, you know?"

Tobias nodded. "All right. I can see that. Connecting with me on that level made you feel... what? Like it used to?"

Phan nodded and then shook his head. He turned to Noah and touched his jaw gently. "I don't feel like I'm his. Didn't even then, that night. You need to know that. I'm visiting. Not staying."

Noah smiled despite the slight uneasiness he was feeling. He wanted Phan to talk, to be honest, to get this stuff out. Whatever issues he, himself, still had could be addressed later. "It's okay, Phan," he said softly. "Just keep being honest; the truth is always okay."

"But you need to believe it, know it's true. I don't love him like you do, and he doesn't love me like that. You two are on a whole other level, okay?" Phan smiled at him weakly. "And it was real nice to touch that. I guess I'm saying that it made me kind of lonely in the aftermath. That the weekend after was... well. And since then?" Phan twisted to look at Tobias, still curled around Noah like a limpet. "Since then I've been foggy and clingy and needy, and you've both done so much. I feel like you're my friends, that I can touch that part of you again sometime."

Tobias looked a little concerned. "Phan, I need to be clear here. Are you asking for our friendship? Because you have that. Are you looking for more?"

Phan shook his head. "No. I thought maybe I was, though. I think I scared Noah."

Noah laughed softly. "For a minute," Noah admitted. He sighed and just gave in a little. "Or maybe more than a minute. Maybe I'm still a little... off balance about it, but I believe you when you say that it's not what Sir and I have. You do love him, though, Phan, and I think you miss serving Sir more than you're admitting now. At least that's how it sounded to me earlier."

"I miss *serving*. And Sir was the best Master I ever had."

Tobias looked thoughtful. "I'll speak to Bradford," he said slowly. "I know that you two don't have that sort of relationship, but maybe if you were doing more of the... mundane acts of service it would help to balance you a bit. Are you subbing at all?"

"I'm supposed to be concentrating on therapy. I can't be flogged 'cause I'm without limits at this point -- it wouldn't be safe."

"That's not what I asked. I recommended Dr. Brewer because she's a submissive -- she lives with it, she knows what it is to serve. It's who you are, Phan, you can't just turn it off to think about something else." Tobias stood up and began to pace. "Damn it, Bradford knows this, she does... what were they thinking?"

Noah raised an eyebrow. "I don't think Phan has mentioned this to them yet, sir."

Tobias waved it off. "That's beside the point -- it's not his job to announce what his therapy should include, it's theirs to design a therapy that works, based on who he is."

Noah sighed. "Sir, if I may, telling Phan that his therapy has been inadequate thus far is probably not helpful right at this moment...?"

"And coddling him is?" Tobias sat down heavily. "Jesus. Phan, come here."

On Noah's lap, Phan shook his head.

Noah raised an eyebrow in surprise but didn't force Phan to move. The poor boy was already reacting physically to Tobias' protectiveness, and if he didn't want Tobias to know, Noah certainly wasn't going to tell him. "If it's all the same to you, he's all right over here, sir."

Tobias looked a little surprised. "I see. Phan?"

"I'd like to stay here, sir. With Noah. Please?" To Noah's

ear he sounded almost desperate under the veneer of respect, but apparently it was enough to convince Tobias to back off.

"All right. I'll talk to Bradford in the morning and see if we can come up with something to occupy the submissive needs you have without getting into physical punishments. I don't suppose it would be tactful of me in any way to ask about sex?"

"Not unless you're offering," Phan shot back. "Sorry, Noah."

Noah shook his head at Phan. "It's just sex, Phan. Answer him."

Phan frowned. "I'm horribly disappointed in you," he said dramatically before settling down. "If you all must know, I haven't been with anyone since before the wonderful weekend in the white room."

"Since the scene with us," Tobias clarified.

"Since the scene with you two." Phan sighed.

"And before that?" Noah asked. The question sort of popped out of his mouth before he thought about it.

"You are a horrible, horrible person. I think I'm going to go sit with Sir now."

"It's just a question," Noah said simply.

"It's a mean question." Phan pouted at him. "Not all of us have... ah, shit." Phan deflated, both literally and figuratively, and slumped against him. "Just over a year, I think."

Noah glanced at Tobias, then back at Phan. "Well, that might have something to do with how intense it was for you, then, yeah?"

Phan shrugged. "Probably. And Sir. Can't forget that."

Tobias stood up and crossed to the couch, sitting carefully at the other end. "I want to help, Phan. You know that, it's what I've spent the last seven weeks doing. But I need to know what you want, as well as what you need."

"I don't know, do I?" Phan said. "I'm just trying to heal."

Noah loosened his grip on Phan a bit. "Don't be defensive with him, Phan," Noah said softly in his ear. "He wants to help."

"Everyone wants to help," Phan said flatly. "But no one knows what to do. There doesn't seem to be much point right now. I mean, it isn't like I'm ever going to be normal, is it? Not like I'll be able to have a real relationship, or find a decent job, or be able to stop aching all the time."

Phan was lifted off his lap so suddenly that Noah wasn't sure what had happened until he saw Phan sobbing in Tobias' arms.

"Call Bradford, please," Tobias said softly. "Tell him we're bringing Phan home and it might be a good idea to call Dr. Brewer."

Noah reached over and picked up the phone, and within minutes arrangements were made and they were all out the door.

4

———

Tobias carried Phan into Bradford's townhouse, trying to monitor both the weeping Phantom and the quietly coping Noah. He hoped Noah would be able to maintain his calm until Phan was under someone else's care; he suspected he'd be taking Noah next door to the club in fairly short order, if only to reestablish a few basic truths of their relationship.

"Dr. Brewer is on her way, Tobias," Bradford said as they came through the door. "Go on into the living room. Hello, Noah. Too much for you tonight, was he?"

"Hello, Master Bradford," Noah said softly and knelt on the floor next to the sofa where Tobias had taken Phan. He looked worried, and Tobias wouldn't have been surprised if there was some guilt in there, too.

"Easy, sweetheart," he murmured, petting Noah with one hand. He shifted Phan to the cushions and off his lap, sitting next to the boy instead of holding him. "Phan, Dr. Brewer is on her way. You must talk to her."

Phan wept and drew himself into a ball. With a sigh,

Tobias looked at Noah and petted him again. "Noah, would you hold him please? Just until the doctor gets here."

Noah complied quickly, climbing up on the couch and pulling Phan into his arms. "I'm sorry," his whispered into Phan's ear once he was close.

Bradford cleared his throat. "I'll just wait outside for Dr. Brewer then, shall I?" he asked, and then he withdrew, leaving the three of them alone.

"It's not your fault, Noah," Tobias said softly, smoothing one hand down Noah's back. "This isn't something you caused or could have prevented. It merely is."

Phan sniffled, his arms wrapping around Noah. "Don't do this," he pleaded. "I don't want to feel like... I can't take the weight of your guilt, Noah."

Tobias shushed him gently, the hand on Noah's back still petting, his other hand wiping Phan's tears. "He means he doesn't want you to feel like it's your fault because it isn't. It hurts him that you're hurting."

Noah nodded. "Okay, Phan, okay," he whispered, cradling Phan in his arms and talking softly. "I know it's not my fault, okay? I just feel bad that you're having to go through this. I'm not hurting, I'm just concerned about you, as a friend, you know? That's all, I promise."

Tobias nodded and pressed a kiss to Noah's forehead. He ached for both of them, and his anger grew with every tear that streaked Phantom's face. Not once had he ever heard Phan say things like it not being worth it, that he wasn't worth it. He'd taken on pain that Tobias could never have carried, but he'd never said it was too much.

Facing the pain appeared to be harder than carrying it.

"Phantom," a voice from the door said, and Tobias looked up to see a woman come in. She looked worried and rushed, and she tossed her coat onto a couch as she crossed the room.

Tobias stood up. "Dr. Brewer?"

"Yes." She looked at him and then moved past him to Phan. "Dr. Vincent, I take it?"

"Yes, and this is Noah." He watched as she smiled warmly at Noah, making no move to extricate Phan from his embrace.

"Hello, Noah," she said easily. "How are you doing, Phan?"

"He's doing just fine," Tobias said acidly.

She stood and turned to face him, one brow up. "I am not your submissive, Dr. Vincent, I am Phantom's doctor. If you continue to speak to me like that, I'll have you removed."

Tobias said nothing, but he stood a little straighter and looked at her, meeting her gaze with a steely look.

"And if you try to top me like that again," she said sweetly, "I won't even speak to you after I talk to Phan. Now," she said, turning to Noah, "if you would be so good as to tell me what happened?"

Noah, clearly concerned about the power struggle, glanced up at Tobias before speaking and waited for his nod.

"Phantom and I were at my place talking, like we do every week, and I'm sure you know that sometimes it's a teary evening and sometimes we just have fun..." He swallowed. "Anyway, tonight we got to talking about New Year's Eve, and a scene that Sir and Phan and I had together, and his feelings associated with that, so I invited Sir over to join the conversation, since it involved all three of us, you know?"

Noah stroked Phan's hair and kissed his forehead. "And maybe it was talking about the relationship I have with Sir that set him off, but then he just got upset and said that it didn't matter, no one knew what was wrong with him and no one knew how to help -- that he'd never have a normal relationship with anyone, and he was always going to be this way. That's when we called you."

Tobias opened his mouth and her hand went up. "After, Dr. Vincent. Right now I think I'd like to spend some time with Phan." She smiled at Noah and nodded. "Thank you, Noah. You've done exactly what he needed. Phan, let go of Noah now, and we'll talk."

Slowly Phan untangled himself. "Noah. It's really not your fault, I promise."

"I know, Phan. I believe you. Honest. Please don't worry about me." Noah touched his face and then got up off the couch.

Tobias held a hand out to Noah, drawing him in. "Phantom," he said before Dr. Brewer could stop him again. "You must tell her all of it."

Phan sat up and stared at the floor. "Yes, sir," he said softly.

Tobias nodded. "I'll be waiting, doctor. You and I need to have a talk."

She looked at him again and then at Phan. With a sigh she nodded. "Within limits, yes. But not until I've spoken to Phan. With all due respect, Master Tobias, get out."

Tobias touched Noah's shoulder and led them out, not really wanting to leave Phan but knowing that they had to, that it was best. As they left the room he sighed. "You did exceptionally well, pet, and I thank you for it."

Noah turned and wrapped his arms around Tobias' waist, pressing his face into Tobias' chest. "Maybe I shouldn't have asked you to come over? Maybe I should have just left it alone when he wanted to change the subject. I only wanted to help, and look at him now. Maybe these visits are a bad idea."

"Tsk," Bradford clucked at him from across the hall.

"Listen to me," Tobias said roughly. "None of that. You did the right thing -- how is helping him hide a good thing? And these visits of yours are the best thing for both of you -- he needs to be friends with someone, he needs to feel safe. I thought you liked spending time with him, pet?"

"I do, but it's never been this bad before, sir. I've never felt like I couldn't handle it." Noah sighed and let go. "I do enjoy his visits. We mostly have fun. He's so sweet, how could anyone do those things to him?"

"I don't know," Tobias said softly. He'd asked himself that time and time again, had even looked into the faces of the people who were supposed to protect the child Phan had been. He hadn't found any answers.

He held Noah to him and stroked his back, hoping to soothe his boy. "Bradford, there's something we should discuss. Phan's not subbing, and it's hurting him."

"You think so? Phan hasn't subbed regularly in a very long time, you know, Tobias. Not since you and he split, as far as I know. He and I have never had that kind of relationship. He came to me to be--" Bradford sighed. "For scenes and that was all."

Tobias shook his head. "Not like that, Bradford. I mean chores, serving. I mean giving him some sort of purpose, man! You are what you are, and he is what he is, and he's had everything taken from him -- even pain. He's without an anchor." He tightened his arms on Noah and took a deep breath, trying to control his temper.

Bradford raised an eyebrow and took a step toward Tobias. He looked Tobias in the eye and his jaw clenched before he spoke. "You need to take a more respectful tone with me, Tobias. You have no right -- no right -- to take issue with me regarding my efforts to help Phantom. I have made myself sick over him. You have no idea. I broke him, I took him in, I have kept him safe and comfortable, I have sat with him through nights of nightmares and tears -- I defy you to tell me that I am not doing enough for him. If you think he needs something more, something else I could offer him, I'm happy to discuss it with you, but leave your anger at the door. Is that clear?"

Tobias let go of Noah and stepped forward. "You defy me to tell you? Fine. You're not doing enough. I spent years taking care of that boy, and you damn well know it. I got him clean, I trained him. Two months after breaking him, your aftercare sucks, Bradford. My anger and I will be outside."

He turned and started to walk away, wondering if he could find cigarettes at the club bar. "Noah, stay where it's warm, pet," he said, grabbing his coat.

Tobias heard Bradford apologize to Noah as he left them and then the sound of Bradford's boots behind him.

"Tobias!" Bradford called, following him. "Wait."

"Not unless you have a bottle and a pack of cigarettes," Tobias called back. Then he sighed and stopped, shoving his hands into his coat pockets as he turned. "Damn it."

"I have both in my office. Will you come sit? I've sent Noah to relax with Nikki and Brian." Bradford gestured toward the back end of the hall and his office.

Tobias felt his shoulders slump. He was going to be making this up to Noah for ages. "I can't promise not to yell. But it's not at you, it's... everything."

"I know, me, too. Come on." Bradford took Tobias' coat and hung it up, then led him back to his office. He closed the door after Tobias came in and went to a cabinet at the far end. "Sit," Bradford said, and returned to his desk with a bottle and two glasses. He slid his cigarette case across the desk.

"Pour," Tobias said, not wasting time as he reached for the cigarettes. "Ashtray?" He looked where Bradford pointed and stood up to fetch it. "I apologize," he said, only slightly stiffly.

"Thank you," Bradford said just as stiffly as he poured them each a drink. "So what is this really about, Tobias? Are you feeling helpless? Guilty? If you think he needs more purpose, I can do that. Thank you for letting me know."

"Oh, don't be like that," Tobias said. "You're no more my Dom than Luca is. Peers, remember? So take that tone and shove it. If I'd known what he needed before tonight I would have told you." Tobias lit a cigarette and inhaled deeply. "And don't glare at me, and don't you dare send me to the wall. I won't go. Not this time."

"Oh, for crying out loud," was all Bradford said before lighting a cigarette himself and leaning back in his desk chair.

Tobias glared at him and raised an eyebrow. "That's it?"

"You're not his Master anymore, Tobias. He's not your boy. He's on his own now and has been responsible for himself for a long while. You can't be the answer to his problems anymore, as much as you'd like to be. You can't hold him and fix it. You can't order him to his knees and center him and fix it that way, either. This time his answers have to come from inside himself. We don't have any choice but to sit back and watch it happen, and that's just frustrating you enough to turn you into a complete asshole."

Tobias took a breath and then followed it up with a drag on the cigarette. That didn't work, so he switched to the scotch. Bradford had a point, and Tobias knew it, but he was wrong, too. Phan was still a sub and he still needed a Dom. He needed it like he needed to breathe.

"He needs me," he finally said, a chill running down his spine at the words.

"Fine," Bradford said, putting his empty glass down on the desk. "Then quit telling me what a lousy job I'm doing with him and take him off my hands."

"I can't." He couldn't. There wasn't any way he could take Phan in. He set his glass down and stubbed out his cigarette. "I have to go. I'll get Noah and leave -- talk to Brewer when she's done, will you?"

"Jesus Christ," Bradford muttered, chasing Tobias back out into the hall. "Tobias. Tobias, damn you, wait a minute. You're walking out on him now? He's going to expect you to be here when the doctor is done with him. I was hoping you'd speak to her with me. Where are you going?"

"I'm going home," Tobias said calmly. He felt amazingly still inside, considering the way his world had just tilted. "As you've pointed out, I can't take him off your hands, so I shouldn't be here." He looked around and shoved his hands into his pockets again, mostly so Bradford wouldn't see them shake. "If you want to call it running out on him, fine. Call it what you want. I call it saving him." He turned and started to walk away, looking for Noah.

Bradford made no reply.

"I thought I heard your voice, sir," Noah said, hurrying to him. He knelt abruptly at Tobias' feet. "I should have waited for you here, I know, but Master Bradford suggested I go in with Nikki and Brian."

"It's okay, sweetheart," Tobias said softly, one hand running over Noah's hair. "Bradford and I had to yell at each other a little." He looked at Bradford and schooled his features. "Are we done?" he asked.

"As you so eloquently pointed out, I'm not your Dom, so I can hardly tie you up to keep you here. I think you're making a mistake in leaving, but my opinion hasn't held much water with you this evening, so -- run if you need to, Tobias, I'll do the best I can here."

Bradford didn't wait for an answer but simply headed back to his office.

"We're leaving, sir?" Noah asked from his knees. "Aren't we going stay to make sure Phan is okay? Didn't the doctor say she wanted to talk to you?"

Suddenly weary, Tobias sighed. "I know, pet. But I don't know if I can deal with this right now. I... I need to make some decisions, and now is probably not the right moment. I seem to be a little worked up."

"If you think that's best, sir." Noah stood and retrieved his own coat.

Best. Tobias stood there for a long moment, fully aware of what he was doing to Noah, to Bradford, to Phantom... to himself. "I don't think it's best," he said softly. "I simply don't know what else to do."

Shaking himself he looked back the way Bradford had gone. "Into the lion's den, then. Come along, pet, you can help me lick my wounds later. If we all survive." He walked to the door and knocked, Noah just behind him.

"Come in," came the voice behind the door.

Tobias opened the door and walked in, holding it open until Noah was in as well. As he swung it shut he said, "What would you have me do? Honestly, how the hell do you see this working, Bradford?"

Noah knelt by the door.

Bradford, damn him, didn't seem the least bit surprised to see Tobias in his office again. "I don't know," Bradford said. "Maybe if we talk it out a bit we'll come to something."

He steepled his fingers and tapped them against his chin. "Moving in with you seems premature, and perhaps ultimately it won't be necessary. I think you're right, though, that he does need a full-time Dom, someone to keep him in his space, to keep him purposeful, to give him reasons to keep doing what he's doing. With your guidance, I will fill that role for now, if you want me to."

Tobias glanced at Noah. "I'm certainly not taking him home," he told Noah. He walked a few steps and turned. "What kind of guidance are we talking about here?"

Bradford looked thoughtful for a moment. "Domestic submission, evening punishment and morning discipline, training, the works if you think he needs it. I'll commit to that for a trial period if that's what we decide he needs, Tobias. No one has suggested that to me to this point, including his doctor."

"Yes, well. His doctor will have a couple of questions to answer." Tobias paced again. "There're too many variables. Too much he's not saying -- and I'd bet lying about. Up until an hour ago, I thought everything was fine."

"Phan lies," Bradford said simply. "He always has. He tells everyone what they want to hear, whether or not it's strictly true. I don't expect his doctor would be any different." He filled their glasses again and sighed. "Tobias, in a perfect world, what would you have happen right now? If it weren't for these other variables, what would you see as the solution?"

Tobias snorted. "Everyone healthy and happy and whole, what else?"

Bradford snorted at him. "That's not a solution, Tobias, that's a pipe dream."

"So I have to choose one? Don't make me choose between them. Noah is my life, you know that. I love him.

He's stronger, though -- don't make me choose being happy with Noah and saving Phan; I can't."

"What?" Noah said looking up from the floor.

"Tobias. I never said you had to choose, did I?"

Noah got to his feet. "What?"

Tobias reached for Noah. "I won't give you up. I won't leave you, and you're mine, do you hear me? I love you. I am not choosing Phantom over you, I won't." He was growling by the end, desperate to reassure Noah, to keep him from leaving. The boy had to believe him.

Noah stepped backward before Tobias could touch him. "Why are we talking about you taking Phan in?"

Tobias stepped forward, keeping the distance the same. "We're not. I'm not taking him home."

Noah looked into his eyes. "It's not all right with me. Don't even consider it, Tobias."

"I just said I'm not, Noah. I won't." Tobias stared into the eyes he seldom got to see. "I won't," he said softly. He felt the burn at the back of his nose and turned his head before Noah could see the tears.

He could feel Noah's eyes on his back, and Bradford's too. No one spoke for a bit, until Bradford finally broke the silence. "You've heard him Noah, he's reassured you several times, hm? Be a good boy and kneel for him again."

Tobias didn't need to turn around to feel the look that passed between them, but he heard Noah go to his knees.

"Tobias." Bradford handed him his drink. "Why don't we wait for the doctor and talk more about this later?"

Tobias nodded and looked at the glass, finally setting it down on a shelf. "Thanks, but no," he said quietly. "For the drink, I mean. Of course I'll wait to hear what the doctor says, but then we'll be going. I don't think I should see Phan tonight." He moved to one of the visitor's chairs and sat, staring at the floor as he waited for the doctor.

Noah moved to Tobias' chair and knelt in front of it, then wordlessly, he leaned into Tobias' lap.

Bradford cleared his throat. "I'll go check on Dr. Brewer," he said, neatly excusing himself from the room.

As soon as the door closed Tobias opened his arms and reached for Noah. "Come here," he said softly, pulling him into his lap. "I love you, Noah. Only you. Do you understand that?"

Noah started to nod and then sighed. "Only me? Are you sure? Are you absolutely sure? Because I don't think Phan is." Noah's insecurity was plainly evident in his question.

"I care about him. I love him on some level, I suppose, but as one does an old and special friend. I feel responsible for him. I worry about him. But you are my heart. My life. My boy. I love you passionately. You are my first priority, my first responsibility, my lover. Does that help?"

"It... helps. Yes. You want to know what I have nightmares about?" Noah asked, rhetorically. "That once Phan learns that he doesn't need the pain, there won't be anything standing between the two of you anymore... but me."

Tobias pulled Noah closer to him and kissed his temple. "It's not going to happen," Tobias said, enunciating every word. "Phan and I have ties, yes. We've been over this, Noah. Phan and I split up over more than the pain, though that was at the root. We... we aren't right together that way. You and I are. You are not second choice for me, Noah Dolan -- you're the only choice. What can I do to prove that to you? What can I do to make you secure in that?"

Noah shook his head. "You can't. I just have to believe it. And I do. I do. Just nights like this and talk like... well, I hadn't expected it, and it threw me." Noah kissed Tobias' neck and sighed. "So, are you all right?" Noah asked, deftly changing the subject. "You've got a horrid temper tonight. I've never seen you and Master Bradford argue like that."

"I'm... I'm not doing so well, no," Tobias said with a grimace. "At least with Deidre I can send flowers; I hate to think what Bradford is going to make me do." He sighed and nuzzled Noah for a moment. "I don't know what's going to happen or how to help, pet, and that's killing me."

"You're not in control of this, I get that." Noah nodded. "But Phan likes Dr. Brewer, she'll help him."

"I hope so," Tobias said. "We'll just have to wait and see what she can tell us. Which, granted, won't be much, given her privilege."

"Hmm, true," Noah said, leaning on him. "He wants this; tonight was rough for him, but I don't think he really feels that it's hopeless."

"That scared me," Tobias confessed. "He's never said anything like that before. I just feel that he's close to something, a breaking point, and whatever happens next is going to be pivotal. It's such early days for him in this process and I... well, I guess I'm wondering if he's going to choose well."

"He's got a lot of help in making his choices." Noah's tone was lighter. "He knows he's not alone."

Tobias didn't say anything, stopping himself from questioning it by the physical act of biting his tongue. Instead, he ran a hand over Noah's back and held him fractionally tighter. "Stay with me tonight?" he asked.

"Thank you for not making me ask first," Noah said with a smile. "I'm not going to work tomorrow, either. I'm too damn wound up."

"Thank you," Tobias said, not bothering to put up his

usual arguments. "I'll call Dee when we get home, see if she can do without me in the morning. We have to vaccinate a small herd in the afternoon, though; I'll have to go."

Talking about work actually relaxed him a little, which he hadn't expected. He also hadn't really noticed it until Bradford walked in with Dr. Brewer and all the tension came flooding back.

Noah kissed Tobias, and then slid off his lap and knelt at his feet as they came in.

"Would you like Noah to go sit with Phan while we talk, doctor?" Bradford was asking as they walked through the door.

"That's up to Noah and Dr. Vincent," she said coolly. "I simply can't tell you that much, to tell the truth, so if he'd rather go cuddle he can -- he'll probably get more details than I can give you."

Tobias stroked Noah's hair. "Up to you, pet. But don't push him for anything." He glared at the doctor. "We only want to help."

Noah was on his feet instantly. "Thank you, sir," he said, and hurried out the door.

"Tobias," Bradford warned. "We're all on the same team here."

Tobias merely looked at him for a moment before shifting his gaze to the doctor. "How is he?"

She sighed, suddenly looking tired. "Well, the good news is that he's fine. Contrite on a couple of matters, swearing to clear the air on one more. The bad news is that you're completely right, Dr. Vincent. That's a sub in need of rules." She held up a hand and said, "However, I would like to point out that I was under the impression he had a Dom."

Bradford raised an eyebrow. "He told you that?"

"You did." She leveled him with a gaze that Tobias found

very unsubmissive. He made a mental note to find out if she had a Master or not, just to see who on earth had to deal with that.

"I? I did no such thing," Bradford protested. "I told you he was staying with me."

"When you called you said, and I quote, 'Dr. Brewer, I have a sub here who needs your help.' You then told me he was living with you, and that you had broken him, calling in Dr. Vincent for support when needed. This, Master Bradford, led me to believe that Phantom was yours. No one dissuaded me from this, and thus I didn't push Phan for things that I should have -- and when I did, he lied. I knew he was lying, and it's on me that I didn't dig; I was unaware that he didn't have a net."

Tobias didn't know if he should laugh or cry.

Bradford sank into his chair with a heavy sigh. "I'm sorry. I ought to have been clearer." He ran fingers through his hair. "Damn it."

"Damn it, indeed," she said. She pulled up a chair and sat, tipping her head back. "All right, gentlemen. I can't tell you much, but you can tell me. Will one of you give him structure for a time? At least... well, a few months, anyway. Phan's got years of work ahead of him, I won't lie. But he really needs structure right now."

"I can't," Tobias said, his voice sounding hollow to his own ears. "Not the way he needs." He'd promised Noah.

"I will," Bradford assured her. "Starting tomorrow morning. I'll talk to him, and we'll sign something to make it official so he takes it seriously."

She nodded. "All right then. Noah. I suggest they keep seeing each other if it works within your relationship, Master Tobias. Phan really likes Noah, and seems calmed by him. However, I'd like to talk with Noah alone for a moment later if you and he decide to keep up the Tuesday evenings."

"It's really up to Noah," Tobias said. "But I'd... well, he seems to like it as well."

"Okay." She smiled a little. "Buck up, gentlemen. It's not as bad as it looked. Some issues came up is all, and he had a crying jag. You called me, we talked, and I got past some fibs. We can move forward now. And, honestly, if Phan is following his patterns, he's about to take a leap ahead." She stood up and stretched. "He's probably asleep by now. Let him rest, and start over tomorrow. Oh, Master Bradford -- no flogging for punishment, keep the spankings light, and let him get off once in a while, okay?"

"Oh, good Lord, I hadn't even thought of that," Bradford sighed. "Do you think he needs a physical relationship as well?"

She shook her head, looking slightly amused. Tobias bit his tongue.

"No. Just... hand him a wipe when he's done and make him clean up." She beamed at him. "And a dildo would be a lovely gift for him to earn. Just a suggestion."

Tobias bit his tongue again, but he thought Bradford saw it.

"Tobias Vincent, I hope you bite that thing off," Bradford said petulantly, but he was smiling. "Oh, all right, everyone have a nice laugh then? I'm exhausted. Take your boy home, Tobias."

"If I can peel him off your boy," Tobias shot back.

Dr. Brewer rolled her eyes. "I have to talk to him anyway," she said, going to the door. "Come along, Master Tobias." She shook suddenly and laughed. "I've always wanted to say something like that. I'm going to be in so much trouble when I get home."

Tobias snorted. "I certainly hope so."

She smiled at him and waved good night to Bradford, admonishing him to be in touch if he needed her.

"I'll be right there," he said, turning to Bradford. "Call me if you need me."

Bradford nodded. "Count on it."

Tobias nodded and turned to hurry after Dr. Brewer, nothing left to say. He was going to tackle the apologies in the morning, or perhaps when dealing with the cows. He managed to catch up just as she was easing the door open. Tobias peered over her shoulder to see the boys curled up on the couch, Phan fast asleep. Noah looked up at the sound of the door and she waved him out, almost backing into Tobias as she stepped back.

She gave him a hard look. "You move fast."

"I have to."

He thought she might have smiled, but then Noah slipped out of the room to join them and she turned away.

"He's asleep," Noah said softly. "He smiled at me when I came in."

"You make us all smile, pet," Tobias said without thinking.

Noah leaned on him. "Are we going home, then?"

"Very shortly. Dr. Brewer would like to know if you'd like to continue seeing Phan on Tuesdays. I said that was entirely up to you."

Noah looked at the doctor. "Yes. Phan wants to, too."

She nodded and glanced at Tobias. "In that case, Noah, I'd like to have a quick word in private. It's just something that Phan wanted me to pass on if you agreed."

Noah glanced at Tobias for permission, and then followed the doctor around the corner.

Tobias tried not to be impatient for them to return, but

found himself glancing at his watch and jingling his keys before Noah rounded the corner again, the doctor behind him.

"Ready?" Noah asked with an innocent look. Damn him.

"Yes," he said evenly. "Everything's settled then?"

Dr. Brewer rolled her eyes and went past. "Goodnight, doctor. I'll tell my Master I finally met you -- he's a big fan."

Tobias almost swallowed his tongue, and he was fairly sure Noah was laughing at him. "Home, boy. I think someone needs some reassurances."

5

Friday night had finally arrived. Lately, Noah felt like he lived for the weekends; he longed for uninterrupted time with Tobias, with his Master, in a safe space. And after the week they'd both had, Noah really needed all of those things. He needed to shake Phan from his mind.

He still felt possessive of Tobias, and he really didn't like it. He and Phan weren't just friendly, they were friends now. They'd talked through a lot of shit together, and Noah wanted to trust him. For that matter, Noah had been through hell this week himself -- a more acute kind of tension than the issues he and Tobias were working through together. Noah hadn't been able to concentrate on anything else all week as he tried to decide how best to handle Phan's current relationship with Tobias. He kept coming back to the idea that a friendship with Tobias' former lover wasn't terribly wise. Reluctantly, however, he had to admit that it was far too late to go down that road now. Phan needed him. He needed all of them.

As the car pulled up the little country lane that led to

the farm, Noah told himself it was time to let it go. Tobias wouldn't want him distracted by anything tonight. There would be plenty of time to talk things out in the safe room tomorrow. When the car came to a stop, he climbed out, tucking his duffel over his shoulder. He smiled up at Mrs. Miller, who was waving to him from behind the storm door where it was hopefully far warmer than it was outside, and climbed the front steps. She opened the door for him a crack and he pulled it open the rest of the way.

"Hello, Mrs. M." Noah smiled and kissed her on the cheek. He only saw her for brief moments these days, usually as she got into the car just after he got out. But she didn't look at all ready to leave the house. That worried him slightly. "Everything okay?"

"Just fine, darling boy," she said as she waved Jorge off. "Tobias had an emergency call and will be an hour or so. Robert will come get me in a bit." She smiled up at him. "Tea?"

"Oh. Oh, well that's a shame on the one hand, but on the other, tea with you sounds very nice, thank you." Someone must have been listening while he was hoping for a distraction. He set his bag down and closed the door against the chilly evening.

"Flatterer," she accused, still smiling. "All right then, come on through. Tell me, did you try the cooked pudding yet? It's tricky."

"It's very tricky. I burned it," Noah admitted, following Mrs. Miller's steps into the kitchen. "Allison shook her head at me."

Mrs. Miller tsked as she filled the kettle. "Nothing to shake her head at; sometimes pudding has a mind of its own. Still, something to treat him with one day." She reached for the big jar that Noah knew full well was stocked with chocolate chip cookies. "Make sure he deserves it before you try again, you hear me?" she teased.

"He's a good man, he deserves dessert," Noah said with a smile.

She rolled her eyes. "Of course he's a good man -- helped raise him up, didn't I? Doesn't mean he should get dessert just for being him." She pointed to the table with authority. "Sit. Tell me how you are, and how your week was, my darling. Eat cookies."

Noah sat as he was told. Far be it from him to disobey the one woman Tobias couldn't say no to, either. He picked up a cookie. It was only the subject matter that kept him from grinning. "Actually, it was a tough week," Noah found himself saying and then instantly regretted it. How he was going to explain it all to her, if he even should, he had no idea. "I've been looking forward to a weekend away from the city." He took a bite of his cookie. It was delicious; a piece of soft, gooey, chocolaty heaven.

"This is a good place to be, then," she said, pulling out a chair for herself. "Are you all right? Maybe you need a vacation."

Noah laughed softly. "Maybe so." He looked at her, deciding to be mostly honest and just hold back the details. "I'm fine. Phantom's been going through a rough time lately and with Tobias' help he's gotten into therapy. I'm just kind of hanging on the edges of that."

She looked at him for a long moment and finally sighed. "His parents again?" she asked, reaching for a cookie of her own.

Noah shrugged. "Well, I think it all comes back to his parents in the end, doesn't it? These cookies are delicious."

"Thank you. And, yes, with that boy it does." She sighed again and went to check the kettle. "It must be pretty bad for

Tobias to get involved again. Don't you let him neglect you, Noah. You're his partner now, not Phantom."

Noah smiled. "Oh, we had that discussion once already this week," he said, sighing. "I felt like an insecure puppy."

"Ah, but you are a pup." She grinned at him. "The trouble with Tobias is that he has a huge heart. He cares a great deal and has a very hard time letting go. But if you feel like you need more of him -- or for him to give less to Phan -- you just say so." She gave him a piercing look. "He loves you very much, and he won't want you hurting."

Noah looked at her for a long moment. She might be over eighty, but she was sharp, and she knew Tobias better than Tobias probably wanted her to know him. "I know he loves me. He's been very good about making sure I know it. And I wouldn't change that big heart of his for all the tea in China," he told her, with a nod toward the boiling water on the stove. "The truth is, whether I like it or not, Phan needs him right now. I don't want to make it harder on him. We'll work it out."

She smiled at him and nodded. "Just so. Your heart is just as big, my darling. Now. Tell me what I can do for our Phan, then. Cake or cookies? And don't tell me that he's not allowed sugar, because I'll have none of that."

"Cookies, then. Chocolate, for sure." Noah laughed softly. "He'll be thrilled."

She smiled and nodded again. "I'll make sure he gets them." She finished making the tea and brought it to the table. "What were you planning for supper tonight? Can I help?"

"I was planning on poaching that salmon I asked you to pick up for me, and some pasta," he said. "Shouldn't take much to put together, so I think I'm all right. Thank you, though." He waited for her to pour him some tea and then picked up his cup, blowing on it to cool it some before taking a sip. "So, tell me," Noah said, setting his cup down; it was still way too hot to drink. "How are *you*?"

She shrugged a shoulder. "Better than I have any right to be, really. Little slow, but I've earned the chance to take it easy. It's nice to have a clean home on Monday morning," she said with a wink.

Noah laughed. "I do my best; I know you're a tough critic."

She grinned. "Tell you a secret -- you keep the place better than I do. Drop by on a Wednesday and you'll see. Don't tell Tobias that, though; he needs a bit of fear in his life. That's my job."

"No!" Noah covered his ears. "Lalalala... I did not hear that," he said with a laugh. "Don't ruin my image of you as the perfectionist he thinks you are."

She laughed, sounding utterly delighted. "I admit I was stern with him when he was young. I had to be -- his mother, too. We had no idea what to do with the lad when he was a teen, and Robert wasn't any help. He came in here one day when Tobias was about seventeen and just stood there looking at me and Tobias' poor mother. Robert was almost thirty, then, mind you. 'Tobias' he said to us, 'Tobias is being... well, James should go home or they'll cause trauma to those horses.' Mary blushed red, and it was up to me to tell those boys to scat. Poor woman never did tell Tobias she knew."

Surely Tobias wouldn't approve of Mrs. M telling him stories about his teenage exploits, but then, even if he were here Tobias wouldn't have been able to stop her. Noah decided to encourage this line of conversation; it was fun. "He was a troublemaker? I should have guessed as much. He had to be a handful at seventeen, I can't even imagine. If he was half as stubborn then as he is now..."

"Oh, stubborn, yes," she agreed, taking another cookie. "But not a troublemaker. More... he had passion, and it could get away from him by times. He was always taking risks, pushing the line. He was never rude or mean -- he's a little too stiff for that. But he'd do things in inappropriate places, just to see what would happen. Like kissing James in the barn when he knew Robert would see. That was for James, and likely to get Robert's reaction as well."

Interesting. He could hardly believe who he was having this conversation with. "He says his parents didn't know," Noah said with a wink. "So I guess his mom knew, and Robert, of course... do you think his father had any idea?"

"Oh, yes, his mother knew," Mrs. Miller scoffed. "She just didn't know what to say, and he never said anything to her about it." She sipped her tea and grinned. "He's never said anything to me about it, for that matter, but I think it's fairly clear by now. Robert, he didn't get comfortable with the idea until after Phantom turned up. And Tobias' father... well, he might not have known at all."

"I hate to break it to you," Noah said and grinned at her, then dropped his voice to a stage whisper, "but Tobias and I are lovers." He laughed and picked up another cookie. "As if anyone could get anything past you."

She grinned at him. "You don't sleep in the guest room? I'm utterly horrified. Really, I am. I thought it was some kind of police program; send an officer to the country to exercise horses, cook, and clean for a cranky veterinarian."

He nearly choked as he swallowed his cookie. "I'm very good with the horses, I'll have you know." He gave her hand a pat. "Well, I'm glad his mother knew. I wonder if he'd like to know that." Noah shrugged.

"I have no idea," she said. "I've never really pushed the issue. How about your parents? Do they know about Tobias?"

"Well, not really." Noah sighed. "I mean, I told my mother, but she has her own special brand of denial. My sister Emily knows all about him, though. She's really happy for me."

Mrs. Miller returned the hand pat. "It can be hard for a family, I'm sure. Just live for you, darling. Life is too short to spend it pleasing too many people."

"Tobias is lucky to have you around, you know." Noah didn't see any reason to hide the rush of sentimentality he was feeling. "You're very sweet, Mrs. M. Thank you for being so kind to me, it's... it's made me feel very at home here."

She looked surprised for a moment and then smiled broadly. "Thank you, Noah. I'm glad you're happy -- he certainly is, and I can't tell you how nice that is to see. You're a good boy, I know. And you'd best get that dinner on now, Tobias will be tired when he gets in." She winked at him again and stood up. "I'll tell him I had the floors done yesterday, so you can have some free time this weekend."

"Thank you, ma'am," Noah said with a wink, realizing that she clearly knew more about the nature of his relationship with Tobias than she let on. He couldn't stop himself from blushing so he stood and took his cup to the sink to cover it. He took a deep skillet from the cabinet and then made his way to the fridge and pulled out the salmon.

"You have a good weekend," she said, still smiling. "Try not to get in trouble." And then she was gone, leaving him there to cook for Tobias. He heard her going upstairs, and he heard her laughing to herself as she gathered her things. Noah decided, grinning despite his embarrassment, that, for now, their conversation would just stay their little secret.

6

They were in the safe room. Saturday stretched out before them, the chores all done and both of them freshly showered. Tobias lay back on the bed, Noah naked between his legs with his head pillowed on Tobias' thigh.

"I'm serious," Tobias said, one hand ruffling Noah's hair. "Anything you want. Your call, pet. Tell me."

Noah thought about it for a bit. "Hmm... something raunchy." His voice sunk low in his chest. "Dirty-feeling. Useable, you know?" He drew a line down Tobias' leg with his finger. "Rent boy?"

Tobias swallowed. "How much? High or low?"

"One of those high priced, no limits boys," Noah said with a growl. "Boy to order."

"Anything I want?" He felt his cock twitch and start to fill.

"I said 'to order,' didn't I?" Noah's tone was playful. "Anything."

"Rough?" Okay, that was more than a twitch; his prick was filling rather quickly.

"Oh, yeah. This boy would love that. Rough, cocky, full-on struggle if you want one."

Tobias rolled over. "Right then. What do I wear?" He got off the bed and crossed to the cabinets. "Suggestions?"

"Well, you've got money..." Noah said with grin, rolling onto his stomach. "Rich, eccentric... Why does this sound so familiar?" he teased.

"Maybe for the same reason that 'rough, cocky, and high priced' does," Tobias said with a grin. "Okay, trousers and a linen shirt, then. I don't want to know what you're wearing. Um. I'm thinking the office, ordering in a nice little snack while I'm working late? Anything I should get from the stables?"

"Cuffs? Or will you be using your own brute force?" Noah grinned.

Tobias growled. "I think I can manage." He would, however, remove a few objects from the room so they wouldn't get broken. And possibly add a few in -- things he'd been unable to actually throw away but could stand to never see again. Like that horrid vase in the living room.

"The lube is in the little cabinet thing under the wall safe." Noah added, sliding off the bed. He was fairly hard himself.

"It is?" Tobias stared. He knew about the one in his desk, but he'd put that there himself.

"It is," Noah grinned. "We're well stocked in every room of the house."

"Poor Mrs. Miller," Tobias said mournfully. "Actually, that explains the looks the twins give me. They do the dusting."

Noah laughed. "What a way to get an education."

Tobias snorted as he finished dressing. "They know quite a lot, I think. All right, then; give me about twenty minutes before you come down, whore." He winked and backed out of the room, watching Noah's cock bob.

He ran down the stairs to his office and surveyed the area from the door for a moment before getting to work. The desk was fine as it was, and he made sure that the lube in the drawer was accessible; the last thing he wanted was to go fishing for it and come up with the stapler. He also retrieved the lube that Noah had stashed and slipped that tube in his pocket.

The large, overstuffed chair was also fine, but the side table was well over a hundred years old, so that got shifted to the living room and replaced with a replica he hadn't really cared for even when he bought it. A few of the finer objects were moved, as well, and, finally, with a glance at his watch, Tobias closed himself in his office and leaned on the desk to wait.

Noah gave him every second of the twenty minutes he'd asked for. He heard stirrings upstairs, finally, the sound of boots on the stairs, and moments later a knock on his closed office door.

"Dr. Vincent?" Noah's voice came through the door, and then another knock.

Tobias walked to the door, a detached look on his face, and pulled it open, ready to outclass any whore, no matter how much he was paying him. The detachment lasted all of the nanosecond it took to actually look at him. Noah wore button-fly jeans, low slung and riding on his hips, and the boots on his feet added at least an inch to his height. The black leather T-shirt was butter-soft, and the V-neck put Noah's silver collar nicely on display.

"Oh, my," Tobias said with appreciation, stepping back to let Noah in. "Truth in advertising at long last."

Noah rolled his eyes as he stepped into the room. He

surveyed the room critically and then turned and let his eyes wander over Tobias with the same interest. "Nice digs," he said, pushing a knickknack out of the way and seating himself on Tobias' desk. "You're taller than I thought you'd be." He crossed his legs and braced a hand behind him on the desk, leaning his weight on it.

"Does it matter?" Tobias asked, stepping close. He leaned in as if to kiss him, but instead swept the arm holding Noah up out from under him. As Noah's back hit the desk, Tobias glared at him. "Chairs are for sitting on. Not desks," he said icily.

"Doesn't matter to me how tall you are, it was just an observation." Noah answered with a snort. "You're paying -- you could be three feet tall and ugly as sin and I'd still be here. This is a very comfortable desk." Noah sat back up, catching Tobias in the groin with his knee just hard enough to get his attention as he did so. "Oops. Sorry about that."

A tight leather shirt wasn't the easiest thing to grab hold of, but Tobias found that if he really dug his fingers in as he lifted Noah off the desk he could manage it. He slammed Noah up against the nearest wall and held him there. "Are you?" he asked.

Noah blinked, quickly recovering the wind that was knocked from him. "Not really," Noah told him in a teasing tone and leaned forward to plant a heavy kiss on Tobias' lips.

Tobias shoved his tongue into Noah's mouth, taking control of the kiss and forcing Noah's mouth to open wider. He kissed Noah hard, pushing against his body with arms and chest, keeping Noah against the wall. "Whore," he growled, leaning back and licking his own lips.

Noah snorted. "Actually, I prefer 'Noah,'" he answered breathlessly. "But, like I said, you're paying." He struggled against Tobias' weight, giving him a taste of his own strength, something Tobias hadn't ever fully experienced. Noah's arms flexed hard and his chest expanded, but he had poor leverage and wasn't able to push Tobias away.

"You like it like this, doctor? A struggle? You like a boy that's strong enough to fight you off?" He grinned. "Fucking pervert."

"That's fucking deviant to you," Tobias corrected. "We're nowhere near the perverted part yet." He slid one hand up to Noah's hair and grasped as much as he could, pulling Noah's head back. "But we're getting closer." He licked Noah's neck, a deep sound rumbling in his chest. His cock throbbed, and he twisted so he could rub along Noah's hip.

With one hand now free, Noah braced it on Tobias' chest and gave him a sharp shove. "Or further," he suggested. Noah's hair was so short that Tobias couldn't keep hold of it and the "whore" skirted around him to the center of the room.

"Depends on your definition, I suppose," Tobias said with a grin. He stalked Noah for a step or two and then stopped as he undid his shirt cuffs and began to roll up his sleeves. "Your mouth was made to suck cock, whore. Not to talk."

"It's Noah. I think I told you already. And you're going to have to do a lot of convincing to get me to touch that thing," he teased, a bit coyly to add insult. "It's huge."

Tobias saw Noah discreetly glance around him, getting the lay of the place for his next move.

"I said 'whore.'" Tobias grinned and took a step forward. "I suggest you head to your right. I'll be pissed if you knock over the chair to the left."

"It is a nice chair, isn't it? Antique. Kind of like you."

Noah darted to his right, pushed the desk chair between them and sat his ass on the desk again.

"Experienced," Tobias countered, his voice like silk. He tugged the chair toward him and to the side, grinning as Noah instinctively moved to the other side. He remained where he was, holding the chair as Noah realized he'd been bluffed and quickly recovered. "Not prone to falling for... tricks," Tobias said carefully. He shoved the chair behind himself and reached out, snaring Noah's pant cuff as he tried to go over the desk. "And? Faster than you, whore." He pulled hard, dragging Noah back across the desktop and using his waistband for leverage. "Now, I believe I said that the chairs were for sitting?"

"Did you? I must not have been listening." Noah plucked at the fingers that held his waistband, trying to get them loose. He gave up on that and reached out a hand, pushing Tobias lightly against the bank of windows behind his desk, and peered up at him with a raised eyebrow. "Come on, old man, surely you can do better than this."

Tobias didn't even change expression as he tore Noah's pants open and grabbed his cock.

"Fuck!" Noah hissed, leaning forward to keep his balance. Tobias grinned as his boy went rigid under his fingers. "Not bad, old man," Noah said, a delightful strain in his voice that wasn't there a moment ago. "You think you can remember what to do with it?" Noah tugged Tobias' shirt out of his trousers and slid warm fingers underneath it, pinching a nipple when his fingers got that far. "I'll be happy to remind you."

Tobias had to grit his teeth to keep from reacting to the fingers. "Now you're giving it away? You're a slut as well as a whore, boy," he said, pulling on Noah's dick.

"That's fairly apt," Noah said as he unbuttoned Tobias'

shirt slowly. "I've some experience of my own." He teased the nipple with his fingers again, grinned up at Tobias, then leaned forward and bit it.

Tobias gasped, hating to do it but having to. He made another effort to pull Noah's hair, cursing as his fingers slipped. With a moan he held Noah's head to his chest and slid his thumb over the head of Noah's cock. Maybe they could just get off fast and then play.

Maybe he was just easy.

Noah slapped his hand away and ducked. "Now who's the slut? Huh? You rich pricks are all the same." He freed himself while Tobias was distracted and took two steps backward, making his way around the side of the desk again, his cock still pointing out of his jeans, taunting Tobias. "Come on, you horny bastard. You want me? You want to stuff that rod of yours in my mouth or up my ass? I don't care what you paid. I don't give it up that easy. You best believe you're going to have to work for it."

Tobias snorted. "Right," he said, walking around the desk and deliberately stalking Noah again, following him around the room relentlessly. "Wave another bill at you and ask nicely. You're a suck-slut. A come-hole. That's all." He let Noah put the easy chair between them and climbed up on the seat. "Like to be hit? Like to feel like you don't have a choice?"

Noah moved to the left and Tobias leapt after him, crashing them both to the floor. "Get your blood flowing?" Tobias asked, trying to climb on top of Noah. Damn boy wouldn't keep still, and Tobias was rather in danger of coming in his pants.

"That's all I am?" Noah spat as he struggled. He was trying to keep Tobias from getting hold of his wrists. "Then why the hell do you want me? Why is it so important to make me yours? Like to throw your weight around with your money, do you? Does it make you feel like a big shot? What's the matter, didn't get a big enough raise this year? Boss' cock bigger than yours?" Noah tried to roll to the side, but Tobias stopped him with his knee. "Get off me, you son of a bitch."

"Not a chance," Tobias said, his voice rough. He straddled Noah's hips and managed to pin one wrist. "That's it, wiggle some more. Feels good, whore." He fumbled for Noah's dick and found it still rigid. "I can tell you hate this."

Noah hooked his free hand around behind Tobias' neck and tugged hard, lifting himself a bit and pulling Tobias down into another heavy kiss. Tobias felt a hint of teeth on his lip.

Tobias answered it with a growl and met the fierceness with his own. The kiss was free of tenderness and wasn't even so much about power as it was about passion; he tasted blood by the end of it and didn't care whose it was.

He let go of Noah's cock and reached up, grabbing the other wrist with a triumphant cry. He pushed his tongue into Noah's mouth and brought both of Noah's wrists together on the floor above his head. "Now we can move on to perversion."

Noah gave him a good fight, tugging on his wrists and trying to get a knee up, but he was unsuccessful at both. "What are you paying for? You want me to beg for it? Or beg to be let go?" Noah asked with a soft growl. "I can do either, but between you and me I can smell your cock from here, and it's hurting for me, isn't it? Straining against your fly, your need making you lightheaded. Come on, old man, admit it."

"Admit what, whore?" Tobias ground down on him, dragged himself along Noah's exposed cock. "Admit I want to shove my dick into a hot hole and come? Sure. Doesn't everyone just want to get off?"

Noah grimaced at the friction. "Do you think your games are new to me, old man? Do you think you're going to hurt my feelings by calling me a whore? You're nothing more than a stiff prick with cash, buddy. Why don't you shut up already and do it? If you can."

Tobias laughed. "You think I care about your feelings one way or the other?" He rubbed again. "Not trying to hurt you. Don't care. Just want it the way I want it, and if I'm a prick with cash, you're a hole taking money to be filled, so just shut the fuck up, all right?" He grinned down at Noah and squeezed his boy's wrists a little. "You think I'm too old to take what I want?"

"I don't think you'd dare," Noah taunted.

Tobias glanced around and spotted what he needed. "You're not very bright, are you?" he asked mildly, leaning over to grab at a light cord, tugging the plug out of the wall. The lamp came tumbling down, the shade thumping on the floor as Tobias wound the cord around Noah's wrists. "Now be a good boy and don't break my lamp while I fuck you, okay?"

Noah looked genuinely shocked for a moment. Without waiting for an answer, Tobias crawled up Noah's body and lashed his wrists to the leg of the desk, his weight on Noah's chest as he did it. "And no biting."

Noah grunted. "Fuck off," he managed to gasp out. He tugged on his wrists, and with a wince he clearly decided that was a bad idea.

"Nope, just going to fuck," Tobias promised. He shifted down and lay on top of his play-whore, making sure he couldn't move. With one hand he held Noah's jaw and licked his neck again. "Tasty."

Noah's hips jerked, trying to throw Tobias off. He kicked one foot, but Tobias was too heavy. "Get off me," he growled. "Fucking pervert."

"Deviant. And how about I just get you off?" Tobias grinned at him. He bit down lightly on Noah's neck, just above his collar. "Ever have a trick suck you off and use your own junk as lube?"

Noah groaned, and Tobias could feel his cock jerk against his thigh. Noah's neck arched, his body betraying him, and Tobias' unwilling whore was suddenly not so unwilling anymore. "Have you always been this sick?" he managed to ask. Noah's voice was tight and husky.

"I think so," Tobias said thoughtfully. "Does it matter?" He moved down Noah's body a little and licked the leather shirt while his fingers found Noah's cock again, playing for only a moment before he shoved the jeans down to Noah's knees. "There. Can't run, can't kick. Well, not effectively."

"You're big as a fucking bear. I wasn't having much luck with kicking anyway," Noah snarled, arching a bit as if he could escape Tobias' hand.

"Aw, thank you. Flattery will get you off. Eventually." Tobias wrapped one hand around Noah's cock and pulled. "So. Is your mouth good at anything aside from back talk, or should I just use your ass? A smart tongue is nice and all, but a tight ass is a treat. Both, whore? Would that do it for you? I bet you'd love that, get cock rammed in you from both ends at once, make you feel like you're really being used to your full potential?"

"Ah... fuck. Asshole," Noah breathed. He flexed his fingers and then clenched them into fists.

"Fuck your asshole?" Tobias studied Noah for a moment. "Damn, tied you wrong for that, hang on." He jerked on the far end of the cord and Noah's bound wrists came free of the desk for as long as it took for Tobias to flip Noah over, his knees in so his ass was in the air. A flip of the cord, and there he was, unbalanced and struggling to right himself as Tobias watched.

"Very nice," Tobias said, slapping one cheek and pushing a dry fingertip into Noah's ass. "Should do you dry."

"Jesus... fuck," Noah growled, still fighting to keep himself upright. He finally settled, panting, and looked over his shoulder. "Don't." His voice had the lovely lilt of begging to it. "Please."

Tobias tilted his head and pushed two fingers into Noah's ass, going deep. "Don't? Are you sure?" He thrust his fingers a little and undid the button on his trousers with the other hand.

Noah hissed and scooted forward, trying to escape the intrusion, but somehow that must have only made matters worse for the poor thing, because he froze and groaned heavily. "Oh, God."

Tobias got his zipper down and fished the lube out of his pocket. No way would he actually hurt Noah -- but he would happily create an illusion. "Something to say, whore? You seem to have changed your tune a little." He twisted his fingers.

"Back off!" Noah spat over his shoulder at him. The words were very convincing. It was almost scary the way Noah could throw himself into a role. Noah, the whore, tried to stifle a moan by biting his lip, but Tobias wasn't fooled.

"No," Tobias said coldly, stabbing his fingers into Noah. He was fairly sure that Noah's cry covered the sound of the lube cap. He slicked himself generously and tossed the lube aside, twisting his fingers in Noah again. "Dry, whore. Going to just shove my cock in you and take you dry."

"No!" Noah begged. He twisted to look at Tobias. "No, please, no..."

The look in Noah's eyes seemed so sincere, but there was no safeword among the words with which he begged so prettily, and Tobias knew them to be only play. "Oh, yes," Tobias promised. He moved closer, right behind Noah, and took a breath. "Oh, yes, my whore, my slut. You know I will." He pulled his fingers out and grabbed his cock, lining up and pushing in as quickly as he dared.

Noah writhed and cried out. He tugged on his wrists and tried to shove Tobias off with his body, but he was well restrained and gave up quickly. "Bastard!" He dropped his head over his arms and panted heavily.

"Pervert, at this point," Tobias corrected. "Oh, God." He'd been so intent on getting Noah in the right mindset that he hadn't really prepared himself for the sensation. Noah was tighter than usual, and with less lube the friction was more intense. "Jesus, you feel good." He thrust experimentally.

Noah moved a bit on him and moaned. "So fucking huge," he said, panting. Tobias could feel him tense a bit, relax, and then tense again, already so close.

"Gonna fill you, whore," Tobias growled, trying to push the fantasy to the end. "Come-hole. Made to take my cock, made to be my fuck toy." He rammed into Noah's ass and reached around to stroke Noah's cock. He found it leaking an almost constant stream onto the floor. "All primed, slut," he murmured, thrusting deep again.

"Jesus. Oh, God, all right, you win! I'll be your whore, your fucking hole. Fine, anything... just don't... don't stop." Noah slipped visibly into the early stages of his climax, arching back to take Tobias deep, grunting and starting to tremble. "Good. Oh, God, so good..."

Grunting, Tobias pulled out completely, leaving Noah to cry out for an instant before slamming back in, going deep.

"Again, again!" Noah screamed.

Tobias did it again, waiting until Noah was moaning from feeling empty before pounding into him. "Take it," he groaned. "Take my cock." The third time he pulled out, he shoved a finger in along with his cock.

Noah shouted, and his hips started to jerk as he finally came, shooting his musk-scented spunk all over the study floor. He tightened around Tobias like a vice. "Oh, fuck, yes, yes!"

Tobias would have shouted his agreement, but he could barely breathe. He rocked steadily through Noah's orgasm, letting it milk his cock, letting Noah's ass massage his dick until he came hard enough that he saw spots. "Oh, God," he finally managed to say, trying not to fall onto Noah's back. "Jesus Christ."

Noah groaned and collapsed over his own knees, panting harshly. It was a couple of minutes before he was able to speak, and the first words out of his mouth were about his fingers. "Sir... lamp cord..." he grunted.

Tobias swore and pulled out, falling to the side as he reached for the cord. "Damn it!" He tugged and Noah's hands came away from the desk, and in another moment he had them free and was massaging the wrists. "Move your fingers for me," he demanded. There wasn't much discoloration, but he'd get the arnica in a moment and some ice. "Are your fingers numb?"

Noah moved them. "They're fine. I'm fine." He leaned into Tobias and gave him a reassuring smile. "They were just now starting to go numb. I'd have used my words if I needed to, I promise. I'm fine." Noah leaned up and kissed him, and Tobias could feel Noah's heart pounding in his chest.

"Okay. We'll take care of it anyway, though." Tobias kissed him back, adrenaline racing. "God, that was good," he breathed. "Better than I thought it would be."

"Fucking hot." Noah grinned. "You're a dirty old pervert. I, of course, had no idea I was such a slut." He winked.

Tobias laughed. "I did. From the first moment, I knew. My slut."

"Yes, sir. Your slut, your whore, whatever you want to call me, I'll answer to it." He was grinning broadly.

"Good." Tobias grinned back at him. "Let's start with 'pet,' and add on 'clean this up after I see to your wrists,' shall we?"

Noah glanced around at the wrecked office so smugly it almost made Tobias laugh. "Yes, sir."

"Yeah, yeah, you did good." Tobias kissed him again and slapped his ass. "I think that's a keeper, boy. And the shirt is yours." Boy, was it his. Tobias smiled and took one more kiss from his slut before finally getting up and going for ice.

He didn't even care if the lamp was broken.

7

This week, Noah had added "fatten up Phan" to his list of things to do. Tonight was comfort food -- grilled cheese, fries, and chocolate milkshakes for dessert. How much really got eaten remained to be seen, but he had a plan. He'd talked to Bradford earlier in the day, just to touch base and make sure it was okay for them to get together, and Bradford told him nothing was going to stop Phan from visiting; he'd been talking about it for a full day. Bradford did ask that Noah try to keep his tone respectful, that Phan was still getting used to curbing his speech again. Easy enough to do.

The doorbell sent Noah jogging to answer it.

"Hello," he said, smiling at Phan as he opened the door.

"Hi," Phan said, his smile almost shy. The smile made Noah realize he'd actually missed Phan of late. "Um. Brought flavored water this time. Bradford said that whatever you had would take care of the caffeine, and he wants me sensible in the morning." The smile widened. "This stuff is loaded with sugar."

Noah grinned. "You're a nut. Come in. Give me your coat. There's comfort food in the kitchen."

Phan tugged his battered leather coat off and passed it over as he moved past Noah in the hall. "Comfort? You mean like popcorn and chocolate? Mac and cheese?"

"Grilled cheese and fries." Noah hung up his coat and herded him along. "And chocolate for dessert." He stopped in the middle of the kitchen and gave Phan a hug. "It's so good to see you. You look great."

Phan hugged him back, his head resting on Noah's shoulder for a moment. "I look like hell," he corrected. "But that's okay. Not a worry, anyway. Thanks for letting me come back."

"Well, okay," Noah conceded, "You do look better than I expected, though. And don't be stupid, you know I like these visits. Sit."

With a snort Phan said, "Yes, sir," and plopped himself into his chair. "Oh, yum. Masses of trans-fats. Yay!"

"Just the thing to put a positive spin on the evening, don't you think?" Noah laughed, and served fries. "So how is Master Bradford?"

"Scary."

"Scary?" Noah raised an eyebrow and sat. "Scary how?"

"Scary the way only a man on a mission can be. He's really intense, Noah. Or maybe I'm just out of practice." Phan reached for a fry. "That's probably it. It's been a while since I had so many rules. He glares."

Noah laughed. "Yeah, he does. And he doesn't budge at all. If he wants you still and you twitch a finger, you're in the doghouse. I remember that about him."

"He sighs a lot, too." Phan grinned and grabbed another fry. "That's worse. That whole 'you aren't paying attention again, Phantom, and you know what that means...' thing. I think he actually has three sighs."

"Oh? What are they?" Noah was genuinely interested. He took a big bite of his sandwich and watched Phan.

Phan looked thoughtful as he chewed, and as soon as he'd swallowed he reached for the water bottle he'd brought. The label said it was raspberry, and it hissed when the top was loosened, the bubbles suddenly active. With a weary sigh, Phan poured a glass. "That's the 'I've told you three times' sigh. It gets followed by 'Phantom. Corner.'"

He winked and drank, then set the glass down carefully. He gave a barely audible sigh and shook his head. "That's the 'Okay, enough for now, you can expect two more strokes' sigh. The last one, though, I hear all the damn time. It's loud and obvious and so put on it makes me cringe."

Noah chuckled and leaned forward to pour himself some as well. "What? What is it?" He was grinning.

"Oh, roughly?" Phan grinned back and then put on a glower. "It means 'Phantom, you are a very naughty boy and I know you can learn, but God didn't have enough patience in his bag to make anyone deal with the kind of shit you give me, so I think I'll just stare at you until you figure out what you've done wrong, apologize, correct the error, and swear to never ever do it again. And then you may push your nose into the carpet 'cause I'm gonna spank your ass in a not fun way.' But just roughly."

Noah covered his mouth. Maybe he shouldn't laugh at that? Except it was hilarious, and he couldn't hold it back. He let himself laugh out loud, leaning back in his chair. "Oh... oh, my side hurts..." he said finally with a gasp. "Oh, Phan, you really are out of practice, aren't you?" His laughter didn't fade one bit.

"I'm almost hopeless," Phan said, giggling madly and

reaching for his sandwich. "But I got three less spankings today than I did yesterday."

The fact that Phan was glad to receive fewer spankings wasn't at all lost on Noah. "Well, that's a start." He was still giggling. "How many total did you get today?"

"Fifteen."

Noah winced. "Damn."

"Uh-huh. Told you he was scary."

"I think the highest number of punishment strokes Sir has ever given me was six? Maybe seven." And Noah had found that to be quite enough, thank you.

"Master Tobias and Master Bradford are... different," Phan said thoughtfully. "Not that one is necessarily a better Dom, but their methods and attitudes about things are their own. And I'm not used to having so many rules. It's been years since I've been under 24/7."

"Even I don't do that... " Noah acknowledged but quickly added, "Yet," with a grin.

Phan grinned back at him and lifted his glass. "Yet," he agreed with a nod. "How are things, anyway? I haven't talked to Sir at all. Has he calmed down any?"

Noah nodded sagely. "Oh, yes, we took care of his tension over the weekend. I suggested a rent boy that liked it rough and let him tie me up with a lamp cord and fuck me." He grinned. That had been so fucking hot. Tobias had been positively animalistic. Noah sighed wistfully. "It was great."

Phan winked. "He does like restraints."

"No restraints. He chased me around his office, called me raunchy names like 'whore' and 'come-hole,' and then forced himself on me. In-scene of course. Tied me up with the cord on that blue porcelain lamp. Jesus, I'm getting hard just thinking about it." That wasn't a lie.

Phan choked on his sandwich. "He what? Jesus Christ,

Noah. Warn me before you say shit like that!" He reached for the water, still coughing. "You're serious?"

Noah blinked at him. "Of course I'm serious. It was just a scene, Phan, he didn't actually hurt me. A couple of bruises, no big deal."

"But he doesn't do that! Well, not that I could ever get him to do, anyway. Not rough like that -- I mean a hard fuck, sure, but nothing like force." Phan looked at him with something like awe on his face. "Damn, you lucky bastard. And thanks, now I've got wood. Prick."

Noah couldn't help the swell of smug pride he felt. Tobias hadn't done that with Phan, even though Phan had apparently asked for it. It probably shouldn't matter to him, but it did. "He loved it. Took him a minute to warm up, but once he was there he was so into it. I am a lucky bastard aren't I?" Noah snickered and munched on a fry.

"Uh-huh. And he really... did he...?" Phan swallowed, apparently forgetting his food. This was becoming a theme, although the flushed skin was new. "Did he really chase you and call you names? Did he... um. Did he pin you down and threaten you?"

Noah nodded, giving up on fighting the rigid presence resting on his thigh. "Knocked over a chair and an end table, swept half the shit off his desk, knocked me to the floor with his weight and pinned me. It was so hot, Phan. He kissed me so hard my lip bled." He was a little breathless after that description, and he reached for his drink.

Phan moaned, his tongue darting out to lick his lower lip. "Oh, man. And you could fight back? You tried, right? I mean, it was a struggle?" He was shifting in his chair.

"I tried to fight back. I'm pretty strong, but he's heavy, you know? We definitely struggled. I got away from him a couple of times, but once he got me on the floor I knew I'd lost, he's just too big. He got the cord around my hands, lashed me to the leg of his desk, and shackled me with my jeans." Noah swallowed, remembering, the words pouring from him completely uncensored. "He fucking skewered me. Just drove in over and over... and then he did this thing, where he pulled all the way out you know? And then slammed back in again? I came so hard I was dizzy."

"Excuse me." Phan carefully stood up, his erection obvious. "I'll be in the bathroom for a moment. Bastard."

Noah blinked as Phan left the room, still half inside the memory himself. He was surprised, shocked actually, to find himself resisting a strong urge to call him back. To blow Phan right there in his kitchen. It took every ounce of his restraint not to chase after him. He thought about how he'd laughed off Dr. Brewer's warning that awful night, about how Phan, unable or unwilling to speak for himself, had asked her to make sure Noah understood the extent of the attraction Phan had for him, and to tell him that he should, please, politely ignore it if Phan got hard while they were together.

He looked out the kitchen door again in the direction of the bathroom, confused by his still-present urge to follow Bradford's boy. Tobias hadn't given them any such permission, and the last thing he wanted to do was be a hypocrite. So he watched Phan go, and then went and stood, absurdly, in front of the open freezer. Jesus. He had to admit that the rough evening in Tobias' office sounded even hotter when he talked about it than it had actually been, if that was possible.

It really didn't seem that long before Phan came back; Noah was still standing, staring at ice cream and frozen ground beef, the freezer only just starting to work for him. Warm arms slid around his waist, and Phan held him from behind. "God," he said, his voice muffled in Noah's back. "That's the hottest thing I've heard in a long, long time, Noah. Almost shot in my jeans, and that just doesn't happen to me."

Noah bit his lip to keep from moaning. "First time for everything?" he offered, suddenly lightheaded. He put a hand on the freezer door to keep from leaning his weight into Phan. Phan smelled good, like sweat and a little musk. A healthy man-smell. "I, uh..." He cleared his throat and tried again. "Want a, uh, a milkshake or something?" he asked, still staring into the freezer.

"Sure." Phan's hand rubbed a circle on his belly. "What do you want?" There was definitely an offer in the tone, but a certain amount of wariness as well, like a tentative pass, if there was such a thing.

God, what didn't he want right then? Phan was warm and right there, and he was so hot when he was on his knees. Noah took a deep breath and exhaled heavily. Then he took Phan's hand in his and gently stepped out of his arms. "I can't, Phan," he said, with a soft smile, looking into Phan's eyes. "But, thank you."

He got a sad smile and a nod. "Yeah. Maybe some other time." Phan turned and went to the cupboards, opening doors until he found the tall glasses. "I'll make the milkshakes. You go ahead."

Noah didn't stick around long, grateful that they could be adult about this. He did give Phan a kiss on the cheek before disappearing into his tiny bathroom. He closed the door and leaned against it, knowing he'd made a good decision but feeling like an asshole for it all the same.

He unbuttoned his jeans, spread his feet wider, and wrapped his fingers around his cock. Phan's offer had seemed completely genuine. Not like a regression thing, or a bid for his attention. There hadn't been any kind of mischief in it or a desire to go behind anyone's back; he was making an affectionate gesture, and a sweet one at that. Noah imagined Phan's mouth, remembering it from New Year's Eve, and was moaning in mere moments. He wasn't sure if this might be a betrayal too, hiding in his bathroom fantasizing about something he shouldn't but could have had.

In his mind, Phan was on his knees, and he was grunting as Noah shoved his cock down his throat. Phan's fingers dug into his ass. "Oh, yeah," he said out loud, though he hadn't meant to. "Fuck, yes." He was already on the edge, brought there by Phan's fingers on his belly. "Oh! Phan!" He grunted and shot, soaking his fingers and the edge of the sink.

He blinked his eyes open, panting, and a little panicked. Quickly, he cleaned himself up and then the bathroom, washed his hands, buttoned up his fly, and splashed his face with cold water. By the time he made it back to the kitchen, Phan had what looked like masterpieces on the table.

"Oh, my God."

"Rich and creamy, and you're now out of chocolate sauce," Phan said, beaming. "I'm gonna be bouncing all the way back to Master's with this much sweet stuff." He picked up one of the glasses and peered at Noah. "You okay?"

"Uh, yeah," Noah said, not actually sure if it was the truth. "A little embarrassed. This looks great." He took a seat and dug in, hoping to God that Phan would change the subject.

Phan winked and picked up a spoon. "Too thick for a straw. And don't be embarrassed -- it was damn hot. Hell, tell Tobias you got off on it again. He'd get a kick out of it, maybe." He winked again and started licking his milkshake off the spoon.

Noah had gotten hard off it, but he'd gotten off on Phan. He kept his eyes on his milkshake and sucked another bite off his spoon. "Maybe," he said. "So, uh, are you and Master Bradford... you know...?" Why had he asked that? Sex was the last thing he wanted to be talking about right now. He worked on his milkshake and didn't meet Phan's eyes.

"God, no!" Phan laughed for a moment. "Not that I wouldn't, but we're not like that. He lets me get off sometimes, though, which is new. All of it's new, I guess. But at least I can react to the spanking now, and not fight on so many fronts at once."

"That's good, right? I mean you're a sub, you should be allowed to, you know, get off on what subs get off on." Noah grinned. "You think it's better for you now? I mean now that you have structure? Do you think it's helping, or is it too soon to know yet?" Noah stuck his straw in and sucked in until his cheeks were hollow, but the shake was still too thick. "Damn, this is a good milkshake."

"Ah, come on, you can suck that up," Phan teased. "I know you can." He laughed and spooned more of his own into his mouth. "I'm not sure if it's too soon or not. I mean, I'm getting a sore ass, so I'm not in the right headspace; things aren't clicking on that level yet. But it's good, you know? I'm getting a routine, and I get to serve. So that's helping, anyway." He paused and looked at Noah with a wince. "I was pretty messed up, huh?"

Noah looked up at Phan thoughtfully. "Yeah," he said gently. "But you'll get past it, Phan, I know you can. And it's going to be so much better when you do. Bradford -- *Master* Bradford... " Noah caught himself, remembering Bradford's request that he show a sub's respect, "is every bit as skilled as Sir is. They have different styles, but they're both very experienced. I was pretty fucked up, too, when I first came to the club, after David and all, and Master Bradford was very helpful for me."

"Oh, Master is a help, that's for sure. And the fact that he's even taken me on after all I've put him through means I'll be grateful forever. I hope that someday I'll be able to show both of them how much I value what they've done. Sir especially." Phan looked down quickly and grabbed his straw. "Time to suck."

Noah knew it was a deliberate distraction; that Phan was closing at least part of the conversation for the time being; but, still, it was hard not to admire the man's technique as he started sucking the milkshake up the straw. It looked like it was taking a certain effort.

He decided it was best to let it go for now. He wasn't a therapist, he was a friend, and it wasn't his job to push.

He also thought it best not admire Phan's technique any further.

He stirred his milkshake up one more time and then made another effort to suck the frozen concoction up through the straw. He managed it this time, and once he got a mouthful he looked up with a grin. "B movies and a cuddle?" he asked, picking up his glass.

"Yes, please." Phan followed him into the living room with his own glass and sat on the couch with his legs tucked up under him. "If I fall asleep just poke me. I have to be back by ten-thirty or Master will be pissed. And, frankly, I don't think I want another spanking today."

"I'll poke you if I'm awake myself," Noah teased. He settled himself on the couch as well, handed Phan the remote, and sucked on his milkshake. A curfew was good; it meant that Bradford would be waiting up for him. Besides, Noah expected that Tobias would keep with tradition and call by then as well. "Maybe you should pick something we can stay awake watching."

Phan giggled. "My default is porn, and that's just not a good idea for us. Maybe something with explosions? Or a complicated plot? 'Gosford Park'?" He sucked on his milkshake until his cheeks hollowed again and set it aside. "Cuddle?" He looked like a little boy when he asked, all eyes and winsome smile.

"I fell asleep watching 'Gosford Park' the first time," Noah admitted. Tobias hadn't been happy with him. "Come here." Noah laughed softly and held his arms out. "Do you do that adorable, boyish thing on purpose, or are you really just that cute?"

"I am just this cute," Phan assured him seriously. He wiggled and squirmed until Noah was about ready to bash him, but then all at once he settled and sighed happily. "Thanks. I've been looking forward to this. Master just isn't a snuggler."

"I wonder if he snuggles with Nikki. I mean, I assume they're sleeping together, right? I can't imagine Nikki not being a cuddler. Not that I want too much detail on his sex life but... doesn't Nikki seem pretty tactile to you?" He'd been curious about that relationship for a long time now, and now that Phan was living there, Noah wondered if he might have some insight.

"Nikki's a screamer," Phan said succinctly. "And probably too dead tired to do more than sleep when Master's done with him."

Noah laughed out loud. "The more I learn about that kid, the more I like him. Comfy?" Noah tucked his arms tighter around Phan and looked at the TV.

"Uh-huh. And Nikki is in total awe of you, you know? Mind, he'd give a body part to play with Sir. You, he likes to look at -- thinks your submission at your collaring was a thing of beauty. And he's right, of course. But Sir made him come in his pants the night he fucked you outside the Domino."

"Oh, my God, the Domino," Noah groaned just thinking about it. "Holy shit, that was incredible. What a night."

"I think that's what everyone says," Phan teased. "But we're doing it again, kiddo. I'm not supposed to be spending all my time with you talking about you and Sir. I'm supposed to be watching movies, cuddling, and being... well, with you. Because you're you and I like you."

"There's not much of me to talk about if it doesn't include Sir," Noah said softly. "I like you, too." Noah kissed him on the top of his head. "I believe I am supposed to be giving you a place to vent without worrying about breaking any rules. Wasn't that how this started? As part of your therapy?"

Phan snuggled in a little more. "Yeah. And now there are just so many rules to break..." He sighed softly. "Sir never had so many."

"Maybe he did, but it's just more work now than it was then, so it seems like more?" Noah asked, noting that Phan sounded sleepy. Well, if he wanted a nap, Noah wasn't about to stop him.

"Maybe. Maybe it's 'cause all my new rules are about the house and not about the other stuff." Phan looked up at him and blinked slowly. "You're warm. Did you know that getting the bath temperature wrong is a spanking offense? And that Master knows precisely how long it takes to let the water cool to just the wrong side of the allowed temperature?"

"You're kidding me. That's just... anal retentive." Noah snorted and grinned. "He lets it cool on purpose?"

"Oh, yeah. Well, no. But maybe. I get it right now. And a

bunch of other things. Actually, I think he hates the rules as much as I do, but it's working. Slowly, but it is. It gives me something to focus on." Phan yawned and pressed closer, his head buried in Noah's chest. "Aside from your fine bod, of course."

"You're really trying to get me in trouble aren't you?" Noah smiled, petting Phan's hair. "I'll make sure you're awake in time," he promised, coaxing Phan to sleep. He picked up the remote and flipped the channels.

He thought Phan might have mumbled something, but as it ended in a soft huffing snore, maybe not.

8

Tobias watched Noah carefully on Friday night. He knew that he'd been far too emotional himself to meet all of Noah's needs since the night Phan had crashed, but things appeared to be leveling out a bit. He was concerned for Phan, of course, but he'd meant it when he said Noah was his priority.

And now, with Phan safely under Bradford's direction as well as his care, Tobias could move past his emotions and begin to repair whatever damage he'd done to his relationship with Noah. He'd thought long and hard about where to start, and when he'd talked to Noah after his visit with Phan, Tobias had reached the inevitable conclusion that everything had to start with truth, from them both.

After supper was done and put away, he gestured for Noah to follow him and went upstairs to the safe room. "Affirmation, pet," he said softly as they walked into the room. "On the bed so we're comfortable -- this could take a while."

He took off his shirt but left his trousers on and had Noah strip to nothing but his collar and rings. Tobias thought Noah was rarely more beautiful than like this, wearing the symbols of his status. Smiling, he sat and opened his arms, drawing Noah near and holding him tight with his own legs and arms until their breathing was steady and measured and he felt Noah relax against him.

"Is there anything you want to talk to me about?" Tobias asked softly. "Anything at all, pet. Tell me, please." It was a leading question; Tobias knew exactly what Noah wanted to talk about.

Noah seemed to think about it a bit before answering. "Yes, sir. I think maybe we should talk about Phan, sir. I've been wondering if his visits with me are a good idea after all." Noah leaned his head back on Tobias' shoulder. "Tuesday was... nice mostly, but it was a little awkward, too."

Tobias nodded, more to himself than to Noah. When they'd spoken on the phone after Phan had gone home, Tobias had thought Noah was a little flustered, but he hadn't pushed to find out why. Some things were better left to process and talk about in person. "What happened?" he asked gently.

Noah sighed. "We were talking about you, and I told him about our session in your office last weekend. Maybe I shouldn't have, but he asks about you all the time and what we're up to, and I didn't see any harm in telling him about something I thought was really amazing. Anyway, he ended up hard and I ended up hard... he excused himself to the bathroom, which was fine and when he came back he..." Noah's voice trailed off. "God, I felt like such a jerk."

Tobias found himself blinking, unsure of what exactly to say -- unsure of what he felt, if he was honest with himself. "Did you have sex with him?" he asked, trying to keep his voice neutral.

"Oh, no. No, sir," Noah answered quickly along with a

shake his head. "But he offered. He definitely offered. I told him I couldn't, and I sort of escaped."

Interesting.

"And how did Phan take that?" he asked, not particularly bothered by Phan propositioning Noah -- they'd all known it would happen. What intrigued him was Noah's reaction.

"I'm not sure. He looked disappointed but like he understood. He said 'maybe next time' and kind of smiled at me. I actually think he... well, I think he took it better than I did. Which is what I wanted to talk about." Noah sighed again. He seemed a little edgy, not as relaxed as he had been a few moments ago.

"Okay," Tobias said slowly. He had a fairly good idea where the conversation was going now; he knew his boy well, and he'd watched Noah and Phan together. "I'm... well, why don't you tell me and we'll go from there, sweetheart."

Noah didn't blurt it out in a rush, he took his time with his confession, speaking thoughtfully, and sounding less worried about Tobias' reaction than just disappointed in himself. "He touched me," Noah told him. "He ran his hand over my stomach and hugged me from behind, and then I turned him down. But when I was finally alone I couldn't stop thinking about him. I... fantasized about him while I jerked off." Noah hugged Tobias' arms to his chest. "I'm sorry, sir."

"For what?" Tobias asked, honestly curious. "You were horny. He was there and offering, and it's not like you don't like him. It's not like you've never had sex with him before. None of us has ever pretended that you two aren't attracted to each other." Tobias thought for a moment, his hands rubbing at Noah's arms. "Would you have felt guilty if I'd been there, or if I'd given you permission?"

"No, if you'd been there I'd have followed your lead. But

the point is that I didn't have your permission and you weren't there. I wanted to take him up on his offer, sir. That's what I feel guilty about. He's working so hard, and I'm supposed to be supporting him, not fantasizing about him. I'm worried that if he hadn't taken it so well, if he'd pushed..." Noah sighed heavily. "I don't know what I would have done. I don't trust myself around him anymore."

"Ah." Tobias worried at that for a moment. "I'm... I'm really not sure what to say," he finally admitted. "Do you want to stop seeing him?"

"No, I want to get my damn self-control back," Noah said stubbornly. "I like spending time with him, and he needs to get away from Master Bradford once in a while, you know? I just... don't want to do something that won't be good for him."

"Okay," Tobias said. "As I see it, I can let this go one of two ways. But I admit that I'm reluctant to... well, to call it as I see it, frankly. Noah, you're my priority, but I don't think you really feel that at the moment, which is my fault, I know. But if I start talking about what's best for Phan, I feel like I'm not talking about what's best for *you*. Does that make sense? If you feel like what's best for him isn't good for you, then I can't encourage you to keep going."

Noah nodded. He seemed to need a moment to process that. "I don't actually know if I feel that I'm your priority right now or not, sir, but that's not entirely your fault. I've been pretty focused on Phan, too, you know?" Noah shifted slightly. "So, why don't you tell me what you think is best for him, and then we'll talk about whether or not it's good for me. As two separate things. Does that work?"

Tobias laughed softly. "I don't know if it will, sweetheart. What's best for Phan at this point might be something you're just not comfortable with me even thinking about. Once it's said, it's out there and has to be dealt with."

Noah leaned into Tobias a bit more heavily, and his sigh sounded worried. "Well. Then I guess you need to decide if you should say it or not, sir. I trust you to know what's best."

Tobias rolled his eyes. So much trust. "I want you to do what feels right at any given moment, pet," he said finally. "Not what feels good, but right. If that means that Phan is needy and clinging and you think it's right to hold him, then do it. If you feel like he's hitting on you because it's a defense against something else, then turn him down. And if you feel like you're getting lost in it all, being forgotten in his pain, then send him away."

"I don't feel lost, sir. I've never felt that way," Noah's tone was cautious. "I do wonder sometimes if he's more turned on by you, or well, by stories about you, than he is by me, though. And that I happen to be there, you know? The whole story I told him about you chasing me around your office -- he kept asking questions about exactly what you were doing to me. I felt a little like he was trying to put himself in my shoes. That was part of what had me concerned."

"That could be," Tobias said, considering it. "I don't know, to tell you the truth. He wanted that, so maybe he was. But he also likes to watch, and he's more than a little attracted to you. You could ask him?"

"I don't know how to bring it up." Noah snorted. "Hey, Phan, are you getting off on me or Sir when I tell you these stories?" He sighed. "Doesn't sound very good."

"So stop talking about me," Tobias suggested. "Or at least about sex with me."

"If you think I should, I will, but he'll ask me why. You're the first person he asks about usually."

"He seems a little... fixated," Tobias said. "I'll mention it to Bradford." He took a breath and decided to trust in Noah's ability to know himself a little longer. With a sense of throwing a lamb to the lions, or perhaps of opening Pandora's box, he said, "Now. Tell me the utter truth, sweetheart. If I gave you blanket permission to do as you wanted with him, what would you do? What would you think and feel?"

Noah was silent for a long while. He shook his head slowly, then finally shrugged. "I don't know. I think it would depend on the moment. This past Tuesday, I'd have still said no. Another day, different reasons, different situation? I really have no idea. He likes comfort from me. He likes me to hold him tightly and let him just be. You know? I could see it happening as an extension of that, the comforting thing, if I thought he needed me. But I'm not sure I could get completely past the idea that I would be betraying you. I'm not sure I could do it and not feel guilty anyway. I know I'd have to tell you about it, talk it out, see if you thought I made the right decision." Noah cleared his throat. "God, it's so complicated."

"That's what I'm getting at, sweetheart," Tobias whispered. "What might be best for him isn't what's right for you. I want what's best for you. Period. Okay? And that's why I'm not going to give you that permission. You can tell him I said no, and that'll be the end of the conversation. Outside of a scene, you may not have sex with Phantom. Clear?"

Noah nodded. "Yes, sir." He seemed greatly relieved, and let out a long sigh before he settled more comfortably into Tobias arms. "Understood, sir. God, that's so much easier."

Tobias nodded and kissed the top of Noah's head. "You're comfortable still seeing him, with that in place?

Because I can talk to Bradford, set something else up. Brian, maybe, or even Nikki."

"I'm fine with it. This is much easier on me, sir. If it's you saying no and not just me saying it, he won't question it, and I won't have to feel bad about turning him down. It solves my own control issues, too. Thank you, sir."

"Self-control, yes," Tobias said. "But it doesn't take away the fact that you want him. Do you want to talk about that?"

"I wanted him then. I don't always. Mostly, I think of him as a friend. But he's so... sexual. He's graceful and fluid, he just... sexy. It's hard not to want him sometimes. I can't imagine I'm alone in feeling that way."

Again, Tobias laughed. "Oh, no. You're not alone. In fact, I think Bradford is one of the few to remain unaffected -- I'd ask him his secret, but I'm not sure I want it to stop. It's almost... fun, wanting Phan when he's trying hard."

"He knows, too. He knows exactly what effect he has on people. He's very clever that way."

"It's what he was taught," Tobias said, fighting the wave of anger that always threatened to overwhelm him when he thought about what Phan was forced to endure as a child. "But after a while one can learn when he's merely playing and when he's hiding behind his sexuality. He's very skilled at manipulating, but a big part of him wants to be caught at it so he can stop. Do you think he was being manipulative when he came on to you, or was he just wanting to take advantage of the opportunity?"

"Honestly? It felt like he just wanted to make me feel good. I actually think it was very genuine. It's possible he was manipulating me and I didn't see it, but no warning bells went off."

Tobias shook his head. "I wouldn't worry about it then,

pet." He stroked Noah's arms again and hugged him a little tighter. "Anything else you wanted to talk about?"

Noah shook his head and shifted slightly so he was lying against Tobias rather than just sitting against him. "No, sir, that was all that was on my mind. You?"

"So long as you're happy," he said softly. "I'm fine."

9

I f there was something Tobias was never sure he'd balanced well, it was where Noah slept. A small part of him, the pure Dom, the part that had ached to own Phan like a possession, wanted Noah on the floor all night, chained to the bed. The rest of him -- the lover, the partner, the top who merely wanted to bury his cock deep in Noah's ass or mouth -- that part wanted his boy in the bed.

He was fairly sure Noah generally preferred the bed, although he liked the chain and was positively giddy about the collar.

Maybe one day he'd get it sorted out to their satisfaction.

Noah was in bed with him this time. They both needed it, Tobias thought, and he slept better with Noah curled against him. He'd been treated to both bath and hot tea, so sleep came quickly, comfortably.

The room was still dark and also slightly chilly when he woke. Or, to be more precise, when Noah woke him. Warm hands roamed over Tobias' skin, stroking his back, his hips, his thighs. He felt hot breath and the pinch of teeth on his ass, and he was hard almost instantly. He bent a knee and

Noah hummed his approval, pushing it up to open him even further, and then circled his hole, gently and deliberately, with his tongue.

"Oh, God," Tobias moaned. He loved this, just loved it. If he was completely honest, this was one of the reasons he really liked having Noah in bed. He could easily order Noah to do this, he knew, but it was just more intense, more pleasurable, when Noah surprised him in the mornings.

He bent his leg even more, rubbing his cock on the cotton sheets as he tried to encourage Noah to go faster. "Please," he whispered.

Noah's fingers dug into his cheeks and tugged them wide. His tongue moved faster and with more purpose. He was licking and biting, teasing sensitive skin, and making soft, low sounds that were partially muffled into Tobias' ass.

Finally, Noah groaned loudly and his tongue dove into Tobias, intruding again and again with relentless, shallow thrusts.

"Oh, God, yes!" Tobias arched his back, wantonly shoving his ass back to Noah. "Please, Noah. God, yes, please." His cock throbbed and he rubbed against the sheets again, trying to get more sensation. He cried out again as Noah's tongue fucked him, and he tried to open himself further.

He couldn't think. He didn't want to think. He just wanted more. "Noah!" he yelled. "Please! God, yes!"

"You are so hot when you scream," Noah panted at him when he came up for air. He quickly replaced his tongue with two fingers and pressed them deep. "Makes me so hard." Noah's fingers thrust in and out, searching for Tobias' sweet spot. "Where is it, baby?" he asked rhetorically. "I want to hear you."

Tobias couldn't breathe, couldn't get enough air into his

lungs, and then -- suddenly -- he could. He screamed, his hips rolling back as he fucked himself on Noah's fingers. More. He wanted more, and couldn't ask for it, so he'd let himself revel in what he was given.

He screamed again as Noah's fingers pushed at the sullen hot spot inside him, sensation shooting through him like lightning. "Fuck, yes!" he cried, one hand reaching for his cock. "More!"

"Jesus..." Noah breathed, his voice sounding heavy and rough. Tobias felt Noah's fingers slip away, and he moaned loudly. "Anything you need, love," his sub-turned-lover said softly. Tobias caught a flash of Noah's hand in the corner of his eye and heard the bedside table drawer open and close. "I want to be everything you need."

Then Noah's fingers were on him again, taking hold of his hips and tugging him partly to his knees. Tobias felt the warm, hard head of Noah's slippery prick press against him and then slowly, very slowly, into him.

"Oh, God," Tobias moaned. He didn't quite dare to believe it, didn't quite know what to do or say. He knew he'd lose what rational mind he had in very short order, so it had to count. "Thank you," he finally managed, shifting his hips and moving back slightly, meeting Noah as he filled him. "Love you."

His head dropped down and he gave himself over to just feeling, loving the pressure and slight burn as Noah slipped into him. He ached for this, welcomed it. "Oh, God," he moaned again. "Yes, please."

Noah pressed deep and held there a moment, leaning partly over Tobias to spread kisses over his shoulders. "I love you so much," he whispered, and then with more voice he added, "Jesus fuck, you're tight."

Noah started to move, keeping hold of Tobias' hips as he

thrust. It started out slow and tentative, more about sensation than anything else, but soon began to build. Thrust after thrust, Tobias sensed Noah's confidence growing, until he was fucking Tobias soundly, plunging into him over and over, his fingers bruising Tobias' skin.

Tobias was almost past words. He repeated an endless litany of begging for more and thanking Noah for what he had, almost hoarse from crying out. He grunted and growled and threw himself back to meet Noah's thrusts, shoving his ass higher as Noah pounded against his gland.

His arms gave out and he sank down onto the pillows, his knees spreading as he let Noah force him closer to coming. He felt like he was a tension spring, coiled to never break, but almost sprung. He began to growl, his voice building to a near howl as he began to move again, working with Noah.

"Oh, baby!" Noah encouraged. He shifted as well, and his thrusts grew faster, one arm now braced by Tobias' shoulder. He was panting hard, his breath hot on Tobias' back. "Close," he groaned. "Tobias... it's so good. Come on, baby, come for me."

The howl grew into a roar and Tobias threw his head back, his eyes shut tight as he grabbed his cock with one hand. He pulled at himself almost brutally, yanking his climax from his body. The world grew hazy as his body started to spasm, his ass clamping down on Noah's cock, keeping him deep in Tobias' body. His roar faded to a whimper as he shot onto the sheets, ribbons of come soaking the bedding as he panted and moaned through his orgasm.

"Yes!" Noah yelled, and his hips jerked against Tobias' ass as he came. Tobias was dimly aware of Noah as he shivered above him, riding out the rush until it left Noah boneless and gasping, hanging over Tobias' back. "Oh, God... oh, God," Noah managed to say as he exhaled heavily. Tobias felt almost desperate fingers in his hair, and hungry lips on his shoulders. "Baby."

"Sweetheart," he whispered. "Oh, God, sweetheart. Love you so much. Thank you." He sank down onto the bed, lying in the mess and not caring. "God, thank you."

Noah settled beside him, curling around Tobias' back and wrapping an arm around to his chest to pull their bodies tightly together. "You're welcome," he told Tobias, "I love you, you know I love you."

"I know you do," Tobias said in a whisper. He didn't trust himself to speak clearly -- already he was feeling overly emotional. "But that... that was wonderful, sweetheart. A gift."

"Mmm," Noah sighed. His voice was soft and lazy. "I'd been thinking about it for a while. I was nervous at first, but your reaction made it so worth it. I'm so glad I was able do that for you."

Tobias would have lifted his head to look at Noah if he'd had the energy. "You have? You were? Yeah?" He blinked and tried again. "You were nervous? And how long were you torturing yourself with that, pet?"

"Oh, God, a long time, sir," Noah admitted, slipping automatically back into sub status with Tobias' name for him. "But don't worry about it, I knew it would happen eventually, I just had to..." His voice trailed off and he shifted behind Tobias. "It's a lot like how I know you'd never have asked me. I didn't know how to offer, you know? Or if I even could."

"Could?"

"Do we have to talk about this right now?" Noah asked,

evading the question. He snuggled closer and ran his hand over Tobias' side. "You feel so good."

"You feel better. And, no, but you know we will soon, if only because you've made me a curious pile of well-fucked flesh." He smiled, fairly sure he wasn't making sense. "I'm going to ache all day..." he said, utterly content.

Noah laughed. "I'll take that as a compliment. I'm hoping that you're happy about that, sir. Are you hungry? I'm going to have to go take care of the horses soon. You want coffee before I go?"

"I'll be asleep before you leave the house," Tobias assured him. "But I wouldn't mind a cup when you get back. Noah?"

"Sir?"

"I love you."

Noah climbed over him and smiled. "I know," he said, and kissed Tobias passionately. After a moment, he pulled away and licked his lips, looking flushed and breathless. "Horses."

Noah slipped out of bed and disappeared into the bathroom.

Tobias briefly considered chasing after him, but even as the sound of water running started up he knew he'd be happier merely lying in bed and enjoying the aches and pains that came from being loved that way. Carefully, he pressed one of the bruises forming on his hip and grinned as his groin tightened in response.

There would be time to chase Noah later; now was for sleep and relishing the sensations still zinging through his body.

Now was for knowing how much Noah loved him back.

10

Tobias sat in the truck and stared out the window until the late February chill had settled into his bones. As he was sitting in the sun, and out of the wind, he assumed it had taken a while, but he really wasn't sure how long he'd been sitting there. With a deep sigh he finally roused himself and went back into the barn to tell Deidre he had to leave for the day and probably the week.

"Are you all right to drive?" she asked him, quiet and serious. "I can call Noah."

He shook his head. "I'll be fine, Dee, thank you. I'll call him on the way to the farm."

She nodded and hugged him hard. "I'm sorry, Tobias. So sorry."

"Me, too."

He drove almost halfway to the farm before he remembered to call Noah. He used the phone in the truck, grateful for both the hands-free system and the digital signal that was coming up strong. He bit his lip and debated between calling Noah's pager and calling his phone, and settled on simply sending the car phone number to the pager; Noah would call when he was alone, and that might be better. Then he called the garage and told them that Noah might be by for the car.

It was about twenty minutes before the phone rang. Tobias sighed, but he answered after a couple of rings. "Noah..."

Noah was using his work voice, that rich, authoritative cop voice, when he spoke. "Sir? I got your page. Where are you? Is this the truck number?"

"Yeah, it is. I need you. Can you get away?" He wondered if his voice was really that tired sounding. "I'm about ten minutes from the farm," he added as an afterthought.

"Uh... sure. Yes, sir. Let me just... you sound awful, you've got me worried. Let me just talk to Carol. Are you all right? Are you driving?" Tobias could hear Noah shuffling in the background and then a car door open and close.

"Mrs. Miller died," Tobias said softly. "I'm going home."

There was a long silence on Noah's end of the line until he whispered, "Oh, God," Noah sighed. "Oh, no. I'm so sorry." He cleared his throat. "I'll come right away. Are you sending a car or...?"

"You can pick it up. You'll come? Right now?" Tobias coughed as his voice started to crack. "I need you."

"Right now. I'm on my way, okay?" He was using that voice again, the strong, capable cop voice. "Get off the road and get inside. I'll be there soon."

"All right. I'm... I'll be there in a couple of minutes." Tobias gripped the wheel a little tighter. He wasn't looking forward to getting there, not sure if Robert would still be there or not. He wasn't sure what would be worse, an empty house or Mrs. Miller's family. "Thank you," he said quietly.

"I love you," Noah told him in return. "I'm going to hang up and go get the car now, okay?"

"Okay. I love you, too." But he couldn't hit the disconnect. "You have to do it this time," he said. "I can't let go." Of the steering wheel, of Noah, of anything.

Noah cleared his throat again. "Get home safely, please. I'll be there before you know it, I promise." Noah seemed to hesitate for a moment, and then the line went dead.

Tobias drove in silence the rest of the way, forgetting about the phone until he pulled into the drive. He powered it off and pulled up to the house, oddly relieved to find cars there. As he climbed out of the truck, the porch seemed to fill.

The twins were there, and Peter, and both Robert and his wife, Sue. A few neighbors, and someone had brought Mrs. Delong up from her farm, though Tobias was fairly sure she wasn't quite over her annual bout of strep.

He walked up the steps and reached out a hand to Robert, unsurprised to find himself pulled closer into a hug; the families had been well tied together by Robert's mother, and though he and Robert had never been close, he knew he was much more than simply an employer. The evidence of that was standing all around him.

"Come on now, into the house," Peter said, taking charge for the first time ever. "There's tea on."

So Tobias let himself be led into the house, let himself be taken care of, and he sat with Robert and Sue to help make arrangements.

The hour it took for Noah to arrive from the city passed quickly with all the company, and Noah did indeed arrive sooner than Tobias expected. He hadn't even heard the car in the drive; he just looked up to see Noah, head to toe in uniform, striding across the living room to him.

Noah stopped short of Tobias, possibly surprised by all the company, and shook Robert's hand. "Robert," he said, nodding. "I'm so sorry." Then he sat on the couch beside Tobias and looked at him. "Nice to have friends around."

Tobias found himself nodding and leaning into Noah. "Better to have you," he whispered. "Thanks for coming."

Noah leaned forward and stroked fingers along his jaw. "I should change my clothes. I'll be back in a few minutes." He stood and greeted the twins as he made his way out of the room.

When Noah returned he was in jeans, a T-shirt, and one of Tobias' sweaters that was slightly too large on him. He took a seat beside Tobias again, slipped an arm through his, and looked at Robert. "Is there anything I can do?"

Robert shook his head, looking faintly amused. "Just take care of Tobias. Can we help you with that?"

Tobias blinked. "I don't need--"

"Oh, yes, you do. At the very least, you need food."

"I think we're all right. Thank you, Robert. Food I can handle," Noah said with a slight smile. He looked at Tobias. "Right?"

"Well, now, yes," Tobias said, attempting to joke. But then it crashed. "Mrs. Miller made sure you knew what I liked." He sat back on the couch and closed his eyes. "Damn."

Noah rubbed his hand on Tobias' thigh, still talking to Robert. "You'll let us know about the arrangements?"

"Most of it's been settled between us all, just have to make the calls," Tobias heard Robert say. "I'll take the twins home to their mother. Peter?"

"Aye."

"Can you drive Mrs. Delong back down?"

"Aye. Sir, I'll turn the horses out tonight. No need for you or... or Noah to bother."

Tobias opened one eye and nodded. "Thank you, Peter.

I'd like to take the morning feed, though. I think I'll be riding tomorrow, too."

Peter nodded, and then people started to move about, gathering coats and scarves and things.

"Did you call anyone else?" Tobias heard Robert ask Noah. "She'd... well, there are people she was real fond of."

"I have a few people in mind to call," Noah said. "I'll make sure they get the word."

Tobias winced at the thought of Phantom's reaction. Standing, he shook Robert's hand again and finally made his way to the door to say his goodbyes. It seemed like an age before they closed it on the last of them and he could turn to Noah. "Sweetheart," he whispered, burying his head in Noah's neck, right there in the front hall.

"Oh..." Noah put his arms around him. "I've wanted to do this since the moment I walked in, but I didn't think... with all those people around..." He sighed. "I'm so sorry, baby. You know I can't say enough good things about her. She was extraordinary."

"She was," Tobias agreed, mumbling the words into Noah's skin. His eyes were starting to burn, and he could feel his chest tighten. "She lived with her whole heart and wasn't scared of anything."

"She was always so good to me," Noah said softly, leading Tobias back to the couch to sit. "She was sweet, kind, helpful, always ready with a cooking tip or an anecdote about you. She really made me feel welcome here."

Tobias nodded. He wasn't sure how long he could do this. "I... oh, God." He coughed. "She was my family." He blinked rapidly, the tears coming up.

Noah nodded and pulled Tobias down to the couch and into his arms. "You loved her, I know." He stroked a hand over Tobias' back and held him close.

"I did. I do." Tobias began to cry, knowing that if there was anyone on the planet who deserved his tears it was Elizabeth Miller.

"I know. She knew it, too. She did." Noah cleared his throat. Tobias felt Noah's hand leave his back for a moment. "She did, baby."

Somehow, knowing Noah was mourning her, too, helped. Having only known her for a few months had affected Noah to the point where he could cry for her as well, and that seemed to loosen even more tears in Tobias. He clung to Noah, let himself cry, let himself feel the loss.

She'd been his mother, his aunt, his guide. She'd never once blinked at his lovers, had welcomed first Phantom and then Noah into her life, had never pried into his private affairs. She'd simply been accepting and strong, teaching class by example, teaching how to love by doing it, and had never once let him hide from a responsibility.

He wept, knowing the world was poorer without her.

Noah held him and rubbed his back, until his shoulders stopped shaking and there was nothing but the sound of their breathing. It was hard to know how long they sat there, Noah being stoic and quiet with Tobias comfortably tucked into his shoulder.

When the sun went down and the house started to get dark and chilly, Noah kissed him on the head. "I should start dinner." He scooted out from under Tobias and fluffed one of the couch pillows for him. "You rest. I'll let you know when it's ready."

Tobias nodded and sank down onto the couch, feeling drained. He couldn't quite get used to the idea that Mrs. Miller was gone, that she wouldn't be back to run the place when he wasn't there. He felt adrift, like his anchor was gone. No, his anchor was making supper, he reminded himself. But something important had been taken from him, and he had to deal with that.

He fell into a fitful sleep, half dreams of his house falling down plaguing him. A stranger living there during the week, making him feel like a weekend visitor instead of an absent son. He moaned and rolled over, waking slightly. He was cold. He could feel fresh tears on his cheeks. He was alone.

"Noah?"

The living room was dark, but there was light spilling into the hallway from the direction of the kitchen, and Tobias noted the warm, homey smell of comfort food.

He sat up and wiped his eyes again, then stood and made his way there. The kitchen was always warm; Mrs. Miller had made it the center of his home. He didn't bother wiping these tears away -- he had a feeling there would be more.

"Noah?" he said again as he walked in. "Where are you?"

"Right here, baby." Noah went to him and slipped his arms around his waist.

"I had bad dreams," Tobias whispered. "And I can't stop crying."

"When my father passed away, my mother told me that tears were good for you. Let's hope she's right, huh?" Noah tightened his arms around Tobias and kissed his chest.

Tobias nodded. Something that felt this horrid had to be good for him. "It's like... spinach then?" he asked, choking out a laugh. He held onto Noah and sniffled a little. "God, I hate this."

"It hurts, I know."

"It does. I want... No. I don't want it to stop. She deserves to have me ache for her, does that make sense? She earned these tears." He felt his chest tighten again, and a sob welled up. "I'm sorry," he said, not knowing why.

"It makes perfect sense, baby, and you're right, she deserves to be missed. She will be, sorely." Noah held on tightly and a quiet moment passed before he finally asked, "Are you hungry at all?"

"No." He wasn't. "I don't know. I don't... I should make some calls."

"Some calls? Who are you calling?" Noah pulled him over to the kitchen table and sat him in a chair. "Have a few bites, you need it." Despite having just been told that Tobias wasn't hungry, Noah went to the stove and dished up some stew and sat it in front of Tobias with a hunk of crusty bread.

"I should call... well, Bradford. Phan will have to know, he loved her." Tobias played with the fork in front of him. "Dee. Um. Order flowers. I have to decide what to do about the house."

"Whoa, hey, all of that can wait." Noah sat at the table with him. "Eat. The house will be fine for a while, I've taken the rest of the week off work. Flowers can wait until tomorrow. I'm sure Dee isn't expecting to hear from you yet, and I can call Phan. Don't push, you're allowed to just grieve, Tobias."

"I don't grieve well," Tobias admitted.

Noah snorted, then shot Tobias a look of disbelief. "Tobias, who grieves 'well'?"

"Well, do you find people to take it out on?" Tobias demanded. "Do you bury yourself in work for months and ignore everyone? Do you forget to eat, and drive yourself so hard that you nearly wind up in a hospital?"

"If you think I'm going to let you do any of those things, you have another think coming, Dr. Vincent." Noah stood and went back to the stove. "And on that note, will you eat something, please?"

Tobias looked at him and managed a weak smile. "If I

was feeling better I'd say no, just on principle. I advise you to lose the 'please' by the day after tomorrow. Maybe Bradford can give you a quick lesson on how to order me around."

Noah turned around and walked back to the table with a quirky grin tugging at his lips. As he leaned both hands on the table, the smile disappeared and he looked Tobias in the eye. "Eat. Smart-ass."

"Spankings and stroke counts are cumulative," Tobias said evenly. He didn't pick up his fork.

"So be it. But I love you and it's my job to take care of you and see to your needs. What you need right now is your strength. So you can levy me *fifty* strokes if you like, but I'm not moving until you pick up that fork and eat something."

Tobias looked at him and finally sighed. "Brat," he said, picking up his fork.

"You're eating." Noah grinned smugly and went to get him a glass of water.

"Yes," Tobias said, taking a bite of the bread. "Be proud of yourself. Now. Are you sure you can take the time off work? I don't want to eat your vacation time; we're still going to Paris."

"I have plenty, and you're exactly the person I want to spend it on," Noah said easily, setting the glass down in front of Tobias. "Honestly." He sat again and crossed his legs.

"All right." Tobias let it go and concentrated on eating everything Noah put in front of him. Fork, lift, chew, swallow. Easy. Mindless. No need to think or feel, only do. He finished everything and finally looked up. "I... I need to go lie down." He felt slightly queasy and suddenly realized he had no idea what he'd eaten.

"Go on upstairs. I'll clean up here and bring you some

tea in a bit. You want a bath?" Noah picked up his bowl and moved it to the sink.

"I... I don't know." Tobias shook his head. "Yeah, I guess so. I'll take care of it, don't worry." He stood up slowly, feeling a hundred years old. "Thank you, sweetheart."

Noah turned from the sink and watched him. "You're welcome, sir. I'll be up soon." He gave Tobias a kiss and another quick hug before sending him on his way.

Tobias bathed mechanically, unable to relax; every time he did, he found himself remembering and tears would well up, or he'd begin to make plans. Neither were the mind-numbing blankness he craved. Once clean and dry again, he crawled into bed and left all the lights on, waiting for Noah to come up.

11

Noah chose these few minutes alone to let his own grief out, letting tears fall as he washed the dishes and cleaned up the kitchen. He needed to keep it together for Tobias. The more off-balance Tobias was, the steadier Noah needed to be. That was understood.

He hadn't known Mrs. M all that well, really, or for very long, but she was one of those people that you couldn't help but love from the moment you met her. And as corny as it sounded, it really was true that she was a big part of what made him finally feel at home in Tobias' house.

He needed to tell Phan. Tobias shouldn't have to make that call, not in his state. So as soon as the dishes were put away and the leftovers wrapped, Noah picked up the kitchen phone and dialed Bradford.

"Hello?" came Bradford's cheerful voice over the line.

"Bradford? It's Noah."

"Uh-oh. What's the matter, boy?"

The informality in his address must have given him away. "I've got some... very sad news, Bradford."

"Oh, Lord, Noah. What is it?"

"Mrs. Miller passed away this morning."

Bradford sighed heavily. "Is he all right?"

"No. No, he's very upset."

"I can imagine. What can I do?"

Noah cleared his throat. Somehow being offered help made him more emotional. "Nothing at the moment, but tomorrow... maybe you could bring Phan out?"

"Oh, damn. Phan."

"I'd like to tell him."

"Sure. Sure, Noah, hold on. And count on us tomorrow."

"Thank you, sir." Noah heard Bradford put him on hold.

Then the line clicked again and Phan's voice came to him, sounding cautious. "Noah? What's wrong? Master Bradford won't tell me."

Damn it, hearing Phan's voice only made this harder. "Oh, Phan... it's Mrs. Miller..." He choked on the words.

"Elizabeth? What?" Phan demanded. "Did she have a stroke? A heart attack? Noah, where is she? Is Tobias with her?"

"Phan, honey, she passed away this morning. I'm with Tobias at the farm."

"Oh!" Phan gasped. There was a long silence and then he asked, "Really? But she's... Elizabeth."

Noah felt a knot form in his chest, and his voice was tight with emotion, but somehow he held the tears back. "I'm so sorry, Phan..."

"Oh," Phan said again. "I'm... wow. Is Sir all right? No, of course he isn't, never mind. Listen to me. Are you?"

"Yes, I'm listening," Noah closed his eyes and nodded, not that Phan could see him.

"She told me once, way back at the beginning when Tobias first took me there, before we were together? She told me a story about him having nightmares when he was a kid.

His parents were away, and she had him at her house for the weekend, and he was missing them. She gave him something, it was a doll, but not a girly thing -- like a charm. About the size of your hand. She called it her good dream doll, and she told me that she let all her kids use it when they had nightmares. It's in her room, probably still on her dresser. It was then, anyway -- she let me use if for about a month. Take it to him, yeah?" Phan suddenly seemed to run out of words. "I... damn it. Thank you for calling. I gotta go."

Noah blinked. He'd never been in Mrs. M's room; he'd been told it was strictly off-limits and had never so much as peeked in the door. "Oh. Uh, sure. Sure, okay. Bradford said he would bring you out to see us tomorrow. Sir did say he'd had some bad dreams while he was napping..."

"Really? We're going out?" Noah wasn't sure if Phan was asking him or Bradford, but he could hear Bradford in the background. "Okay, yeah," Phan said, and then he sniffled. "Take care of him, Noah," he said softly, his voice starting to break. "And don't forget you can cry, too. She loved us all, and we'll all miss her."

Noah took a deep breath and sighed. Funny that Phan of all people was telling him it was okay to cry. "Oh, I've done a good bit of that, and I don't imagine I'm done yet." He coughed. "So uh, take care of yourself too, Phan, okay? See you tomorrow."

"See you, Noah," Phan said softly. The line went dead with a soft click, and then there was nothing left to do but go up the stairs.

12

Tobias was staring at the ceiling when Noah came in. He hadn't heard Noah moving about the house, hadn't heard his step on the stairs or anything. He sat up slightly and blinked, not sure what he was seeing. "Is that... is that?" he started to ask after a long pause.

"Her good dream doll." Noah said with a nod. "I talked with Phan." He placed the doll in Tobias' hand. "He told me to get it for you. He and Bradford are going to come out and visit tomorrow." Noah tugged his sweater off and sat on the edge of the bed.

Tobias stared at the doll. It was made of thick cotton and had a painted-on face that he'd always thought looked particularly kind without being saccharine. The clothes had changed a couple of times over the years, but the little yellow suit it had on was the one it had worn when Mrs. Miller gave it to Phan. It didn't look like a child's doll, and it wasn't a plaything, but something indefinable instead.

The last time he'd had it given to him had been by Mrs. Miller, the night his parents died.

"Thank you," he whispered. "This is perfectly right." He set the doll on the night table and turned to watch Noah get ready for bed. "How did Phantom take it?" he asked, feeling guilty for not calling Phan himself.

"He's hard to read. He did a good job of covering it up by worrying about you and telling me it was all right to cry." Noah shook his head and shucked his jeans. "And then he suddenly had to go."

Tobias sighed and nodded. "That sounds right. Bradford was right there?"

"Right there, I'd told him first." Noah stepped into the bathroom and turned on the light. "I'm sure Bradford will take good care of him," he said loud enough to be heard over running water.

"Yes," Tobias called back. "He'll be fine." Now all he had to do was worry about Noah. He sighed and looked at the doll again. Maybe it worked for two. "Will you ride with me in the morning?" he called. "Or will they be here early?"

Noah poked his head out of the bathroom. "I don't think Bradford knows how to get up early," he said around his toothbrush. "And I'd love to ride." He disappeared again, and soon the water stopped, the toilet flushed, and then Noah was climbing into bed.

"Great," Tobias said, waiting for Noah to slip into his arms. "Crispin needs a workout."

Noah pressed against him and kissed him. "Sounds good. Some air will be good for us."

"Yes," Tobias agreed, taking another kiss. And then another, his tongue pushing into Noah's mouth.

Noah opened his mouth and yielded to him easily, cupping his jaw with cool fingers.

Unexpectedly, Tobias found himself achingly hard, kissing Noah like his life depended on it, depended on the passion behind every breath. "Oh, God," he said when he stopped to breathe. "Oh, God."

Noah rolled onto his back and pulled Tobias over him, his hands roaming over skin down his back to his ass. Noah's lips found Tobias' throat.

Feeling utterly out of control, beyond it, Tobias thrust against Noah. This was rutting, though he tried to make it more than that. It was feeling and sensation, and it was pure hunger. "Noah," he growled. "Need." He moaned and bared his neck for more of Noah's mouth, needing something powerful.

"Yours, baby," Noah replied. He continued to explore Tobias' neck and shoulder with his lips and teeth. He rolled his hip into Tobias' erection and held it there as he reached into the bedside table for lube. "Better in a minute, promise," he panted and flipped the cap off.

"Hurry," Tobias groaned. "Hurts." And it did, if felt like his heart was pounding in his dick, like if he didn't get off he was going to explode, shatter, scatter, splinter and fragment. He keened and thrust against Noah again, looking for friction.

Noah reached down and slicked Tobias' cock quickly, his hand warm and strong against the rigid flesh. He held Tobias off with his hip just another moment, shoving those same slick fingers into his own ass. He groaned and his brow furrowed for a moment, and then he rolled flat, raising his knees. "Come on... come on, it's okay."

Tobias shook his head no and shoved his cock into Noah's ass anyway, plunging into him and going deep with a grunt. Noah was tight around him, too tight, but he felt so good, so hot and alive, that Tobias almost didn't stop. He managed to freeze before pulling back, staring down into Noah's face.

Noah gasped and grimaced, but it was nothing Tobias hadn't seen before and, he knew, nothing that Noah couldn't handle. Warm fingers reached up and tugged his face lower, catching his lips in a hard kiss. Tobias felt Noah relax a bit, and Noah's ankles crossed at the back of his thighs.

As if something inside him had snapped, Tobias started to thrust, stabbing into Noah again and again, harder and harder. He gripped Noah's hips, pulled him up onto him, and growled. He felt like he could go on for hours, although logic told him that was impossible.

Noah grunted and whimpered. One hand reached up and gripped the headboard and the other seized his cock, stroking himself in time to Tobias' thrusts. "Sir..."

"Go ahead," Tobias said, not stopping or slowing. "Come. It'll relax you." He felt rather clinical about it.

Tobias had no idea if Noah even heard him. "Oh, God," Noah panted. He let go of the headboard and plunged his fingers into Tobias' hair. "I love you."

"Love you, too," Tobias whispered, grinding his cock into Noah's ass. "So much."

Noah whimpered, then shivered and shot upwards, slicking Tobias' belly. The look on his face was pure pleasure, as if he'd been waiting all night for this moment. A couple of deep breaths later, Tobias wasn't surprised to find that he was right, Noah's body relaxed around his cock and Noah moaned softly. "Jesus."

"Love you," Tobias whispered again, his hips driving. "And I'm going to hurt you, I'm sorry." He could feel a tear track down his cheek. "Love you, love you," he chanted, thrusting into Noah again and again.

Noah reached up and slid his fingers across Tobias' cheek -- a surprisingly tender gesture in contrast to the strength and urgency of Tobias' own need. "I'm yours, Master," Noah told him quietly. Sincerely.

Tobias shuddered. "Again," he demanded, his rhythm faltering.

"Yours. Only for you," Noah panted. "I am yours, Master." Noah gripped his shoulders and arched his head back with a groan.

"Ah, fuck," Tobias groaned, his hips stuttering. He could swear he felt his cock swell further. "Mine," he said, slamming into Noah, balls deep.

"Yours to--" Noah hissed, twisting his hips a bit. "To fuck, to have, to please you. Your boy. Oh, God."

Tobias nodded, past words, and pulled almost all the way out of Noah's ass before going deep again. He wanted to come. Needed to. And he had no idea how to get there. He fucked Noah hard, finally bending to kiss him, to taste his mouth.

Noah opened his mouth for him and accepted his tongue, caressing it with his own as they kissed. Fingers dug hard into Tobias' arms, hard enough to leave bruises if they stayed there too long. "Master," his boy gasped between kisses, and Noah's body started to move. He locked his thighs around Tobias' hips and clenched hard around his cock, restricting Tobias' ability to thrust.

Only able to push in a little, Tobias growled. Noah had given him something to fight against, something to battle and overcome, and he reveled in it. He could feel his balls pull up as he moved harder, rocking more than thrusting. He sucked on Noah's tongue and panted into the kiss, his body sliding along Noah's wherever they touched, sweat making them both slick.

"Mine," he growled again, breaking the kiss. His orgasm started to roll through him, fire roaring through his veins.

Noah arched and groaned, fighting to keep his grip on Tobias' hips and on his cock. His eyes were closed, and the grimace on his face proved to Tobias that every bit of him, physically and mentally, was wrapped up in this moment, that he'd committed himself to Tobias' release as much as Tobias himself had. "Sir!" Noah gasped and whimpered at him.

"My boy," Tobias said again, still coming, still filling him, still lost on another plane of existence where all that mattered was sensation and connecting to the one in his arms. Nothing else mattered, nothing else could touch him, nothing could hurt him. "Love you," he whispered, finally falling forward onto Noah and panting, tears pricking the back of his eyes.

Noah relaxed as he did and opened his arms, wrapping them around Tobias' shoulders as they settled back together. "Yes. I love you," Noah whispered, pulling Tobias into his chest.

"I know you do," Tobias said softly, not even bothering to try to catch his breath. His panting was rough and harsh, his throat aching. "I'm sorry, baby," he said. "I must have hurt you." Carefully he pulled out, wincing himself. "Oh, God."

Noah's voice was soft, soothing. "Shhh. Right now I feel great, we'll see what tomorrow brings."

Tomorrow. He didn't want to think about tomorrow. He didn't want to move, didn't want to clean up, didn't want to do anything but sleep and hold on to Noah. He heard a sound and knew it had to be a whimper; after a moment he decided it had to have been him. He closed his eyes and held onto Noah, hoping the good dream doll would do its work.

13

The sun was streaming in the window when he opened his eyes again, and Noah was smiling down at him, a cup of steaming coffee in his hands. "Good morning, sir," Noah said, waiting until he was sitting up to pass him the mug.

Tobias took the mug gratefully and drank half of it before taking in the state of the bed and himself. Noah was suspiciously clean. "Couldn't take the mess?" he asked with a grin. "Can't say I blame you, I'll be showering before and after taking care of the horses." He looked at Noah with a keener eye. "Are you all right?"

Noah grinned, looking smug. "I'm pretty sore, sir. Riding will be... challenging."

Tobias shook his head. "And you're okay with that? I'm not going to make you ride if you'd rather not." He finished his coffee in three quick swallows and swung his legs out of bed. "Ew."

"Let me start a shower for you," Noah said, turning to head for the bathroom. He had a couple of thumb-size bruises on his ass that Tobias didn't recall making, and he seemed to have a light hitch in his step. "I'd like to ride, I need the air. Really, I'm fine."

"You're hurt!" Tobias walked after him and crowded Noah into a corner. "What did I do to you?"

Noah blinked at him, grinning. "You fucked me, sir, and quite well. I'm not hurt, I'm sore. A little achy is all; I'm fine."

"Really?" Tobias asked. He knew he'd taken Noah hard, knew he'd needed to, but he hadn't quite expected Noah to be so... happy about it. He felt a little swell of pride rear up and squashed it firmly, or tried to. It was kind of nice to know he could still do that, though. "You're okay?" he asked again, this time more to distract himself than from any real worry.

Noah leaned up and kissed him. "Promise. Now, please, sir, may I start a shower for you? You stink."

Tobias looked down at himself and grimaced. "God, yes. Thank you." He really needed a shower. He didn't waste time in it, however, and within fifteen minutes he and Noah were dressed and on their way to the stables.

The morning chores went quickly with two sets of hands. They fed everyone first and then spent some time cleaning out stalls other and barn chores. By the time they had Crispin and Dianna groomed and tacked up, the horses had had plenty of time to digest.

Dianna, Tobias noted, wasn't as ornery around Noah as she used to be. Whether that was because of his presence or because of some understanding the two had finally come to, Tobias couldn't be sure, but he was glad of it all the same. They rode out into a bright, sunny, still morning. Noah took Crispin into the ring to warm up and appeared to be fairly sure of his seat despite his aches.

It was a good morning. Tobias felt better, as if the shock was wearing off around the edges. He supposed that being so physical helped the psychology of it -- fucking Noah, riding, raking stalls, moving so much -- it all served to remind him on every level that he was alive, that he had work to do.

Missing Mrs. Miller was something he had a lifetime for, and he knew he'd use it. Dealing with the loss in the immediate timeframe was his goal.

They rode out into the fields for a while, the biting February wind keeping the outing shorter than he would have liked, but he also didn't know when Bradford and Phan were going to arrive, or if others were going to stop by. Mrs. Miller had been popular, and her home would serve as a stopping point, even if her son and daughter-in-law lived down the road.

Tobias expected it to be a busy few days.

"Let's head back," he said to Noah, considering just that. "Get some lunch on for people."

Noah turned Crispin around and brought him up alongside Dianna. "Right... visitors," he said with a nod. "Race you back?"

Tobias considered Noah's challenge a moment and then gave Dianna a squeeze with his thighs. Off she leapt, like the big-hearted, long-legged lady he knew her to be, racing him back toward the barn over hard ground and through the frigid air. He could hear Noah behind them, shouting something about his start not being fair, and he grinned, sitting deeper into the saddle and giving Dianna her head.

By the time they'd reached the barn, both horses needed a bit of a walk and Tobias and Noah were both breathless. But they were warm, Tobias noted, so there was something to be said for the workout.

"You cheated!" Noah said in an accusing manner, walking Crispin around the yard to cool him down.

"Oh, sorry," Tobias said mildly. "Had a little trouble catching up, did you? Next time I'll be sure to give you a count of three and a warning."

"Crispin has shorter legs. You hurt his feelings," Noah said petulantly, but he was grinning. "She goes beautifully, that mare of yours, I must say."

"She's a cranky bitch," Tobias said with a smile and a nod, "but she knows how to move. She's a bit like me."

"No kidding."

They walked their mounts out a bit longer and then led them back into the barn. Noah took their tack while Tobias groomed them again and wrapped them up in their blankets, and then the two men headed back up to the house.

"I think we should get a soup on," Tobias said, pulling his boots off. "Which means you get a soup on; use the biggest pot you can find. Showers first, and I'll get some quick bread started. God knows how many people are going to wander through here or how long Bradford and Phan will stay."

The showers were fast. Noah seemed a bit worse for wear after the ride, but he still wasn't complaining. Tobias watched as Noah limped his way down the stairs in his blue jeans and yet another too-big borrowed sweater. At least this one had a nice V-neck so Noah's collar gleamed for all visitors to see.

Noah had a rich tomato and vegetable stock going in record time and began adding everything but the kitchen sink to it. As it turned out, their haste was warranted, because before long a black car pulled into the driveway, and the smartly dressed driver opened the door to let Phan and Bradford out.

Tobias waited on the front porch, watching Phan's face as the two men walked to him. Phantom had dark circles under his eyes but seemed okay otherwise, if a little pale. Bradford offered his hand as he climbed the stairs, and Tobias shook it solemnly before opening his arms to Phan, unsurprised when the boy flew to him, burying his face in Tobias' chest.

"How was he last night?" he asked Bradford, rubbing Phan's back.

Bradford sighed. "He was very upset, of course; he loved her. He cried on and off all night. I let him sleep with me... he needed comfort." Bradford looked at Tobias critically. "How are you?"

"Better than I was yesterday," Tobias said. "Not as good as I will be." He rubbed Phan's back again. "Come on in, both of you. Noah's got soup on, and we can be warm."

Against him, Phan nodded, but he didn't let go. Tobias rolled his eyes at Bradford and eased the boy into the house, finally giving up and calling for Noah. "Can you... um, take him for a moment? Just so I can check the bread and get Bradford a drink."

Noah nodded. "Yes, sir." He slid a hand between Tobias and Phan and drew Phan over to the couch. "It's okay, Phan."

Tobias watched Phan go to Noah, easily transferring the clinging hold he'd had. With a rueful smile he inclined his head to Bradford and gestured for him to follow into the kitchen.

"Tea, coffee, or something stronger?" he asked, peering into the oven.

"Coffee." Bradford pulled a chair out from the kitchen table and sat. "He's exhausting."

Tobias snorted and reached for the grinder. "Tell me about it." Measuring beans into the grinder, he took a closer look at Bradford. "How are you coping? With Phan in general, I mean."

"In general just fine, I suppose. It's not what I'm accustomed to, and poor Nikki is feeling a bit put out, I'm afraid; but as far as Phan goes, it's helping, I think. He makes enough mistakes that he has something to think about constantly. Did he always have trouble retaining things? I mean, is that just in his personality, or might that be a symptom of his therapy?"

Tobias thought about that as he ground the beans and got the coffee maker set up. "Well, I'm not sure," he said. "At the start it was like training a raw sub, which I hadn't expected because he'd been on the scene a while. But by the time we signed the slavery contract he was doing fine, rarely made any mistakes at all unless he was acting up on purpose. As a slave it was the same thing... a rough start. So maybe it's his pattern? Do you talk to Dr. Brewer at all?"

"She and I touch base every week. She says he's frustrated with what he perceives as 'too many rules' but that he's interested and genuinely trying, so I suppose things are fine on his end." Bradford crossed his legs. "Could just be his pattern; he is improving quickly."

"Hmm. Anything in particular he's having trouble with? Maybe Nikki could help?"

"I am a creature of habit. I like my routines. Maybe I'm fussy and eccentric, that's not out of the realm of possibility." Bradford said in a self-deprecating tone. He shook his head. "He hasn't picked up on the routine quite yet; it's difficult for him to remember and anticipate me. It's not really his fault. In a perfect world I would set him up with someone that suits his style better; we're a little like a round peg and a square hole, but we manage."

Tobias sighed. He'd never had trouble fitting with Phan, not until things started to fall apart. He flipped the switch on the coffee maker and fetched the mugs, letting his hands do the busy work of getting the tray together. He paused, looking at the sugar bowl, and smiled.

"He gave this to her," he said softly. "The first Christmas he was here. He'd broken one the week before, and he dragged me all over the city to find the perfect one to replace it. This bowl cost me almost eighty dollars, the brat."

"Which brat? Phan? He's sweet. He really is. He has a huge heart and has no earthly idea what to do with it."

"I know," Tobias agreed. "She knew that, too, and just sort of... took him under her wing. It was amazing to watch. She didn't spend nearly as much time with Noah, and I kind of got the impression that she knew he didn't need her the same way. She was like... Phan's grandmother, really. She taught him to cook, and she scolded him, and she wouldn't put up with any backtalk. They adored each other."

"Noah is completely different," Bradford agreed. "Night and day, really. He's earnest, wears his heart on his sleeve, but he knows what he wants and insists on getting it."

"Oh, he does that," Tobias agreed. He finished getting the tray ready and added, "He's damn pushy sometimes. God, I love him."

Bradford grinned. "He's a better balance for you than Phan was." He stood and made his way over to lean on the counter. "I didn't know her that well, but you know you have my deepest sympathy, Tobias, as a friend. As more than a friend. I know this must have affected you deeply, and I am here if you need to blow off some steam, all right?"

Tobias nodded. "Thank you. For the sympathy and the offer. This is... well, frankly, it's pretty horrible. Mrs. Miller took care of me for thirty-six years -- I had her longer than my parents."

Bradford nodded and touched Tobias' shoulder. "I know. Was it quiet for her? Gentle at least?"

"Very," Tobias said softly. And he thanked God for it. "She just... didn't wake up in the morning. The poor twins who come to dust knew something was wrong when they got here and the doors were still locked. They called Peter down from the barn, and he went in. Said she just looked like she was sleeping." He lifted his hand to wipe at his cheek, unsurprised that it was damp again. He cleared his throat. "Robert told me that she didn't have any pain at all. Really, it was the best any of us can hope for."

"We should all be so lucky. She deserved it to be that way, Tobias, be happy for her." Bradford gave Tobias' shoulder a squeeze and backed off a bit, giving Tobias more air. "If I make it to eighty I will consider myself a very lucky man."

"If you make it to eighty we'll all be considered lucky, Bradford."

"Let's hope we get there together, then. We can be dirty old perverts and sit around drinking port and watching the young men strut around my club." Bradford winked. "Is that coffee ready? I haven't warmed up yet. It's cold outside the city."

Tobias grinned and poured the coffee into a carafe. "You're a pervert; I'm a deviant," he corrected, picking up the tray. "Shall we go find the pets?"

Bradford laughed. "Semantics. Yes, let's go."

"Ah, it's an important distinction," Tobias said, leading the way into the living room. "It's also a good comeback with a mouthy sub." He glanced at the boys on the couch and smiled. "Which neither of them is at the moment, seeing as how they're asleep."

Noah had Phan mostly in his lap, with Phan's head resting on his chest as they leaned back into the couch. One of them had pulled a blanket over their legs and one of

Noah's arms, and it looked like they'd made themselves a nice little nest.

"Are we going to let them sleep?" Bradford asked, amused.

"Phan probably needs it. And Noah's body could use the rest." He set the tray down on the coffee table and looked at the boys, smiling.

"Kept him up late, did you?" Bradford grinned.

"Not late so much as..." Tobias shrugged one shoulder. "Well. Let's just say that my subconscious made an effort to prove I was alive. I was a little surprised he was fit to ride a horse this morning." He poured the coffee carefully and handed a mug to Bradford. "I feel a little guilty about it, actually."

"Don't," Bradford said decisively. "You're his Master, you had a need, and he fulfilled it for you. That's his responsibility, and I'm sure it made him happy to be able to do it." Bradford took the coffee and took a long sip. "You wouldn't feel guilty if you'd felt the need to flog him."

"No, I suppose not," Tobias said. He wouldn't have. He thought about it for a moment, deciding that Noah's smug attitude in the aftermath meant he really and honestly didn't have anything to be guilty about. "Maybe I'll do that later, as a reward," he added with a smile.

"Good man." Bradford winked. "He's really come a long way with you, Tobias. I'm very impressed, you know. I'm thinking of holding some workshops over the summer, and I hope you'll accept an invitation to be one of my instructors."

Tobias raised an eyebrow and tried not to smirk. "That sounds interesting." He glanced and Noah and his smirk grew. "And what shall I instruct on?"

Bradford laughed. "I'm sure you'll think of something --

or someone." He let silence fall while he took another sip of his coffee. "So, you'll be thinking about contract renewal soon?"

Tobias nodded. "Of course. I suspect we'll work out the fine details in Paris. I've been thinking about a few things I want added."

"Really? I suppose that's good." Bradford stood and moved to the boys, adjusting the blanket that had slipped off Phan's feet. He lowered his voice a bit. "What sorts of things are you adding? Has he made any mention of wanting to alter the contract at all?"

Tobias shook his head, smiling at the boys as well as Bradford as he cared for them in his own way. It was a comforting picture. "I doubt he'd ask for the big things, and he hasn't talked about any minor changes." He sipped his coffee and watched as Noah's grip on Phan tightened a little in his sleep. "I expect he'll want to drop a few of the restrictions, based on the trust level we've established, but the big changes will have to come from me."

"I'd ask what those are, but I really hate to sound like a busybody," Bradford said with a grin as he made his way back over to sit. He picked up his coffee again. "But Paris sounds like a good time. Such a kinky town. Has he ever been?"

"No. Actually, I'm pretty sure he hasn't traveled a lot. And you don't have to worry about sounding like a busybody," Tobias admonished. "I value your opinions, you know that." He took another quick swallow from his coffee cup and set it down. "In fact, you'll probably have a lot to say about it, even if I don't want to hear it; it usually works that way." He smiled to take any sting out of his words and winked at Bradford, wondering how long he could dance around the conversation before he actually had to ask Bradford what he thought.

"Usually does. And generally it's for the best, even if you disagree." Bradford winked right back. "So are you hedging because you think the boys are eavesdropping, or because you're genuinely concerned about what my opinion is going to be?" Tobias caught the grin on his lips before Bradford hid it with his coffee mug.

"Bit of one, bit of the other," Tobias said with a smile. He looked at Bradford appraisingly and lowered his voice. "I'm thinking of some changes to our living arrangements. And..." He paused for a moment, considering his words. "And I'm going to suggest we make the timeframe of the next contract indefinite and long term with smaller negotiations occurring as issues or changes come up."

Bradford looked thoughtful for a moment. When he responded, his tone was questioning and he said only one word. "Interesting."

"You don't like it," Tobias observed.

"Well, if you want my opinion, the adjustment to your living arrangements is certainly something to be discussed, but a live-in arrangement may require more significant alterations to the existing contract than you think." Bradford shifted in his chair. "As for the indefinite contract length, I think reviewing it 'as things come up' is dangerous, frankly. If you desire an open-ended contract I would build in a mandatory review period monthly or quarterly, something that will both empower Noah to speak up and force you to allow him to do so. It's not that I doubt your integrity..." Bradford's words trailed off as he took another sip of his coffee.

"Whoa!" Tobias sat up and shook his head, trying not to smile. "I really do get it both barrels, don't I? One thing at a time, okay? I'll give you a mandatory review time being a good idea, but let's talk about the live-in. What's the issue there?"

Bradford chuckled softly. "Sorry," he apologized and leaned forward a bit. "Noah is a very... independent sub, Tobias. At this point, I'll grant that you know him far better than I do, but I also know that his work is important to him and you're going to have to build in a way for him to keep that independence and still serve you twenty-four hours a day if he moves in. I assume you're talking about him moving in? It seems complicated to me, but maybe you and he can work it out."

Tobias sighed and looked around at the house he'd grown up in. "His work is pretty much all that's keeping me from moving out here full time, to tell you the truth. No way he could commute, and I don't think he's that comfortable in the condo. I'm thinking about looking for a building downtown, really. Something that can be reclaimed, closer to his precinct." He trailed off, knowing he sounded unsure of himself. "And I'll have to sign the condo over to Phan," he added as an after thought.

"That sounds reasonable." Bradford nodded. "And you're willing to do that? Move farther downtown, live the city lifestyle for him?"

"Of course," Tobias said, surprised. "The condo is just... an apartment. It's got a nice view, but it's not like here. Here means something; the condo doesn't. Well, to me anyway -- I'm sure that it means something to Phan, if only because it's his, too."

"Phan's always got a place with me," Bradford offered. "If he ever needs somewhere to go. I really am happy for you, Tobias. You've been very good for Noah; it's obvious how he feels about you, and he's been good for you, too. You've clearly given this more thought than I'd given you credit for. I'm sure the two of you can work out living arrangements that will fill both of your needs."

Tobias shrugged. "We'll sort it, I know. Right now there are other things to think about." He sighed heavily and forced himself not to sink into grief right then. There was plenty of time to deal with that later -- and he was fairly sure that he'd be doing a lot of it. Gathering his thoughts again he said, "I'd like to clarify some rules as well -- public scenes, rules for playing with others, that kind of thing. Noah tends to be happiest when the rules are laid out and very clear."

"Because he can just follow them and he doesn't have to think or worry about it. He doesn't have to make heat-of-the-moment-decisions." Bradford grinned. "He's a good boy."

"He is," Tobias agreed with a smile. "And sometimes he does make good decisions under fire." He winked, remembering the feel of Noah in him. He tried not to move around his chair.

"Um, I think I should warn you I'm awake now, sir," Noah said softly from the couch. He grinned and ran his fingers through Phan's hair.

Bradford looked at him. "How long have you been awake, boy?"

Noah blinked. "I just woke up this minute, Master Bradford. Honest."

Tobias decided to take Noah at his word; if he'd heard more than gentle praise, they'd talk about it later, in the safe room. "How are you?" he asked instead, watching to see if Phan would wake up also.

"I'm fine, sir. Sorry I dozed off, Phan is just so warm when he snuggles."

Bradford snickered. "He is at that."

Tobias snickered. "I was wondering if you snuggled. You don't seem the type."

Bradford laughed. "Not hardly. But tell me, how do you spend any significant time around Phan and not find yourself snuggled with?" He grinned.

"'M not that bad," Phan said, his voice muffled by Noah's chest.

"Yes, you are," Tobias corrected gently. "But it's not a bad thing."

"You're like a cat, Phan. And I mean that as a compliment." Noah smiled and continued to play with Phan's hair.

"A big, hedonistic cat," Bradford added, still laughing.

"Now you're just making fun," Phan grumbled, but he stretched and wiggled, snuggling Noah even more completely. "Besides, he's just the same."

Tobias assumed Phan meant Noah and not Bradford. "No, not really," he said with a smile. "He likes his cuddles, but not quite to your level." He looked at them critically. "But, then, he doesn't ever seem to mind you crawling all over him."

"What's to mind, sir?" Noah asked, grinning as Phan practically climbed him like a tree.

Tobias just laughed and shook his head again, watching Phan play. He knew very well that Phan was acting up to avoid talking about things that hurt, and he also knew he couldn't let it go on for long, for his sake as well as Phantom's. "Have some coffee, boys," he said softly. "And then maybe Noah can take Bradford to see the horses."

"Thank you, sir," Noah said extracting himself carefully from Phan. "You want some coffee, Phan?" He made his way over to the tray and offered Tobias and Bradford warm-ups before filling a mug for himself.

"No, thanks," Phan said, sitting up. He sighed, and Tobias watched him shift gears, reacting to the change in the room, the shift of the mood. He looked around the room and finally got up, moving past Noah with one last pet to sit at Bradford's feet, his head leaning against the man's knees. "I'll just... wait."

Bradford stroked a hand across Phan's head and let it rest on his shoulder. "Do you feel any better after your nap, boy?" he asked softly.

Phan shrugged. "A bit, I guess. I'll be able to eat later, I think."

Tobias gave him a hard look. "You'll eat."

"I tried!"

"I'm sure you did, and I'm sure Bradford did his best to make sure you did -- I'm just saying that you're here... you'll eat. Noah's got soup on."

Tobias saw Bradford raise an eyebrow, but the man said nothing.

"You'll like it," Noah assured Phan softly. He looked at Tobias. "I can take my coffee out to the barn, sir, if you'd like me to show Master Bradford around."

Tobias nodded, standing up. "If you don't mind," he said to Bradford. "I'm not trying to step on toes, I just..." he shrugged helplessly. "I need some time with Phan. And I think he needs some time in her kitchen."

Bradford shook his head. "My toes are fine," he said as he stood, then he looked at Noah. "Come along, boy."

Noah stood as well, taking one more sip of his coffee and apparently deciding just to leave it behind. "I'll get your coat, sir," he said as he led Bradford out into the foyer.

Tobias looked at Phan, still sitting on the floor. "Come on," he said gently. "Time to eat. We can talk in the kitchen."

Phan sighed again and followed Tobias into the hall and

then down to the kitchen. "Are you okay?" Phan asked as they went into the wide, inviting room.

"I will be," Tobias said, yet again. "But at the moment, not really. It's... I think it must be because it was such a surprise. She was in such good health, I didn't really think of her as being as old as she was."

Phan nodded as he pulled out a chair and sat down at the table. "I never thought of her as being old enough to die," he said softly. "She was too vibrant for the idea of it to really cross my mind. But really -- I mean, I knew she would, some day."

"Just not *this* day," Tobias agreed. He got a deep bowl and ladled some soup for Phan, adding a good many vegetables but making sure to get out as many carrots as he could. He made up for it with the peas and corn. The meat he wasn't so picky about; he just didn't want to give Phan an excuse to pick at his meal. "Bread?" he asked, setting the bowl down in front of Phan.

Phan looked up at him, his eyes wide. "God, I'm sorry. I should be doing this--"

Tobias waved it off. "Sit. Eat. It's been a hard day or so."

Phantom picked up his spoon under Tobias' watchful eye and started eating his soup, making an appreciative sound. "It's good," he said, taking another spoonful.

"I know," Tobias said with a smile. "Noah's getting to be a wonderful cook -- he takes lessons."

Phan nodded. "He told me," he said, slurping more soup. He glanced around the kitchen and tilted his head. "Elizabeth taught me to cook."

Sitting down, Tobias shook his head. "She refined you a bit. You could already cook."

Phan smiled sadly and ate more soup, finally emptying the bowl. He pushed it away and bit his lip, his shoulders starting to shake. "Remember the sugar bowl?" he whispered.

"I was just talking about it," Tobias said softly. He got up and rounded the table to put his arm around Phan. "She loved it."

"It wasn't as nice as the one I broke."

"She liked yours more."

"You bought it."

"You picked it out. You spent a weekend chained to a wall for being clumsy. You wanted to replace it. You thought about her feelings. Her tastes. Her needs. You made it up to us both, but it was her you apologized to."

Phan turned and buried his head in Tobias' chest, sobbing quietly. "I miss her. I miss... everything. I miss you."

Tobias nodded, not surprised that one thought led to the other. "Shh," he soothed. "It's okay to miss her. She loved you -- called you her sweetie pie."

Phan's shoulders shook and his arms went around Tobias' waist as he cried. Tobias stood in the kitchen, more Mrs. Miller's than his own right then, and held him, his own tears falling silently until there was a quiet knock at the kitchen door.

He looked up and nodded at Robert, but didn't let go of Phan as the neighbors started to arrive. They could see to themselves, and Noah would be back to help before long. He had a boy to take care of, if only for an afternoon.

14

Tobias was well aware that in the few short weeks since Mrs. Miller's funeral he'd relied on Noah to be many things. Sub, lover, partner, and friend, Noah had really been exactly what Tobias needed, when he needed him to be it. Tobias had also spent more time with Phantom than he had been, and while he knew that Noah understood, he also knew that there was a time when certain things were going to have to be underlined once more.

Like the fact that Noah was his, he was Noah's, and that Tobias wasn't the only one with issues.

The weekend of Noah's thirtieth birthday, Tobias had plans to give his boy a monumental gift. Intangible and horrible, the gift was one that Tobias hoped would lead Noah past one of his deepest limits.

Friday was passed in the usual way, with added teasing as Noah prodded him for hints about his present. All that Tobias would tell him was that Saturday would be long and intense and that dinner was being catered.

Saturday morning, while Noah saw to the horses,

Tobias made a few changes in the ring, adjusting the furniture to suit his needs. Satisfied after he'd pulled a few of the trunks to the walls, made sure he'd gathered all the first aid equipment, and put his cell phone on the library table, he went back to the house to wait for Noah in the safe room.

Noah's shower seemed longer than usual, but he appeared soon enough, naked except for his collar and his rings. His hair, which Tobias had noted Noah had allowed to grow longer in recent weeks, was still wet and combed neatly.

He made his way into the safe room silently and knelt in front of Tobias' feet.

"Good boy," Tobias said softly. "The horses behaved?" He fingered a leather lead as he spoke, twisting the braid through his fingers.

"Yes, sir. They were less than happy to be turned out in the cold, but they'll warm up soon enough. It's really raw out there this morning. Windy."

"Then you'll have to wear more than just a harness out to the stables," Tobias noted. "I had thought about attaching this to clamps, but I think a harness will be better -- pick one out, please, and something warm to wear over it."

"Yes, sir." Tobias watched Noah look the lead over curiously before making his way to the armoire. He spent a few moments considering the several harnesses there and then picked one, taking it off the hanger.

It was made of smooth, wide, sturdy leather in front, where all the leather straps were permanently attached at the sternum to a flat piece of metal that had a round ring hanging from it. The back was fastened to a D-ring snaffle bit. Horsey, kinky, and, Tobias knew, one of Noah's favorites.

As the fasteners were all in the back, Noah pulled it over

his shoulders and then knelt with his back to Tobias for help.

Tobias bent and began to thread the leather through buckles. "We're going to work hard today, pet. It's time we made progress on something for you... time I pushed a little. I need you to really try. I need you to do your very best today." He kept his tone low, his voice quiet and serious. Noah had little trouble finding his subspace these days, but what Tobias was going to do needed him deeper.

Noah nodded. "All right, sir," he answered, and Tobias felt him take a deep breath under his fingers as he fastened the last buckle. "May I ask what you have in mind?"

"You can always ask," Tobias said with a smile. "But this is one of those times when I won't tell." He stroked a finger along the harness and nodded to himself. "Stand, please, and face me."

Noah moved as ordered, automatically assuming his display position as he did so, neatly clasping his arms behind his back and lifting his chin. His eyes, of course, remained low.

Snapping the lead on, Tobias admired his boy. "What are you, pet?" he asked. "Tell me your place."

Noah licked his lips and then answered. "I'm your sub, sir," he said easily. "It is my place to please you, to serve you, and to fulfill your needs."

Tobias began to move around Noah, pacing and touching him randomly. "Correct. And to do that you fill any reasonable request I have, is that also correct?"

"Yes, sir. I am yours to use as you wish." Noah's skin pimpled with goose bumps where Tobias' fingers brushed him.

"You are," Tobias agreed softly. "And I will. But first, you will help me dress. Then we will transform you, pet. It won't be easy." He touched Noah again and stood in front of him. "You will be scared."

"I will try my best to please you, sir. I know that you'll keep me safe." Noah spoke just as softly, but his voice held confidence that his words were true.

"Good boy," Tobias praised him, and rewarded him with a kiss on his forehead. "Very good."

He took a step back and looked down at himself, dressed in jeans and a sweater. "This won't do, pet. Fetch my boots and the boot hooks while I change, please."

Noah nodded and turned, not rushing as he did as he was told, simply moving efficiently. Tobias stripped and began to dress in his black leather pants, pleased but unsurprised when Noah helped him without being asked. Noah really was a good boy.

Once he was wearing the tight leather, Tobias slipped on a leather vest and sat down so Noah could help him with the jackboots. Finally, he stood and picked up a crop.

"Get the cloak, pet, and something warm to cover your legs. I don't want you damaged on the way over."

Noah fetched the cloak and tugged on a pair of loose sweatpants for the walk. It didn't exactly make the outfit, but if it was as cold as Noah said it was, fashion was a secondary consideration.

Noah waited as Tobias took the lead in his fingers and then followed fairly well at heel down the stairs.

Tobias made sure Noah had warm shoes on and put on his own overcoat, not for the first time wishing that the stable were closer to the house. "Come, then," he said, and tugged a little on the lead as they went out the door, just to see if Noah would move closer and how long it took him. He was reasonably pleased with Noah's reaction, and hoped that it boded well for the afternoon.

He brought Noah into the stable and they took a moment or two to run through their routine. Noah put their outerwear away and Tobias turned up the heat a little and played with the lights until he had what he wanted. In this case, he lit the whole ring and the hall leading to it; there was no need for dramatic lighting at all.

He took up the end of the lead again and started down the path to the ring. "Simple heel training to start," he said softly, knowing Noah would see the cage and the supplies the moment he happened to glance up from the floor. He was well aware of Noah's change in posture behind him, but it wasn't as extreme or as long-lasting as the last time they'd done this exercise. It was just a few awkward moments before Noah seemed focused again, and he never completely lost his concentration.

"Very good," Tobias praised softly. "A little closer now." He walked Noah in a smaller circle, and then took him within ten feet of the cage before leading him away again.

The closer they got to the cage, the more Tobias sensed Noah forcing himself to concentrate, forcing himself deeper into his space. He was walking right at Tobias' heel, so close that Tobias could feel Noah's breath on his shoulder, and his eyes were fixed straight ahead. He was not allowing them to linger on anything at all, including the cage.

Tobias stiffened his resolve. He had to do this to Noah, had to do it *for* Noah. He walked him to the cage and stopped. "Look at it," he ordered, trying to make sure his voice was calm and clear, not in any way something other than the one he used to say "I'd like some water, please."

Noah stiffened, but he did as he was told, if briefly. He turned his eyes on the cage and held them there for a moment before lowering them to the floor.

"Nothing will happen to you," Tobias said, his voice still

calm and soothing, pitched for the most effect. "It's steel bars, and nothing more. It's smooth, there are no snags. I will not leave you. Nothing will happen to you. Look at it, and we'll touch it together." He held out his hand, waiting for Noah to take it in his own.

When Tobias felt Noah's trembling fingers in his, he reached down and pressed their hands against the cool steel. Noah's breath caught and the boy cleared his throat. They stood there quietly, moving their hands over the steel and exploring how it felt, until, quite unexpectedly, Noah went to his knees beside Tobias and curled his fingers around one of the bars on his own.

"Oh, good," Tobias breathed. He knelt down next to him, one hand solid on Noah's back. "That's it, just hold on for a moment. It's just steel, there really is nothing here that will hurt you. Good boy."

He waited for a long moment, rubbing a slow circle on Noah's back. "All right so far?" he asked. Tobias assumed that by now Noah understood what he was in store for. His breathing wasn't quite steady and he hadn't entirely stopped shaking, but he seemed to be reasonably stable.

"Nervous, sir," Noah admitted quietly. "Apprehensive. But I'm all right."

"You're doing just fine," Tobias said softly. "I'm right here and I won't leave. There's no rush. Touch the cage... look at it. Move around it, examine it. It's just steel bars. It can't hurt you. I won't leave." Tobias put a slight cadence into the repetitive words, and he slowly backed away a foot or two, no more. He was there, right there, but Noah could move without bumping into him. No matter how much Noah was going to try to cling, it was important that he take steps by himself.

All the same, Noah looked over his shoulder as Tobias

moved away and didn't look back at the cage until he seemed sure that Tobias was going no farther. When he turned his attention back to the cage, he added a second hand to the first and held on to both bars. He gave a light tug against it as if testing its weight. He stood and walked a painfully slow circle around it, his eyes riveted on the cage and his arms crossed tightly over his chest, his lead gathered up in one hand. Every so often he'd wince, as if he were working through his memories. Finally, he ended up back at Tobias' side, kneeling and staying close and tight to Tobias' calf.

"I don't think you're ready, pet," Tobias said softly. He wasn't, Tobias was sure. If he ordered Noah in now, it would get messy fast. "Examine it some more. Touch it. Get used to it."

Noah took a deep breath and sighed heavily. But he got to his feet and moved back to the cage as Tobias told him to and then moved to the far side. He circled it again, bending slightly to trail his fingers along the top edge.

He stopped, and Tobias watched his face as Noah wrapped his fingers around the bars again and seated himself cross-legged beside it.

Noah stared into the empty space inside the cage and his brow furrowed. "It's just steel, I know. Steel bars alone can't hurt me," Noah whispered. He seemed to be talking primarily to himself. "I have a scar or two, but it wasn't the steel of the cage that hurt me before. Not really." Tentatively, he slipped one hand through the bars and into the cage as far as he could manage. His eyes narrowed, but he kept his arm there until his fingers stopped trembling.

"It was never the cage that hurt me, sir," Noah said again, loud enough to be well heard this time. "It wasn't this... contraption, it was... it was the people that put me in it."

"Exactly, pet," Tobias said. His voice was soft because that was what Noah needed, but inside he was yelling, cheering Noah on. "Exactly."

Tobias walked forward and around, keeping his steps just as slow and measured as he'd kept the entire process. With one hand he gently swung the cage door open. "When you're ready," he said, trusting that Noah understood he meant that afternoon, not months from now.

Noah withdrew his arm from the cage and turned to face the open door. He'd gone pretty pale since they'd started this, but the look on Noah's face wasn't really fear anymore. Nerves, worry, to be sure. But not fear. Tobias had seen fear in Noah's eyes before and this wasn't it.

Tobias didn't want to push him, but it did seem like forever before Noah finally moved around in front of the open door. He traced the contour of the locking bolt with his fingers and otherwise procrastinated for a bit before concentrating on the inside of the cage again.

By Tobias' estimation, it took him three honest attempts before he was really moving. By his third try he was trembling again and angrily wiping tears from his eyes. But he managed it, crawling through the open door and completely into the cage, his leash once more clutched tightly in one hand. Once inside, though, he froze.

"I'm right here," Tobias said immediately. He crouched down by the cage and kept himself in front of Noah, taking further care to stay at eye level. "You are not alone," he said. "You are not in danger. I'm right here. You are not alone."

Noah nodded and swallowed hard. Part of him, Tobias could tell, was keeping an eye on the still-open door, as if he might bolt at any moment.

With what looked like great effort, Noah forced himself to sit down on one hip. He leaned back, resting his back against the bars at the far end of the cage. His breathing was shallow and he blinked tears out of his eyes again, but he seemed better with Tobias in his line of vision.

"You're doing fine," Tobias said, sitting on the floor. "I'm right here. I can see you, you can see me. It's just steel. I won't hurt you, you know that."

Tobias watched carefully, but he was feeling more and more confident every moment Noah remained there. He wasn't panicking; he wasn't hurting himself to get away. He wasn't comfortable, but he was light-years from where he'd been.

"I will never damage you," Tobias said again, his voice soft and careful as he stayed exactly where Noah could see him.

"I know, sir." Noah closed his eyes and took several long, measured breaths. "I trust you, I do." Noah shifted again so he was sitting upright. His head just barely cleared the top of the cage. "It's not the cage. It never was the cage," he whispered again, reassuring himself perhaps, or just trying to stay grounded. Either way, it was an important distinction, and one he hadn't made until today.

"I've tried not to blame Brett," Noah said softly after a long silence. "I... I know he didn't mean to hurt me. But he was careless and he did. It wasn't my fault I lost my balance -- lost my headspace -- it wasn't my fault for not trusting him enough. It was his fault for leaving me there... right? It's not that I was wrong to be afraid. It wasn't wrong to fight it and not just wait for him to come back, was it? I've always felt like I let him down, that I should have shown my trust for him and tried harder..."

"It wasn't your fault," Tobias said matter-of-factly, his voice quiet. "He didn't earn the trust you still want to give him, and he messed up. You paid for it. It was not your fault in any way, pet."

Tobias had a great deal more to say on the subject, and maybe someday they'd get to that. He knew very well that Brett was a good man, a kind man, but he'd had no business messing with Noah's mind when he had. Tobias also knew that Brett had never gotten past the incident, and that fact alone softened his opinion. At the moment, however, all of that was beside the point. He had Noah in a cage and he had a job to do.

"It was never your fault," he whispered again, watching Noah closely.

Noah nodded again and sighed. Silently, he reached over his head and traced the bars with his fingers, out as far as he could reach, then down the sides to the barred floor. He slid his fingers along the floor as well.

"I'm okay, sir," he told Tobias softly. "My heart is still pounding a little and my stomach is tight, but it's like those knee-jerk reactions I used to have. It's not rational, it's emotional."

"You're doing well," Tobias encouraged him. "Do you want some water? I'd like you to stay there for a little bit, see if we can get you totally calm."

Noah blinked. "Oh... yes, please, sir." The small offer of comfort seemed to rally Noah a little. "My mouth is pretty dry."

Tobias nodded. He moved carefully as he stood up, watching as Noah tracked him with his eyes, turning his head to keep Tobias in view. Tobias walked the three steps to the table and got a water bottle, relieved that he'd not needed any of the first aid equipment or the cell phone. They weren't done yet, but the worst part was done.

He walked back to the cage and handed Noah the water

through the open cage door. And then he carefully swung the door closed, not latching it. "I'm right here," he said yet again.

Noah took the water calmly enough, but his eyes widened as the cage door closed and he dove for it, grabbing hold of the door with one hand. He clearly wanted to shove it open, everything about his posture said so, but Tobias was pleased to see Noah fighting to regain control.

Noah took several deep breaths and, as his trembling subsided, he let go, moving stiffly to the back of the cage again. His eyes never left the door, however, even as he opened the bottle of water and took a long gulp.

"It's the same place," Tobias said as soothingly as he could. "It's still just steel. I'm still right here. And I am not going to leave, I promise. I will never hurt you. It's just steel bars. You're doing well, pet. You're okay." He kept up the litany as he sat down on the floor, right in front of Noah, on the other side of the door.

"Okay," Noah said softly when he could speak again. "Okay."

Noah sipped his water more slowly as they sat there. He watched Tobias the whole time, but his posture did relax little by little. When he'd finished the water he reached forward and handed it back through the bars to Tobias.

"Thank you, sir." He sounded better.

"Thank you," Tobias replied softly. "Do you think I can lock the door for a couple of minutes?"

Noah chewed his lip and his brow furrowed but he nodded slowly. "You'll stay right there, though?"

"Of course. I will never leave you like this." Tobias had a sudden thought and added, "And just in case you had a fear growing in the back of your mind, I will never use a cage in a scene with you. This is just to push the boundary. Do you understand?"

Noah sighed and seemed to relax a bit more. "I understand, sir."

"Good boy." Tobias settled himself a little more, and reached for the cage door. "Just a few minutes, pet," he said, as he flipped the catch to lock the door. "I won't padlock it." He slid the bolt through its eye.

Noah didn't move, didn't stir, and Tobias was starting to wonder if he was even breathing until he licked his lips and swallowed hard. "I trust you, sir," Noah said, speaking carefully. "You've never betrayed that trust, never hurt me, never given me any reason to doubt you. I really..." His words trailed off, and he swallowed again. "I really can't tell you what that means to me -- how grateful I am."

Tobias shook his head. "Thank you, pet, but really... don't think about me right now. This is for you. You're doing a great job, you're meeting your fear and you're getting through it. Pleasing me isn't the issue here, although I appreciate that you want to. Just be who you are, what you are. Feel what you feel. You're scared and you're upset, but you're coping. You're not panicking. Be proud of yourself, boy."

Noah bit his lip and blushed, and then Tobias caught a hint of a smile. "Thank you, sir," he replied, more confidently than he'd said anything since he crawled into the cage.

"Oh, well done, pet," Tobias praised. His heart lightened as he watched, noting all the changes in Noah's posture and how far he'd come since the first time Tobias had pulled the cage into the ring. He really was exceptionally proud of Noah, and he could feel pride beginning to stir in him. He himself was becoming part of the experience, and that was a signal to begin the end.

Slowly, he retracted the bolt and unlatched the door. "Ready to come out?" he asked casually, swinging the door open.

"Yes, sir." Noah shifted to his knees again and crawled toward the door once Tobias had it open. He still didn't like the cage, obviously, but he wasn't rushing or panicking at all.

Tobias smiled and moved back, giving Noah room to crawl right into his lap. "Come on, then," he said. "Let me hold you for a bit."

"Thank you, sir," Noah whispered as he settled against Tobias' chest. He pressed close and sighed, and although he seemed to be relieved to be rid of the cage, he wasn't trembling like he was before he went in. "Thank you."

"Happy birthday," Tobias whispered, holding Noah tight to him and rubbing his back. "I'm so proud of you. I can't even begin to tell you how much." He couldn't find words for the way his blood was surging, Noah's victory charging through him. It was a Top's high, without doubt, and he wasn't terribly sure it was appropriate, but there it was. He felt fiercely that Noah had outdone himself, exceeded any expectation either of them had, and the Dom in him was shouting for joy at the success. He pressed an almost chaste kiss to Noah's forehead and said it again. "So proud of you."

Noah was grinning now. "That wasn't too bad, was it? That was okay. I wasn't a complete wreck, you know?" He laughed softly. "God, I feel so good. So strong. Thank you so much, sir." He took a deep breath and let out his remaining tension as he exhaled. "What a perfect gift."

"I'm glad you think so," Tobias said, a little embarrassed by the growl creeping into his voice.

"I wasn't sure at first, sir, and you scared the hell out of me when you closed that door." Noah lifted his head and kissed the underside of Tobias' chin. "You're so good to me."

"Didn't mean to scare you," Tobias said. He took Noah's chin in one hand and held him there for a long, deep kiss. "Never mean to scare you," he said when he came up for air.

"I know, sir." Noah shifted slowly in Tobias' lap so he was on his knees facing Tobias and straddling his hips. "I am what I am. I am able to do these difficult things because of you. I am your boy. I know I'm growing personally, too, but if I make you proud, Master, it's because you have given me what I need to do it."

This time, Tobias actually felt the growl rumble in his chest, and with an effort he squashed the urge to merely dump Noah on his back and attack him. "My boy," he said instead, his voice tight. His hips rolled up of their own accord, and he tugged at Noah's lead with one hand, pulling him down for another kiss.

Tobias felt warm fingers through the leather of his pants, pressing his cock and lower, rubbing at his balls. Noah leaned heavily into him, and Tobias went backward to the floor, fingers still tightly gripping the harness.

Quickly, Noah undid his vest and pushed it open, then Noah's lips were on him -- warm and wet on his neck, his shoulders, teasing a nipple.

"God, yes. All mine," Tobias groaned. With his free hand he grabbed at Noah's ass, the smooth skin feeling slightly cool. His hips pushed against Noah's hand and he groaned again.

Noah said nothing; he just kept right on doing what he was doing. His teeth closed around the other nipple. His fingers rubbed and tugged at Tobias' cock and finally started to undo his fly.

"Not here," Tobias managed, even as his cock pushed past the zipper and into Noah's hand. "Table."

"Yes, sir," Noah said in his silkiest bedroom voice. He gave Tobias' prick a swift, hard tug and then got to his feet. He left Tobias where he was and slowly made his way over to the table. Tobias was grateful for the view, and he knew Noah's movements were deliberate. Finally, Noah placed his hands on the table edge, looked over his shoulder toward Tobias, and shoved his ass out, his erection now much more evident.

Tobias lay on the floor for a moment longer, wondering what he'd ever done to deserve such a sub in his life. "You're going to kill me one day," he said, rolling to his feet. He snatched the lube off the table and waved it at Noah. "But not before I manage to fuck you stupid."

"I think you've said that before, sir," Noah teased, spreading his legs just that much wider. "The stupider, the better; it's my thirtieth birthday, after all."

"Happy birthday," Tobias said again, shoving two slick fingers into Noah's ass. He leaned over Noah's back and bit down on his shoulder, rubbing his cock shamelessly on Noah's butt while he fingered Noah open.

Noah's head dropped forward between his arms and he groaned, long and low. Tobias felt Noah relax around his fingers and press back to meet them in his usual shameless way. "Yes..."

"You're such a slut," Tobias chuckled. He added a finger and rubbed against Noah's gland. "Think I can make you shoot before I fuck you?"

"Oh, God." Noah glanced over his shoulder and moaned. The answer was perfectly obvious; he didn't need Noah to tell him he could push his boy anywhere he wanted him to go.

Grinning, Tobias moved his fingers again. "You're so hot when you come," he said, making his voice as throaty as possible. It wasn't quite talking him into an orgasm, what with his fingers up Noah's ass, but it was close enough. "I love watching your cock when you shoot, you know that? The way it throbs and jumps and the way your balls pull up -- that's part of why I like watching you jerk off."

Noah whimpered, and the fingers of one hand moved to his cock. "Sir... love your voice, to hear you talk dirty, so hot." Noah moaned and kept talking, his words tumbling out of him. "Fingers are so good. Want to ride them, can't wait to feel your cock in me. Hard, deep... Oh, God." He started to pant, his fingers pumping his erection slowly.

"That's it, pet," Tobias growled. "Touch yourself. Talk to me. Make it feel good..." He rubbed against Noah again, leaving a slick trail as his own prick leaked.

Noah moved on Tobias' fingers and fisted his cock. "So good. Always so good. You make me so hard. Want you in me, need it, need you, Master, like air, like breathing. Need you... oh, oh, oh, yes, there!" He arched his back and then went still, letting Tobias continue the thrust of his fingers.

"Come for me," Tobias urged, driving his fingers deeper and stroking over Noah's gland again and again. His gaze was fixed on Noah's cock, waiting for the swollen head to pulse, waiting for Noah to come.

Noah gasped, ducked his head and grunted, and his fingers sped on his prick. In moments he was pulling release from his body, moaning and spilling milky spunk across the heavy table. "God yes... Sir!" he babbled, squeezing every last drop from his cock before his shoulders slumped and he sighed, fully spent.

Tobias groaned, his own cock leaping in sympathy as he slowed his hand and let Noah come down a little. "Going to fuck you," he whispered. "I'm going to bury myself in your ass and fuck you hard."

"Yes. Yes, please, Master," Noah encouraged, lifting his head and looking over his shoulder. "Want you, want to feel you, want to still feel it tomorrow."

"You will," Tobias promised. He pulled his fingers out of Noah and reached for the lube again, slicking himself efficiently. He was harder than he could remember being in a long time -- weeks -- his dick rigid and red. He caught sight of the cage out of the corner of his eye and growled again, his hunger building even more. "So fucking proud of you," he said, grabbing Noah's hips.

"Best birthday ever," Noah breathed, pushing back toward Tobias' cock. "Do it, please. Take me!"

Tobias pulled Noah back onto him, sliding in hard and fast. "Just because you asked so nicely," he said roughly, starting to thrust. He felt Noah grab the table with both hands and slid one of his own around to Noah's cock. "You're still hard," he said with a tight smile. "Slut."

"Want you," Noah grunted, his fingers going white knuckled on the table edge.

"You better." Tobias bit down on Noah's shoulder again and thrust into him with tiny, shallow strokes, purposely missing the hot spot more often than he hit it. "Love your ass. Love feeling you around me."

Noah collapsed at the feeling of Tobias' teeth, bracing one elbow on the table and leaning into it. He reached back with his other hand and managed to get a grip on Tobias' thigh. "Jesus!"

"More?" Tobias asked, trying to sound like he was merely making a polite inquiry, but he thought he was probably betrayed by the need in his voice. He wanted Noah to come again, wanted to feel Noah spasm around his cock, but he wasn't sure he could hang on that long. With a groan he thrust harder, deeper, his body forcing him to up the pace.

"More! Harder. Please!" Noah shifted, changing the angle, trying to guide Tobias to the spot, as if Tobias didn't know perfectly well where his buttons were.

Tobias grunted and slammed into Noah's ass. "Harder? More? Here?" he asked, starting to fist Noah's cock with each stab into his body.

Noah whimpered, arched, thrust into Tobias' hand.

"Want to feel you," Tobias hissed into Noah's ear. "Want you to come on me, pet. Want to fuck you through another orgasm and then I'll shoot in your ass, fill you up--"

Noah was well beyond words and didn't seem to know whether he should thrust back to Tobias' prick or forward into Tobias' hand. His hips jerked and thrust erratically and he grunted and whimpered until a second climax finally took him. His body went eerily still, and Tobias collected a fistful of come before he felt Noah go tight around him, choking his cock.

"God, yes!" Tobias cried out, his head falling back as he pushed deeper, worked against Noah's orgasm to pull his own out. "Fuck!" He shook and pushed and tried to get as far into Noah as he could as he started to come. His head came down and he tried not to bite Noah's neck, but he wanted to, wanted to mark him.

Noah was his.

"Mine."

He kept coming, his cock throbbing and pouring spunk into Noah's ass. Fire raced through him, ecstasy floated in his blood, and he shuddered again and again, finally pushing Noah flat on the table and falling across him, spent.

Underneath him, Noah was panting hard. Tobias felt his chest expand and contract as he struggled to regain control.

They were drenched, both of them, slippery with sweat and come, pliable in the wake of their efforts. "Master," Noah breathed. "Love you."

"God, yes," Tobias whispered. "Love you so much, sweetheart." He lifted himself up and off, pulling out carefully with a low moan. "Jesus. I'm too old for this."

Noah laughed, turning himself around and pulling himself up to sit on the table. "Too old for what exactly, sir? Fucking me stupid?"

"Yeah, that." Tobias looked at him and shook his head. "You can sit? I'm doing something wrong."

"I won't be able to in an hour. Hurts so good." Noah grinned, tugging Tobias closer. "Kiss me."

"Oh, all right," Tobias said, feigning reluctance. He leaned forward and shoved his tongue into Noah's mouth, his arms going around to pull him close.

Tobias felt Noah grin around the kiss. Noah sucked Tobias' tongue briefly and then released him, still grinning, his eyes remaining low. "Just bars." He shrugged. "What are you going to do with me now?"

"Take you to the house and give you your birthday spankings, of course."

"Thirty is a lot of spankings... you'll have my ass on ice tomorrow," Noah teased.

"Probably," Tobias agreed happily. "A nice rosy ass... one of my favorite things." He stood up and redid his fly with a grin. "And then there's the presents..."

Noah hopped off the table, wincing a bit as he hit the floor, apparently discovering that he shouldn't be hopping around for a while. "Presents!"

"Presents," Tobias confirmed. "All good boys get toys for their birthday."

"I better get to cleaning up in here then," Noah said coyly.

"That's a good idea," Tobias said, walking away. "I'll be in the shower. With your new dildo."

Noah blinked and stuttered. "My...?"

"Your." Tobias stopped and turned around. "You really should hurry, or I'll be forced to start without you."

T obias looked at the folder on his desk and sighed. The file held a list of all the possessions in the farm house that belonged to Mrs. Miller, and he'd just spent an hour walking through every room, making sure that her things had gone to her family.

His house felt oddly off-kilter, despite the fact that the things she'd kept in the common areas were few in number. In fact, the one thing that took up the most room, a long hallway table that she'd loved, was still there. Robert and Sue had insisted he keep it, saying it just looked best there. They'd also insisted that he keep many of her favorite kitchen items, claiming that there was no need to duplicate things in their own home.

Gone were her personal things, everything from her bedroom, and the little knickknacks she'd wanted to go to various family members. Still, there were a few things like the sugar bowl, which Tobias planned to make sure went to Phan.

The house still bore her mark, but it lacked her energy,

and Tobias found himself sighing again before closing the folder.

"All right, Tobias?" a voice asked from behind him, and Tobias jumped.

"Fine," he said as he turned to face Peter.

"Sorry about that," the man said. "Thought you heard me knock."

"Should have," Tobias said with a slight smile. "I was just cleaning up the last of Elizabeth's things. Making sure Robert and Sue didn't miss anything."

Peter shook his head. "They wouldn't be upset with you if they did, man. They'd just mention it. Everyone knows you're family, near enough."

Tobias smiled sadly. "You're right, of course." He picked up the other file on the desk and a pad of paper. "Let's go into the kitchen and have some tea."

Peter nodded. "Right enough. I've got some ideas for the back fields this season, and what we should leave fallow."

Tobias smiled. Peter ran the farm, really; this conversation was a mere formality so Peter could tell Tobias what he was doing and so they'd both know where the money was going. It was an annual event, and had been for years. Peter would also let Tobias know when he'd hired on help, when the hay was due to be cut and come in, and everything else.

It was Peter's farm, really.

"So, you're off to Paris next week?" Peter asked, sitting at the table.

Tobias nodded. "Yes, it's a gift to Noah. He's never been."

Peter smiled. "Hope it's a good trip for him."

"Me, too. We need the break, after this winter."

Peter nodded. "It's been a hard one, aye. How's Phantom?"

Tobias blinked. "Phan?"

Peter shrugged. "Mrs. Miller sent him cookies a few times. Said he was having a hard time."

Tobias really should have known. "He's doing better," he said, gathering things for tea. "Thanks for asking."

Peter just nodded calmly, and they spent the next couple of hours planning for the farm and going over accounts. Tobias found the process very close to setting his affairs in order; perhaps he'd been thinking too much of such things.

"Should I keep it?" he asked suddenly, leaning back in his chair.

Peter didn't even ask what he meant, merely nodded. "Aye. You love it, you can afford it. Tobias, you lost family this year. Don't be thinking of losing your home, too. Decisions made in haste and all that."

Tobias nodded slowly. "But it's losing money."

"Does that matter to you?"

He sighed. "Not really."

"So you'd sell and regret it. And who would you sell to? Developers?"

Tobias stared at him. "Never. The last thing I want to see out here is a development. That's not what we need, what the people around here want." He couldn't do that. And he couldn't really imagine giving up the house, the horses. The stables.

Peter nodded. "You're tired, Tobias. Take Noah to Paris. Enjoy the sights. Come back and get back to your life. Things will even out."

Tobias sincerely hoped so. And if nothing else, he had a week away with Noah ahead of him; the thought cheered him immensely.

The plane was small, but not tiny. It was, after all, a jet used for business, and a jet used to impress.

Noah seemed impressed.

Tobias was rather impressed himself, and he'd been on it before. The pilot and the co-pilot had been full of apologies on behalf of the owner about the lack of steward, but Tobias was willing to forgive anyone for getting the flu. Plus, with no one wandering about the cabin, he got to enjoy it all with only Noah for company, and that was perfect, really.

He watched as Noah looked around again, taking in the casual seating of a few fixed chairs and the long couches. There were tables -- real ones, not those on the back of a chair in front of you -- and even a bar, which they both ignored except for the bottled water.

"Like it?" Tobias asked with a grin once the plane had leveled off and they could move around freely. He stood up and stretched, touching the curve of the roof over his head. "It's kind of nice, don't you think?"

"It's amazing, sir," Noah said, his eyes still wide. He wandered around the cabin, literally touching everything --

the mahogany bar, the leather bar stools, the shiny table tops, the smooth suede and leather seating. He looked out the window. He opened a door. "Oh, my God, have you seen the bathroom?" Tobias was sure Noah had almost squealed. Grinning, Noah turned back to Tobias. "This is incredible, sir. This is a dream. Pinch me, this can't be happening."

"Oh, an invitation," Tobias laughed, slipping an arm around Noah's waist. He goosed him and grinned. "So you approve, then. I'm glad. The trip is a little longer this way, but worth the time, I think."

Noah's grin was coy, and he slid a finger across Tobias' chest, tweaking a nipple through his shirt as he went. "Gee, whatever are we to do with the time?"

"I assumed you'd come up with something," Tobias said dryly. "Play cards, perhaps? Discuss the latest fashions or movies?"

Noah snorted. "Oh, yes. Cribbage. I'll deal."

Tobias laughed and rubbed his hand over Noah's ass. "You can if you want. Your trip, your plans. Well, right now, anyway."

"What?" Noah grinned again. "I'm in charge? Well, in that case, I lost the cards and current events are boring. I think you should let me blow you right where you're standing." He slid fingers along Tobias' thigh. "Slow and hot. We have hours to kill, after all. Did your flogger make it through customs?" Noah laughed softly.

"Sadly, no. I didn't even try a flogger... but I have great success with leather belts." He cupped Noah's ass again and squeezed. "Want to arrive in France with a glowing butt? Of course, if you'd rather just suck my cock and bend over a table, that could work, too."

"Can't we do all of those things? I'd love to get my ass whipped at thirty-five thousand feet. That would be one for my journal." Noah's hand pressed into Tobias' groin. "And just think, the co-pilot might come back to use the head at some point. He was pretty hot, too." Noah's voice got gravelly, and Tobias couldn't be at all sure that Noah was joking.

Shaking his head fondly, Tobias chuckled. He pressed into Noah's hand and let him grope for a moment, enjoying it quite thoroughly. "You want to be whipped, I'll whip you," he said, his own voice rough. "But I don't think I'll let the co-pilot play. Maybe he'll just watch. Would you like that?" he teased.

"He's probably happily married with a wife, three kids, and a golden retriever," Noah said with a chuckle. "This is nice, though." He squeezed Tobias through his perfectly-pressed dress pants. Evidently they weren't going to arrive in Paris that way.

"It is," Tobias agreed, pushing back a little harder. "Couch? Floor? Bathroom?"

"Not the bathroom, it's nice, but it's... pointy," Noah's nimble fingers unfastened Tobias' belt.

"Pointy?" Tobias asked with a choked laugh as Noah's fingers skimmed his length. "That's a new one."

Noah shook his head. "Lots of corners, small space," he explained.

"Ah. And here we have... leather. Couches." Tobias tried to nod wisely, but Noah's hand was finally slipping into his pants, and he got a little sidetracked. "Okay, you have me," he said, a little breathlessly. "Now what are you going to do?"

Noah stepped closer, forcing Tobias to step back until his knees hit one of the wide leather lounge chairs. "Guess," he breathed huskily and gave Tobias a light shove into the chair.

"Oh, let me see," Tobias pondered with a grin. "You're going to quote poetry to me?"

"Sure," Noah winked. "How shall I suck thee. Let me count the ways."

Tobias started to laugh, unable not to. "Oh, sweetheart," he finally managed. "I love you." Deliberately, he shoved his trousers down his hips and palmed his cock, stroking it loosely.

Noah was sporting a permanent grin. He tugged his sweater off over his head and then his T-shirt after it, tossing them both onto one of the tables. He knelt, and with both hands, he pushed Tobias' shirt up and licked across his stomach. "You're so hot," Noah said, his lips moving against Tobias' skin.

"Feeling rather warm, yes," Tobias said unevenly. "I suspect it's the altitude." He pulled his cock again and moaned, letting his legs fall apart. If they timed this right, he could come down Noah's throat and have time to get hard again. Maybe while whipping Noah's ass. The thought made him moan again. "Pet," he whispered.

Noah's lips moved over his skin, ignoring Tobias' cock for the moment and heading for his balls. Noah tugged them free of his pants and then began to bathe them slowly and with a great deal of attention paid to each. He took one and then the other into his mouth and rolled them with his tongue, his hands still resting warmly on Tobias' abs.

Tobias knew that he'd felt this needy before, and recently; he always did when it came to Noah. Usually he tried to tame the feeling, to give back as much as he was given, but this time he decided to be a little more selfish than the norm. He lifted his hips and pushed his trousers and shorts farther down, one hand going to the back of

Noah's head to encourage him. "Yes, pet," he moaned. "Like that."

Noah pushed Tobias' thighs wider and engaged his teeth lightly on the sensitive skin, teasing. Then he shifted and licked up the underside of Tobias' cock, all the way up his length to the head. He circled it with his tongue and then licked his way back to the base. "Like that?" Noah whispered, doing it again. "Like this?"

"Yes," Tobias hissed. "Any way. Don't care. Just want you."

Noah moaned this time, then opened his mouth and took Tobias in, once, all the way to the back of his throat. He released him right after, going back to licking and nibbling. "Taste so good, Master," Noah said in his hottest, deepest cop voice.

Tobias growled and tugged at Noah's hair with his fingers. When Noah's mouth opened, his eyes dancing with laughter and dark with lust, Tobias shoved in, pushing his cock deep again. "Suck me," he rumbled, his stomach tightening.

He caught Noah off guard, and it took a moment for him to catch up, but Noah followed Tobias' orders not only willingly but with an enthusiasm all his own. Without any hint of urgency, he took Tobias deep down his throat and then pulled back until only the head remained between his lips. He swallowed Tobias down again and pulled back, repeating the pattern evenly and moaning hotly when he was able to get air.

"Jesus," Tobias groaned, watching his prick slide between Noah's lips. "God, yes, pet." He tried not to thrust, not wanting to choke Noah again, but his hips were rocking, and he could feel his orgasm building. "Soon, pet."

Noah nodded slightly and picked up his pace. He shortened his strokes, sucked harder, swallowed Tobias over and over, encouraging Tobias with his moans and strong fingers dug into Tobias' thighs.

Tobias groaned and tried to keep himself quiet, but as the engine roared and the plane vibrated around them he decided it wasn't that important and let his growl grow a bit. He firmed his grip on the back of Noah's head and fucked his mouth, diving into the wet heat with a rising urgency until he felt his balls draw up tight.

"Now, Noah," Tobias ground out, his head falling back and his eyes closing as he started to come, his cock pulsing and throbbing as he shot down Noah's throat, his hips stuttering and losing any rhythm he'd had.

Noah shoved him back into his seat with both hands and swallowed him down, sucking and working his prick with his fingers until Tobias was spent. He sighed, bathing Tobias with his tongue. "So good."

Tobias merely rumbled and ran a hand over Noah's head, stroking the short hair and petting him for a job well done. He felt utterly boneless, content, and satiated. "Nice," he managed to say after a little concentration.

Noah raised his head and licked his lips, his eyes lifting just about to Tobias' chin but no higher. "I'm sure you say that to all the boys who blow you on the way to Paris."

"Hmm. As a case study of one, I'd have to say you're correct," Tobias said, grinning. He stretched, only slightly annoyed at finding his trousers in a tangled mess, and made himself presentable in short order. Completely ignoring Noah's obvious excitement, he removed his belt and placed it conspicuously on the back of the couch. "Could you get me some water, pet?" he asked politely.

Noah had followed the placement of the belt with his eyes and seemed genuinely startled by the request. "Oh, yes, sir." He stood and made his way to the bar, his erection clearly pushing at the fly of his jeans. He stepped behind the bar and found a bottle of water in the refrigerator, then returned slowly, kneeling by Tobias' feet and holding the bottle about head height for Tobias to take.

"Thank you," Tobias said, taking the bottle and opening it. He took a long drink, downing about half the bottle in a few swallows. It was important to stay hydrated. With his free hand he petted Noah's hair some more, just touching him while he finished the bottle of water. When it was gone, he leaned forward and put it on the table. "Okay, take off your pants," he said casually.

Noah seemed to have been eager for that request. He stood and shoved his jeans down and his briefs with them, toed his shoes off, and kicked everything out of the way.

Tobias shook his head and bit his lip to keep from laughing. "Such an eager boy," he commented, reaching for the belt. "Now, I'm fairly sure that I'll be fucking you at some point, so I suggest you prepare yourself..."

"Yes, sir." Noah nodded and stepped past Tobias to his carry-on bag, from which he produced a tube of lube. He came back, offering the bottle to Tobias first.

"You do it," Tobias purred.

Noah nodded and set the bottle down on the table next to the couch. He slicked his fingers and then lifted one foot and braced it on the couch between Tobias' thighs. Noah's hand disappeared behind his back as he leaned toward Tobias just slightly and then he sighed and moaned and his head bent forward.

Tobias raised an eyebrow. "Feel good? How many fingers?" he asked politely.

"One just now," Noah replied in response, already a little breathless. "Feels great, sir." He shifted and his hips pushed back a bit. "Wait... there. Two, sir. Just a little stretch, it's nice."

Tobias smiled and sank farther into the couch. "Just make sure you can take me, pet. I won't want to waste time."

"I can always take you, sir," Noah assured him. He worked himself a moment longer until he groaned, low and deep in his chest. "Mmm." He slipped his fingers free and swallowed, blushing. "I... think that's probably good enough, sir," he said, obviously trying to look contrite.

"Enjoyed that, did you?" Tobias asked rhetorically. "Well, I'd say your spanking is off to a fine start then." He grinned and slapped the belt into his hand. "Across my knees, ass high. No coming until I say so, understand? I'd hate to arrive in Paris with come stains on my trousers."

"Yes, sir. I understand." Noah bent over Tobias' knees and braced his hands on the floor. His heavy cock hung neatly between Tobias' thighs. No ring, Tobias mused; that would have been quite a thing to explain as they went through the metal detectors.

"Good boy. And try not to scream -- I'm not sure how much the pilot is willing to ignore." And with that, he brought the belt down on Noah's ass, leaving a nice red stripe.

"Ah, God." Tobias felt Noah's cock twitch as he hissed through the sting. Noah relaxed a little and sighed. "Try not to scream." Noah snorted. "Yeah, okay, sir."

Tobias grinned and lifted his hand again. He'd have to go gentle on Noah's ass -- not only did he prefer not to put on a show for the men in the cockpit, but the luxury of the couch meant he couldn't get a good swing if he'd wanted to. So, he played. The leather of the belt stung and snapped but didn't bite, and the blows landed solidly instead of flicking. Noah's ass would soon be hot and red, and the effort would be minimal; Tobias only hoped that he would hold on long enough for Tobias to recover his erection.

Noah was a trooper and held his climax back, quietly, just as he was told. He moaned a lot and the fingers of one of his hands dug into Tobias' thigh instead of supporting his weight. The pinker his ass became, the more Noah whimpered, until he was reduced to lovely, pitiful begging. Even the effort of keeping that soft seemed to be difficult for him. "Sir... Master. So hard. So fucking hard, please..."

Tobias moaned with him, his cock filling rapidly. He was getting harder with every slap, every snap, and every moan. The leather of the belt was warming, adding its scent to Noah's, and Tobias shifted, his leg bumping his boy's cock. "Soon," he promised. "Soon."

Noah shivered and whimpered again as the belt made a satisfying slap against his skin. "Is it red?" he asked, panting. "Are you hard, sir? You like it? Swollen and pink and yours to have... Sir... please, Master, fuck me, please!"

"Soon," Tobias said again, his voice tight. "You're a lovely shade, pet. Red and hot, and I'm going to part your ass and push right in, rest my hips on you." He dropped the belt and slapped Noah's upturned and glowing ass with his hand, feeling the heat pouring off it. "On your hands and knees. Now."

Noah slid awkwardly off Tobias' knees to the floor with a grunt. He shoved his rosy ass back toward Tobias shamelessly, begging softly like there was nothing else he could say. "Please, please, please."

Tobias didn't say anything, merely tore at his fly and shoved the fabric out of the way for the second time since takeoff, his cock hard and almost as red as Noah's cheeks. He forced Noah's knees apart a little more and plunged two fingers into him, making sure he was slick. "Ready?" he demanded.

Noah shivered. "Yes! Yes!"

With a sound that was more grunt than anything else, Tobias forced his way into Noah, pushing hard at his hole and not stopping until he was balls deep. "Oh, God," he moaned, trying to catch his breath. "Tight."

"Huge." Noah gasped. Tobias felt him trying to relax -- trying not to come. He controlled his breathing carefully and went nearly silent.

"Good," Tobias tried to praise. "Make it good." He took a breath and slowly began to pull out, his breath catching. "Oh, God."

Noah moaned softly, in time with his breathing. He wanted to scream, Tobias knew, and he wanted to come. But he wouldn't. Noah would wait until he was given permission; He always had, after all. Noah arched his pinked ass higher and braced himself on his forearms, moaning low, over and over.

Tobias fucked him slowly, skating the edges of his own need. Having come only a short while before, he knew he was good for a long time; he had a choice to make. He could torture Noah and make it last as long for them both as he could, or he could speed up his own need, timing it so he could slam into Noah roughly after he'd shot and was pleasantly relaxed.

He wasn't sure which would be better.

He looked up, his fingers digging into Noah's hips. "Do you suppose," he said only slightly breathless, "that there are security cameras?"

Noah lifted his head and looked over shoulder with a slight grin. "You think they're watching?" he asked breathlessly. With Tobias taking it slow, Noah seemed to be getting a better handle on his own need. "Maybe they can give us... a copy of the tape when we're... uh... when we're done. Oh, God, so good."

With a grin Tobias rocked into Noah again. "You'd like that?" he asked, knowing very well that Noah would. He loved an audience, even a pretend one. He'd also been the one to comment on the co-pilot... "Maybe they're whacking off, watching," he mused, speeding up a little.

"Just so long as we don't crash... oh, Sir." Noah groaned and rocked with him, forward and back and forward again as Tobias thrust. "Tell me you're going to fuck me in public in Paris."

"Only if you're a good boy," Tobias said. He started planning the event right then, running through unlikely places they could go, and what he'd make Noah wear. "Oh, God." He sped up, pushing hard into Noah and circling his hips. "Ride me," he ordered, letting Noah dictate the pace for the moment.

Noah ground backward, twisting his hips as he moved. "Yes, sir, yes. Yes." He rocked and twisted, keeping the pace even for the moment.

Tobias groaned and watched as Noah moved on him. He watched Noah's muscles working, watched his back arch and his legs flex. But mostly he watched Noah's ass, watched his own cock, and suddenly he was there, right on the edge and hard as hell, just aching. "Come for me," he whispered.

Noah grunted and slammed back onto Tobias' cock once, and then again. He took hold of his cock as he came, going even tighter around Tobias' prick and shooting hard into his fist. "Thank you, sir! Oh, fuck, yes."

Tobias moved with him, fucking him through it, and shoved deeper with every tight spasm. Tighter than anything, clinging and massaging him, Tobias was sure that

Noah would pull him over, but he held on. Like a machine, he pounded into Noah again and again, even when he felt Noah go limp under him. "Still with me?" he asked, his hips driving in once more.

Noah nodded and groaned, but he pressed back again, mustering what Tobias needed.

"That's it," Tobias said, tugging Noah back onto him. "Love the way you feel around me. Love your ass, love fucking you." He growled and slapped Noah's ass, slamming into him and pushing his head down, forcing Noah's ass even higher. He felt like he was dancing on the edges of his awareness, and suddenly he was right there. On a plane, over the Atlantic, halfway to another continent. Hard and hot and inside his sub, a few feet from strangers, and on his way to Paris to, in effect, get married.

"Noah!" he yelled as he started to come again. "Jesus, yes."

Noah groaned and shoved back at him hard, matching Tobias' forward thrust and making them both go still. "Oh yes, sir -- yes, baby, yes..." He rolled his hips up and down as Tobias filled him, and he reached back to take hold of the hand on his hip, tangling their fingers tightly.

"Love you," Tobias whispered, still shaking with his release. "So much, sweetheart."

Noah was still catching his breath himself and so he didn't answer Tobias with words right away, but he squeezed Tobias' fingers again and whimpered softly. He hung there, hunched over his knees, head down, until his breathing came easily. "Fuck, sir. That was great."

Tobias laughed, the sound dry as he panted. "Glad you liked it. Not buying you a plane for a repeat. This is possibly the most expensive fuck you'll ever have." Grinning, Tobias eased out of Noah and fell to the side, not caring that his dick was hanging out of his pants. "Dead now."

Noah flopped on his back. "There's always the ride home," he said with a laugh.

"True," Tobias admitted. "But I was kind of planning on you being too sore by that point."

"There's a goal," Noah grinned. He pulled himself up and sat with his back against the couch, then winced. "Jesus, this carpet is murder on my ass," he said with a hiss and switched to the couch itself instead.

"I thought it was the belt," Tobias grumbled, trying not to sound as good-natured as he felt. "I'm out of practice, you say?"

Noah laughed out loud. "No! No, sir. I'm saying my ass is so sore from your expert ministrations that sitting on that industrial carpet is like rubbing my ass on sandpaper."

"Uh-huh." Tobias eyed him skeptically. "So, my arm is adequate? And if I were to visit a few shops I know of, looking for new toys... you would be happy enough to come along so I could try them out?"

"I wouldn't want Sir to buy anything that wasn't exactly to his liking." Noah grinned impishly. He must have learned that look from Phan.

Tobias nodded and finally did up his pants, though he remained stretched out on the floor. "And if I took you out to these shops in... say, your collar and little else? As a reward, perhaps. You would behave and take your whipping as I ordered?"

"You know I would do exactly as you asked of me, sir. Eagerly." Noah's voice was still playful. "You like that idea? Leading me around Paris half-nude at your heel? I'm not likely to run into anyone I know in Paris."

Tobias grinned. "I am."

Noah laughed. "Oh, my God."

"Oh, no, they never call me that anymore." Tobias finally had to laugh, long and loud. He pulled himself up to sitting and then onto the couch where he wrapped himself around Noah for a long kiss. "I will show you off, pet. Just wait. But for now? You need to dress, clean this up, and get more water. Earn your praise, my peacock."

17

If the pilots had any indication of what had gone on in the cabin during the flight, they didn't let on. Tobias thanked them and tipped them generously, and then it was off to their hotel. Noah spent most of the lengthy cab ride alternating between leaning out the window and pointing at things and trying to swallow Tobias' tonsils. He was electric -- wound up like a clock, eyes bright, and completely unable to decide what to do next.

Tobias thought his reaction to be rather adorable.

Dinner that night was light, and Tobias couldn't recall the last time Noah had crashed so hard, falling asleep almost before his head hit the pillow.

They slept in, indulging themselves in the luxury of the large bed, the lush room, and the oversized tub and shower. They ate breakfast in their room, taking in the view of Parisian rooftops and planning what to do first. Noah had really needed his morning spanking to settle him down, but after that he was more than ready to sightsee.

They walked a lot, down quaint narrow streets and through busy markets, and eventually they ended up where

Tobias had intended, outside Notre Dame. They took the tour, inside and out, with Noah snapping pictures whenever he could. He commented, as another American tourist took their picture with the gates of the huge cathedral in the background, that it was the first time they'd ever had their picture taken together. Tobias just smiled at Noah's sentimental streak, thankful that he had it.

Toward the later part of the afternoon, they took the Métro to the Trocadéro and walked from the Palais de Chaillot to the Seine, taking in the long view of the Eiffel Tower. It was a lovely walk, and Noah kept hold of Tobias' hand the whole way, probably enjoying being able to do so openly. After crossing the Pont d'Iéna they headed for the tower itself and waited in line with the rest of the tourists to climb up and get a view.

Tobias' timing had been deliberate. The view from the tower was best right before sunset, and they were not disappointed. The air was clear and the panoramic view was just what he'd remembered it to be. Noah took a few more pictures, but mostly he just leaned on the railings and stared. It took nightfall, and Noah's own growling stomach, to finally convince him that it was time to go.

Tobias had chosen a quiet restaurant, one that his local friends had taken him to years before, and they sat at a small table off in a corner. Though their combined understanding of French was barely above high school level, they wrestled with the menu and managed to place their orders without too much difficulty. Noah had even convinced him it was all right to sample a glass of French wine.

"I've never been anywhere so... old," Noah said after the waiter had left them. "So historic. It really makes you realize how young America is, you know?" He poured water from a bottle into his glass and took a drink. He'd been insistent from the moment they left home that they not drink the water. Apparently his sister had told him horror stories.

Nodding, Tobias sipped the wine and smiled. "It does. However, there are truly modern parts as well, though hidden away. Well, the ones I mean are hidden; not unlike our club, which attempts to look older than it is."

"And when will we be visiting these hidden away places?" Noah asked coyly. He lifted the napkin off their basket of bread and offered some to Tobias.

"After some shopping -- you have nothing suitable to wear, pet." Tobias smirked and tilted his head, considering the question. "A couple of days, I expect. I'll have to make some calls, get the necessary approval."

Noah raised an eyebrow over his water glass. "Nothing suitable to wear? My, my, I am intrigued. I can't wait."

"You'll have to," Tobias teased. "Because I won't even give a hint. Now, what would you like to do this evening? Any ideas, anything catch your eye in a brochure or something? I was thinking we'd try for an early morning, however, so keep that in mind."

Noah squinted at him but didn't say anything more about not getting a hint. "Well, sir, if you want an early morning, then maybe we should just take a nice walk near the hotel to digest, have a cafe au lait and turn in early. I want to thank you properly for showing me that beautiful view from the tower. I really hope my pictures come out."

Tobias hoped the pictures turned out, too, but he was far more interested in the view across from him. "And what would a proper thank you be?" he asked, leaning forward slightly.

"Something slow," Noah suggested, leaning forward a bit himself and grinning. "Something unhurried and hot and all about you. Something that involves, let's say, my tongue and your ass?"

Tobias raised an eyebrow for show, but he was fairly sure they both knew that the walk had just been curtailed to a brief stroll. His cock twitched and began to fill. "I see. I do believe you know me rather well," he said, his voice dropping a little. "A thank you that will benefit us both, if the current state of my interest is any indication."

Leaving without embarrassment would be an issue if he wasn't careful.

"That's good to hear." Noah winked, leaning back again. "I heard the hotel has a sauna, maybe we could check that out after. Oooh. Food." Noah moved his hands from the table so the waiter could set their plates down. "Smells so good. Doesn't look like what I ordered, though; I must have misinterpreted something. Oh, well! I'm sure it will be delicious." He laughed and grinned across the table. "Think you can eat?"

"Of course I can eat. I just can't walk." Tobias picked up the escargot fork and gestured with it. "Behave or you'll be getting your ass warmed before you..." He trailed off and smirked.

"Oh, and that would be such a shame. I'll be good, sir." Noah smirked right back and picked up his fork. After a bite he added, "Oh, it's some kind of fish. It's good."

"What were you expecting?" Tobias asked curiously. He lifted a morsel to his mouth and had to stifle a moan as the rich flavor exploded across his tongue. "Oh, my."

"I thought I'd ordered lamb. So much for my French. But this is..." Noah took another bite. "Perfect. Yummy. Want a bite?" Noah held his fork out to Tobias.

Tobias smiled and leaned forward to take the offered bit

of fish. Noah didn't feed him at home, and Tobias found the entire thing oddly romantic and little amusing.

"Oh, it's good," he said, tasting the lemon and delicate seasonings. "It's trout." His smile widened. "Even better than the one we shared the first time we met."

Noah grinned and raised an eyebrow. "Just about six months ago now, wasn't it? I remember my first impression of you very well." He sat back and sipped his water, then set it on the table again. "I thought you were handsome, eccentric, and had a huge ego." He laughed. "Little did I know how well you'd earned the ego. I found that out that very evening, didn't I?"

Grinning, Tobias nodded. "You thought I was eccentric? I thought you needed to learn a fast lesson. And I thought you were in desperate need of grounding, and of being taken down a peg or two." His smile broadened and he reached for his wine glass again. "Just look at us now, pet."

"Indeed, look at us now," Noah said, raising his eyes to meet Tobias' for a brief moment, and giving him a sentimental smile. "Look at us now." He cleared his throat, then lowered his eyes again and tucked back into his dinner. "I still think you're eccentric, sir. You've brought me to Paris in the most pampered and indulgent manner possible, after all. In your case, a little eccentricity is a good thing."

"I'm not eccentric, but I am indulgent," Tobias said easily. He sipped the wine and set his glass down carefully. "You, however, just earned yourself a stroke of my crop -- when I can get a new one." He smiled to himself, mostly just enjoying the ease of conversation, but also anticipating both the flogging and the shopping trip that would precede it.

"Yes, sir," Noah acknowledged, but he didn't seem terribly repentant. They fell into a comfortable silence, both enjoying their food for a bit. There was more of that sentimentality in Noah's voice when he spoke again. "It seems like it's been longer than six months, doesn't it, sir? What a ride."

Considering that, Tobias continued to eat his beef dish, relieved that it was, indeed, beef. "It's been intense," he said. "Wonderful. You've really come a long way. We have, together." He glanced across the table and cocked his head to the side, wondering if they were about to start the dance of negotiations, if they should.

"You know, if you had told me that first night that I'd be in that cage by my birthday, I'd have probably not signed on with you in the first place." Noah grinned. "But Bradford promised me my trust would be well-placed with you, and he was right. He was absolutely right."

"He usually is," Tobias said dryly. "And we're usually happy with it." He set down his fork and pushed ahead with the topic frankly. "So, is there anything like that which would keep you from signing with me now? Any more cages lingering in your mind?"

"No, sir. Nothing of that magnitude." Noah said immediately. "I'm sure you'll set aside some time to discuss this thoroughly, but as things stand, I have every intention of signing with you again if you'll have me. I'll be interested in hearing your thoughts and discussing them."

Tobias relaxed slightly. "I'm pleased to hear that," he said softly. "I admit I'm looking forward to discussing the terms of our new contract, to setting out what we're hoping for." He picked up his fork again and began to eat, a warm feeling forming in his belly.

Noah took the last bite of his fish and set his fork down. "I'm sure we'll come to an agreement easily, sir," he said almost absently as he picked up the dessert menu. "Oh, my God, chocolate."

"Don't eat so much you make yourself sick," Tobias cautioned before he could stop himself. Quickly, he added, "And, yes, I'm sure we'll agree -- but I actually enjoy the process of talking it out."

Noah raised an eyebrow and glanced over the top of the menu in Tobias' direction, but he was careful not to raise his eyes too high. "I think this thing is called a 'chocolate volcano.' I think you should split it with me, sir. It sounds gooey and messy."

Tobias tried not to snort. Noah really liked gooey and messy. "No, thank you," he said. "I'm saving room for something else."

Noah froze with a grin on his lips. "Oh?" He set the menu on the table. "Maybe I'll hold off on the sweets," he said coyly.

"Up to you," Tobias said with a teasing smile. Walking was once more going to be a problem. "Don't let me stop you -- you can eat whatever you want." The last comment was delivered with as much sly innuendo as he could manage, given the setting. He would not intentionally get them in trouble or cause a scene -- but he'd certainly torture them both as much as he could.

Noah coughed and sipped his water. "I think you were right, sir." He set the menu down carefully on the table. "I wouldn't want to overdo it, given that I have an evening nosh waiting for me at home." He set his water glass down with intention, licked his lips, and ran his finger lightly around the rim.

"Oh, you tease!" Tobias laughed and finished his water, then reached for the bottle to pour more. "Just for that, I'm going to take my time with the rest of this and make you sit there. No talking, unless it's about something other than getting your tongue in my ass and my cock in yours."

"Sir!" Noah gasped. He blushed and seemed caught between horror and laughter. He actually looked around as if to make sure no one had overheard.

"English, pet. And even if they did understand, does it matter that they know we like to fuck?" He watched Noah's color carefully, trying not to laugh.

Noah's lips twitched, and he hid behind his water glass and took a quick sip. "No, sir. I suppose it doesn't matter if they know that we fuck, what with this being the city of indulgence, but... well, I've been ordered to silence on the subject. Jesus, you could make a sailor blush."

"Thank you," Tobias said happily. "I do try. Oh, and getting used to silence might be a good idea, boy."

"As you wish, sir," Noah said and nodded slowly. He picked up his water glass and took another sip.

Tobias shook his head. "Not for me, pet. I like talking to you. It's just that one of the places I want to take you requires that the submissives don't talk. At all."

"Oh." Noah smiled. "Well, that sounds like a very deep evening for me. I look forward to it."

"It should be fun," Tobias agreed. "For me, anyway. Some of the people who should be there I haven't seen in ten years, and it will be nice to show you off. They take a submissive's demeanor very seriously, though, so watch your eyes and your posture. I won't hesitate to correct you -- immediately, harshly, and publicly."

Noah nodded. "I will do my very best to make you proud, sir, as always. Especially around people you haven't seen in so long."

"Of course you will. I don't doubt it at all -- if I did, I wouldn't be taking you, and possibly wouldn't have brought you to Paris at all. I know what you are, Noah, and I know what you can do, how wonderful you can be. We've found your limits, yes?"

Noah smiled and nodded. "Yes, sir. Thank you."

"Which brings us back to thanks..." Tobias said with a grin. He raised a hand and signaled for the check. "Shall we race back to the hotel, or do you have your heart set on that stroll?"

"What? You can walk?" Noah asked with a grin. He folded his napkin and placed it on the table.

"I have better control now that I'm an old man," Tobias said dryly. "Can you? Or are you hard for me, pet? Is your cock full and heavy between your legs? Are your balls aching? Or are you sadly ready to simply stand up and wander out of here, which would, of course, crush my soul? No pressure."

"What in the world was in that wine?" Noah laughed. "I'm hard, sir. Something about your cock in my ass got a rise out of me not long ago. I'd prefer a cab."

"I suppose it would be terribly unfair of me to award you a stroke for that?"

Noah blinked. "For being hard or for asking for a cab, sir?"

"For talking about my cock in your ass, pet," Tobias said clearly as the waiter handed him the bill.

"Oops," Noah touched a finger to his lips and grinned. "No, sir, you did tell me to be silent on the issue, didn't you?" He stood and held the back of Tobias' chair for him.

"I did, but I also teased you," Tobias said with a smile as he stood up. He winked at the waiter, who very properly didn't even blink. "So I leave it to you -- was that worth a stroke?" He began to walk away from the table, slipping his credit card back into his wallet and trailing Noah along behind him.

"Disobedience. Absolutely, yes." Noah followed him at heel.

"You are so easy." Tobias grinned at him as they left the restaurant. "You really like having a warm ass, don't you?" Never mind that he liked warming it. He pointed down the street toward the corner where they could see a cab stand and started walking that way.

"When I'm permitted to, yes, sir. Besides which, you enjoy it." Noah took a deep breath and exhaled in the cool night air.

"I do," Tobias agreed. "I'd like to mark you, actually. Nice solid lines on your ass that will stay for more than a weekend." His prick throbbed at the thought.

Noah peered in his direction around his shoulder. "Are you asking my permission, sir? Or just talking out loud?"

"I'm not sure, really, so I suppose just talking. Saying that I want it. I don't mean whip marks that will bruise so badly they linger, I mean... stripes from a cane, maybe. Something that will be clear on your skin for almost a week, something that you'll feel for a time." The cab pulled up and Tobias stepped to the door, not looking at Noah to see his reaction. He preferred to hear Noah give his opinion in words this time.

Noah reached around Tobias and opened the door for him, holding it while Tobias got in before sliding into the backseat beside him. He was silent as Tobias gave the driver their destination, and for several minutes thereafter. "I suppose then, sir," Noah said finally, his voice slipping into that low register of his. "I suppose it's a happy coincidence that you have me for a week, isn't it?"

"Is it?" Tobias asked softly. "Do you think it's wise to go into a negotiation where we will be equals when you can feel the sting of my cane on you? It won't... be too much a hold on you?"

"Hmm." Noah nodded thoughtfully. "I hadn't considered that." He was quiet again, and leaned on Tobias lightly, somewhat reminiscent of their contact in Affirmation. He sighed before speaking. "Perhaps if it were merely part of a session, and not something dealt as strokes in discipline?"

Tobias ordered his own thoughts. "I think that if I were to do this, I would want it to be a claiming. My boy, my ass, my stripes. But that would bring us back to you feeling it for days, four at least. We'd have to time it well, to avoid you feeling claimed when we're talking about a new contract. It wouldn't be fair."

"Perhaps." Noah nodded slowly. "But, sir, I told you I plan to sign with you again. There is no question that I am yours. I don't see being able to completely table that notion for a negotiation in any case."

"And if I suggest rather substantial changes you won't be at all swayed by the feeling of stripes?"

Noah glanced in his direction. "You have *substantial* changes in mind, sir?" Noah sounded surprised.

"Oops."

"Well." Noah sighed. "That could change things, then."

Tobias sighed, cursing himself. "Nothing bad, pet. At least, I hope not." He took a breath. "You should think about it for a while, anyway, so I guess there's no harm in telling you now. I'm intending to ask you to move in with me." He didn't hold his breath, but it took a certain amount of concentration to keep his breathing regular.

Noah turned his head in Tobias' direction again, studied Tobias' chest for a moment, and then looked back out the window. He took full advantage of the control being a sub allowed him. "Good to know."

"Just... think about it," Tobias said, completely thrown for perhaps the first time since he'd met Noah. He had no idea what his reaction meant and found himself both amused and worried about it. He pushed the matter aside for the time being and watched the Paris streets slip by as they neared the hotel.

As they pulled up at the front door he reached for his wallet again and counted out the euros to pay the driver. "Did you want to see if they have café au lait in the hotel lounge?" he asked.

"No, I'd rather just go fuck, sir," Noah teased. "Unless you wanted to talk more...?"

"Fucking is fine," Tobias assured him with a laugh.

The cab driver, unlike the waiter, stared and looked mildly annoyed. Tobias added a generous tip and urged Noah into the hotel with a swat on his ass and a teasing glare.

Noah made his way through the lavish marbled lobby to the elevators and hit the call button, staying close to Tobias' side. He got frisky in the elevator, pressing close and kissing Tobias hard until another couple got on.

Tobias ignored the surprised look on the man's face and returned the woman's smile. She seemed to find it rather cute to have the elevator open and see two men making out. "He's a little excited to be on vacation," Tobias said in a confidential tone.

To his surprise, the woman nodded and said, "Lucky you," with a sideways glance at the man with her, whose look turned embarrassed and then speculative, which made Tobias stifle a laugh.

The elevator carried them quickly to their floor and they got off with cheerful wishes for a good night, and then Tobias hustled Noah down the hall with unseemly haste.

"Inside, now," he growled, sliding his key card through its slot.

Noah went right in and took off his jacket in the foyer of their suite. He turned to face Tobias and went right to his knees.

"Good boy," Tobias praised, ruffling his hair as he walked past him. "Stay." He went through to the bedroom and checked to make sure there was lube by the bed and that there were water bottles in the refrigerator, and then he went back to Noah, taking off his dinner jacket on the way.

"Now," he said as he tossed his jacket over the back of a chair. "There was mention of giving thanks." He undid his shirt cuffs and loosened his tie.

"Yes, sir. Would you prefer I take orders or take initiative?" Noah's voice was low, but his words were playful.

"It's your thank you, I think you should give it however you want," Tobias said, his voice getting thicker. "Which is not to say that you should discount any... suggestions I may have."

"All right." Noah stood and moved quickly to Tobias. His fingers curled tightly in the fabric of Tobias' shirt and he tugged Tobias down into another kiss.

Tobias fell into the kiss, pulling Noah tight to him and holding him in place with one hand on Noah's ass. His cock was filling nicely, but the erection Noah was rubbing on him felt like he was getting close already.

"Do you have a ring on?" Tobias asked as he shifted his hand to stroke Noah through his pants.

Noah groaned. "Yours, sir, of course."

"I mean one that will keep you from coming, not just look pretty on you." Tobias undid Noah's button and zipper and tugged his trousers down.

"Not at the moment, no, sir," Noah answered, his fingers

working Tobias' shirt off of his shoulders. "There's one in my suitcase." He pushed his hips into Tobias' fingers.

"Never mind," Tobias said. "I'll take care of it." He picked Noah up and carried him to the couch, tossing him down none too gently, then crouched beside him and stroked his cock again. Before Noah could do anything more than gasp, Tobias bent low and licked Noah's cock, tracing around the swollen head with the tip of his tongue.

"Wait... this was supposed to be my... thank you... oh, shit," Noah shivered and let his legs fall open.

"It will be," Tobias said, lifting his head for only as long as it took to explain. "And soon, I suspect. At the moment, I'm just taking care of your little urgency problem. You'll get it back up, I assume?" He dipped his head again, sucked Noah's prick into his mouth, and began to bathe it with his tongue.

"Sure, sure, okay," Noah panted. He threw one arm around the back of the couch and lifted his hips slightly, letting his head fall back. "Oh, my fucking God."

"Uh-huh." Tobias would have grinned, but he was too busy sucking Noah's dick to bother. He played with Noah's balls and traced the steel cock ring, his head bobbing as he worked with Noah's thrusts.

Tobias could sense all the things Noah wanted to do. He wanted to thrust with his hips, he wanted to tug on Tobias' hair, but instead he remained as polite as possible apart from the swearing. He groaned and panted and shuddered. Tobias was unsurprised to find Noah hovering on the edge of his climax just moments after he'd begun.

"Oh, God. Yes, yes." Noah babbled and whimpered until Tobias tasted the first drops of Noah's come on his tongue. "Yes!"

Tobias moaned around Noah's cock, sucking hard. He

felt him swell further and knew Noah was about to come, so he slid his fingers over Noah's balls again and back a little farther to tease at his boy's hole.

"Oh, fuck!" Noah went tense and still, gulping air as he came, Tobias swallowing around him. Noah's fingers rested on Tobias' head, tangling and untangling in his hair until he was spent. "Oh. Jesus. Thank you, sir."

Tobias wiped at the corner of his mouth and grinned. "You're welcome," he said, standing up. "My turn." He walked toward the bedroom and yelled back, "Bring water, when you can walk."

Tobias stripped quickly, then sprawled on the bed. Noah still looked flushed as he came into the bedroom, his cock hung thick and half-hard against his body, and he was grinning as he set the bottles of water down on the table beside the bed.

"Your turn, sir," Noah teased, climbing slowly onto the bed with Tobias. His mouth went to work right away, moving over Tobias' shoulder to his chest and settling to nibble and lick and tease a nipple.

Tobias bit back a groan -- he wasn't as easy as all that. Really. Also and further, he had not been hard for this from the moment Noah mentioned it. Nope. He was a man of the world, utterly in charge, and not one for begging. "Pet," he growled, a hint of warning in his voice that he sincerely hoped Noah would interpret as "hurry the hell up."

"Master," Noah answered softly. He slid warm fingers around Tobias' cock and gave it a tug. "Mmm. You want me," he observed in that husky bedroom voice. His fingers moved on to fondle Tobias' balls and then slid even farther back to stroke over his hole. "Roll over, sir." There was no question that was a heated order and not a request. "Roll over," Noah said again, darkly, using one knee to encourage him.

Tobias rolled, his legs spreading wantonly as he lifted himself onto his knees. A tremor ran up his spine as Noah's hands moved over his ass. "Oh, God," he groaned, his head hanging between his arms. His legs shook and his hips rolled.

"You have such a hot ass," Noah hissed behind him. He gave both cheeks a squeeze and then pulled them apart with his fingers. He dove in teeth first, nipping and biting inches from the target, teasing Tobias even further. His tongue moved unpredictably, first here then there, until it finally found the sensitive skin around Tobias' opening.

Noah licked around it in a circle, flicked at the tight ring of muscle with the tip of his tongue, and then started to work him, alternately shoving his tongue part way in and feasting on the puckered skin around the outside.

Tobias made a noise that sounded partly like a gurgle and mostly like a whimper. "God," he said again, shoving himself back. "Oh, God, yes." His cock was rigid, and every nerve ending he had felt like it was on fire. He was sure he could feel every loop and whorl of Noah's fingerprints as keenly as the breath on his ass. He shuddered again, trying to hang on and enjoy it before he inevitably gave in and started to beg.

As Tobias felt his body wanting, relaxing into the welcome intrusion, Noah's tongue pushed in even farther. He thrust it in and out with the relentless effort of someone that was really enjoying what he was doing.

"More, sir?" Noah asked, his fingers massaging gently. He was panting a bit himself. "Anything you want. You want more of this? You want me, yet? You want my ass?"

"More," Tobias ground out. "God, more. Please?" Part of him hated asking and part of him loved it, got off on it. It wasn't something he ever longed to do, but begging for

Noah's tongue, his mouth and fingers, was almost a release in and of itself. He took a shuddering breath. "More, pet. Now, please -- just... more."

Noah groaned. He obliged, giving Tobias more, and harder and faster to go along with it. He made enthusiastic grunting sounds as he tasted Tobias again and again. Noah's fingers brushed roughly over Tobias' balls, stroked down his cock, and then disappeared again to dig into his hip.

"Yes!" Tobias yelled. He fell forward, his ass high as his arms gave out. He reached for the headboard and braced himself, shoving back as his legs shook and spread and he tried to get more sensation. His cock was leaking a steady stream onto the bed, and his balls were almost tingling. "More," he panted. "Noah, please!"

With a growl, Noah tightened his fingers around Tobias' balls and squeezed and then moved to his cock. Noah stroked him fast and his teeth sunk hard into the flesh of Tobias' ass.

Tobias cried out and came hard, his hips pushing wildly as he tried to thrust into Noah's hand. The bite sent shockwaves through him, made lights dance behind his eyes as he shot. His eyes rolled back and he had to fight to breathe, his voice harsh as his cry became a near scream at the apex of his climax.

And through it all, while Noah's hand still teased, still stroked him with a slick fist, Tobias' erection hardly flagged.

"Jesus," Tobias growled, pushing himself up on his hands again. "Pet."

"Sir." Noah licked up Tobias' spine. He gave Tobias' cock another squeeze.

Tobias' growl grew and he heaved himself up, turning to face Noah. He pulled him close and kissed him roughly, one hand going to Noah's erection, the other swatting Noah's hand away from his own shaft. "On your back," he ordered when he let Noah breathe again.

"Pleasure, sir," Noah answered breathlessly, not bothering to hide the grin on his face. He shifted and rolled onto his back, planting his feet flat on the bed and spread wide. "I'm yours, sir," Noah told him, as if he needed reminding.

"Mine," Tobias agreed, grabbing the lube. He squirted a handful into his own hand and started working his cock, keeping himself hard. The tube he tossed to Noah. "Get ready," he said, his voice gruff.

Noah flipped open the tube and slicked his fingers, then pulled one knee up almost to his shoulder and held it there while he pushed two fingers into his own ass. He groaned and dropped his head back into the pillows. "Want you, sir. Master. Want you," he babbled as his eyes closed and his cock stood even more upright.

"You'll get me," Tobias promised, his gaze fixed on Noah's hand and ass. His own cock was still heavy, swelling back to full hardness as he watched and hit every hot spot he had. "Talk to me," he said, stroking over the head of his dick. "Tell me how you want it."

"Deep," Noah breathed at him. "Want to feel it in my spine. Want you buried in me." His fingers moved faster, deeper. "Want you to crawl inside my skin."

"I live in your skin," Tobias said, his hand slowing, making his strokes longer and smoother. "I live in you, own you. You can feel me in you whenever you want, pet. I know you can."

Noah panted, his voice was soft and low, one of many indications that he was securely in his space. "If I close my eyes, if I just listen to your voice, I can."

"Good boy." Tobias moved closer and slipped one of his

fingers in with Noah's, stretching him a little and reaching for his gland.

"Sir!" Noah gasped and arched, using the foot he had still on the bed for leverage. He exhaled in a long groan. "Master, please!"

"Please what, pet?" Tobias asked, draping his boy's other leg over his shoulder. He held his cock and waited.

"Please fuck me. Please, I need you, sir. Want you. Aches..." Tobias watched Noah grind onto their fingers, watched his body shiver. "Please!"

Tobias tugged his hand away, pulling Noah's fingers out with his own. "Good," he said, lining up his cock and pushing in. "Love it when you beg for me."

Noah relaxed around him, letting him slip in, balls deep. "Oh, yes," he panted. "So good." His hand moved to grip Tobias' shoulder, and his ass tightened maddeningly around Tobias' cock. "Deep, sir, please. Yours."

With a grunt Tobias thrust hard, pushing deeper. "Want it rough?" he asked, licking Noah's neck. Without waiting for a reply he pulled out and plunged back in, shoving his cock as far into Noah as he could, grinding against his hips.

Noah groaned and nodded. His lips moved and his mouth seemed stuck open, as if he were trying to speak but couldn't get the words out. The hand on Tobias' shoulder went to Noah's cock instead, and he stroked himself in a jerky, uneven manner.

Tobias stopped him, grabbing his wrists and pinning his hands down. "Not that way. Just from this. Just from my cock, jammed up your ass."

"No, no. Sir!" He tugged on one wrist and then the other, fighting Tobias' grip and whimpering. His hips rolled to one side and then the other, but Tobias had him well pinned. "Please, please..."

Tobias tightened his grip and snarled. "Mine!" he said fiercely, fucking Noah hard and fast. He was tuned to hear Noah's safe word, but unless he heard it, he wasn't stopping. He held Noah down and took him harshly, roughly, pounding into his ass. "Whore," he spat at Noah. "Slut."

"No!" Noah shouted at him. "Please. Please! Oh, God!" Tobias felt Noah starting to tense and tremble. He fought hard, tugging on his wrists and twisting under Tobias in an effort to get free. "No, no, no... God!"

Tobias was tempted to find out what a slap across his boy's face would do, but reason took over and insisted that hitting was something they really should discuss beforehand. Instead, he bared his teeth and squeezed Noah's wrists again, surely causing pain this time, and stabbed into his body again. "Take it," he said. "It'll be worse if you don't. Ride my cock, whore, or I'll beat you fucking senseless."

"Fuck you," Noah spat back, lifting his head so it was just inches from Tobias' face. "You'll be sorry." Another hard thrust and Noah fell back to the bed and rolled his hips. "Stop, please. Oh, God."

"Not a chance." Tobias rolled his own hips and grinned. "You love it. All you whores do."

"What the hell do you know?" Noah growled, but his body was betraying his words. He tensed again and very obviously panted through what should have been his climax. "Oh, fucking hell. Get off me!" Noah made one more effort to shake Tobias off.

"Jesus!" Tobias said, Noah's arching finally getting to him. His dick was harder than ever, his balls tight, and he hoped to hell that Noah was going to come soon, because he was about ready to pop. "Shut the fuck up!" he yelled, letting go of Noah's wrists and raising his hand as if to backhand his boy.

Noah reached up and caught the back of Tobias' hand with both of his. Tobias felt him start to twist his arm, but he was interrupted by his sudden orgasm, which this time he couldn't seem to hold off. "Oh... fuck!" Noah shrieked and came, shooting hard enough to soak Tobias' stomach and chest. He let go of Tobias' arm as his strength gave out and let his hands fall on either side of his head. "Ohhh, yeah."

"Yes," Tobias agreed, his breath catching. "Oh, fuck." He threw his head back and thrust wildly, his hips stuttering as his orgasm began to roll through him. He looked at Noah at the last moment, his cock beginning to pulse. "Sweetheart," he whispered, his eyes fluttering closed as he came, his body braced on hands hastily thrown out for balance.

Once the shuddering stopped, Tobias could feel Noah's fingers sliding lightly along his arms. Noah twisted gently so his leg fell free and he lowered it to the bed, then pulled Tobias down and into his arms. He was still catching his breath; Tobias could feel his chest heaving as Noah took in air. "Jesus," he said, and moaned softly in Tobias' ear.

"Um, yeah." Tobias could only agree. He wanted to ask if Noah was okay, but what came out was, "That was... better. Without a set scene. God." He panted again and rested his forehead on Noah's shoulder. "Christ."

Noah turned his head and kissed Tobias' hair. "I'm glad I've learned to read you; it didn't take me long to figure out what you wanted."

"I knew you could," Tobias murmured. "Though, to be honest, I didn't realize it was going to be quite that intense. You really like the struggle; we'll talk about that sometime. I almost had to hit you, you know. I'd made a threat I couldn't back up yet."

"Hey, as long as the shiner is gone by the time I have to go back to work..." Noah grinned, but it faded quickly. "If I'd had any problem with what you were doing, you know I would have used my words, sir."

"I know, sweetheart." Tobias smiled and kissed him softly. "I was counting on it. Mostly, I just didn't want to hit you barehanded without there being some sort of understanding about it; an impromptu scene like that raises issues, and that's good." He grinned. "Gives us something to talk about over breakfast." He sat up, groaning. "I am far too old to be raping and pillaging. Thank God I'm not a pirate."

"How about a hot bath for the aching back?" Noah suggested, also sitting up. He didn't seem uncomfortable in the least, but he had red finger marks where Tobias had been holding his wrists. "And maybe a call downstairs for some clean sheets."

Tobias looked at the bed and nodded. "Sheets would be good. Ice for your wrists, too." He crossed to the phone and picked it up, then glared at Noah. "I mean it, pet. Wrists first, then run the bath. I'll be right in."

"Ice first, sir." Noah agreed.

Tobias grinned, getting a good look at Noah's ass as he slipped out of the room. He shook his head then called for clean sheets and put a standing order in for a set to be left each day. Noah was going to kill him one day, but it wouldn't be in Paris.

18

I n the morning Tobias made sure they both had a fairly full breakfast, heavy on the fruit instead of the crepes Noah insisted he wanted. "You'll just go back to sleep," he said with a smile. "Don't think I didn't notice you wanted the ones with chocolate and not berries. Eat your melon like a good boy."

Once he'd managed to get Noah sufficiently full of nutritious food and strong coffee, they began their morning out by going to the Louvre, where Tobias fully intended to spend the greater part of the day. As he'd expected, there was a line to see the Mona Lisa even before opening; it had been that way when he'd last gone to see it, as well.

After seeing the painting and once more reaffirming for himself that there were a lot of other things he preferred to look at, they toured gallery after gallery, taking a break at lunch to eat and chat and compare thoughts on various works they'd enjoyed. Tobias rarely felt compelled to discuss art, but as he'd immersed them in it, the topic seemed natural and easy. His usual objection to discussing paintings instead of music was that his knowledge was sparse; Noah didn't seem to mind, and they talked of color and light rather than brush strokes and mediums. All in all, he found it a relaxing and pleasant experience.

That he was sharing the day with Noah made it even more so.

In the afternoon they enjoyed some of the less crowded galleries, holding hands and whispering to each other, ignoring the other patrons and the lone artists working on their impressions of the great works before them. After coming out of the Boucher Room, Tobias glanced at his watch and smiled. "Time for a nap, pet," he said. "And then shopping."

Noah raised an eyebrow but agreed easily enough, and within an hour they were back at the hotel and asleep, curled up on the expansive bed together. Tobias woke up at about five and made a phone call, happy to discover that the shop he wanted to visit still existed, and was still in the same place. He left Noah sleeping and showered, dressing himself casually in trousers and a light sweater before laying out Noah's clothes for the shopping trip.

He leaned over Noah and kissed him awake with a smile, enjoying the sleepy way Noah stretched before opening his eyes.

"Mm. Time to get up?" Noah mumbled, pushing his pillow away and sitting up in bed. He blinked a couple of times and then seemed to remember where he was. "Oh... sorry, sir." Noah grinned and rubbed his eyes. "Damn, I was really asleep. Are you dressed already, sir?" He scratched his fingers across the top of his head. "Are we late?"

"Not yet, no. Get undressed, please." Tobias stood back from the bed, one hand on the clothes he'd picked out for Noah, the other holding a leather cock ring. "We have to get you ready."

Noah cleared his throat and slid off the bed, tugging off the T-shirt and briefs he'd slept in. He took another step forward and waited while Tobias fastened the ring in place. "What are your plans for tonight, sir?"

"Well, first we're going shopping," Tobias said as he played with Noah's cock, stroking his fingers over it as it filled. "And then we'll see." He teased Noah again, watching the erection in his hand begin to strain toward him. "And you get to work very hard for me, pet. I want you to maintain this lovely hard-on for me. I don't care what you have to do -- stroke yourself, think about whatever you want. The more turned on you are, the better. If I so much as glance at you, I want to see this fighting to get out of your jeans." He let go and tossed a plain white T-shirt at Noah. "You can do whatever you need to -- just don't come. Understand?"

Noah took a deep breath and cleared his throat again before speaking. "Yes, sir," he answered. If he was at all embarrassed or self-conscious he didn't let on. He slipped the T-shirt over his head. His voice was tight, and his cock filled even further. Whatever he'd chosen to think about seemed to be quite sufficient.

"Well done." Tobias handed him his socks and jeans, waiting as Noah carefully buttoned himself up, arranging his erection to be shown off but not pressed painfully on a seam or zipper.

"And now we shop," Tobias said with a grin. "Quickly now, into your shoes and coat, there's a car waiting by now, I think."

Noah smiled and gave Tobias a nod. He seemed eager to see the shop himself. He did exactly as he was told -- slipped into his shoes, and made his way into the foyer to get his coat. As they left the suite for the elevators, Noah was firmly at heel.

In the cab, Tobias amused himself by staring at Noah's crotch. "When we get there," he said quietly, "you can speak as freely as you can at any scene function we've attended. You'll act every inch the submissive you are, but you're not ordered to silence. That won't hold true if we're allowed to attend the club tonight, however. The man who runs the shop is British, so there won't be any trouble with the language -- that's actually why we're going there, in a roundabout way."

He looked out the window for a moment and then returned his gaze to Noah's lap. "When I was here ten years ago I needed a few things and found his place entirely because I needed an English speaker. We got along, and he introduced me to a few other people, and then I was permitted to go to the club -- it's associated with his shop somehow, though I'm not clear on the details."

The car slowed to a stop on a narrow street and Tobias nodded. "Here we are." He paid the driver and climbed out of the cab, Noah right behind him. "All right?"

Noah reached down to adjust his erection after they got out of the car, and Tobias watched him give himself a squeeze through his jeans. He didn't seem to care that they were standing on a public sidewalk. "Understood, sir," he said, breathing through the slight discomfort.

Tobias nodded and walked to a nondescript door, pushing it open without bothering to ring the bell. As he'd remembered, the outer room was so barren that a casual or mistaken visitor would turn around and leave again, thinking they had the wrong place. He smiled to himself and led Noah to the inner door, where he paused long enough to knock before nudging the door open.

"Un moment, s'il vous plait," a voice said as they walked in.

Tobias looked at the man's head, bent over his desk, and murmured, "Of course."

The head snapped up and Gregory beamed at him, instantly giving Tobias all of his attention. "It was you!" he cried, coming around the desk with his arms out. "Tobias Vincent. I thought they were having me on."

Tobias smiled and returned the affectionate greeting. "No such luck; I finally came back," he said, kissing Gregory's cheek.

"And you brought a present, too!" Gregory said, looking Noah up and down. "My, my."

Tobias rolled his eyes. "Just to look at, Gregory."

"It's enough. Tell me, boy. Does that lovely cock always stand so proud for your Master, or is this a special occasion?"

Noah smiled, keeping his eyes respectfully low. "Paris happens to be a special occasion, sir, but it's never far from making its presence known when Sir is near, even when he doesn't specifically request it," he replied smoothly.

Both Gregory and Tobias laughed. "Well done, pet."

Noah's smile grew broader. He turned slightly toward Tobias. "Thank you, sir," he said, and then he turned his attention back to Gregory. "Master says the two of you go back a very long way. It's a pleasure to meet you, sir."

"And you," Gregory said smoothly. "I'd tell you stories, but I suspect I'd better not."

"That would be wise," Tobias said, just as smoothly.

Gregory's smile grew and he nodded his head sharply. "Shall we, then?" He moved back behind his desk and opened a drawer, pulling out a file folder. "I believe we've got it right for you, Tobias."

Tobias moved to the chair in front of the desk and sat, pointing at the floor. "Noah." He smiled to himself as Noah immediately sank to his knees, his arms going behind his back. "Good boy," he said softly, reaching down to pat Noah's erection. "Keep it up for me while I look at the pretty pictures."

Tobias could sense that Noah was curious and wanted to look as well, but he was a good boy, of course, and instead he knelt calmly at Tobias' side, with only the occasional movement to palm himself through his jeans.

Tobias leaned back in the chair and flipped the file open, nodding with approval at the first image. When he'd called from the hotel he'd only had the sketchiest idea of what he wanted; Gregory had really come through. "These are in stock?" he asked, moving to the next picture.

"Certainly. He can be fitted as soon as you've decided; Andre is especially eager to work on the last -- there are two styles there for you to look at. Oh, and the harness can be adjusted in multiple ways, depending on how many D rings you want."

Tobias made an appreciative sound as he took out the last two images, considering the options. The harness shown on the model in the first picture would do nicely, and he had more elaborate leather at home, but the chaps were going to be a work of art. The first of the two images he had in his hand was quite basic, but made of a super soft leather he knew from experience would fit like a second skin and warm nicely from Noah's body heat.

"This second is rather... obvious, isn't it?" he asked, looking at the image. The leather was less tight, though not so loose as the chaps Tobias had for riding. They did, however, have studs down the sides that Tobias could see no use for, and laces along the front edge. In the picture, the model had a red and swollen erection tied up rather prettily in the laces, his cock held in place where the laces wound around the head and were then fastened back into the chaps.

"Obvious is the point," Gregory said easily, his eyes drifting to where Noah was once more playing with himself.

"Point taken." Tobias closed the file and pushed it across the desk. "The simple harness, leather cuffs for his wrists, and the second set, I think. If they can be made a little tighter -- not as tight as the first, though."

Gregory beamed at him. "Lovely. I'll fetch Andre, and the boys can go play while you and I go look at toys upstairs. You said you needed a--"

"Crop," Tobias said firmly.

"A crop." Gregory smiled and stood up. "I'll be right back," he said as he walked around the desk. "You're a lucky boy, lad."

"Always, sir," Noah agreed, moving his hands behind his back again. His gaze followed Gregory's feet as he left the room. He glanced in Tobias' direction, and then seemed to sit up a bit straighter as if he might be able to see what was lying on the desk.

"You'll see soon enough, pet," Tobias said, amused. "Tell me, what have you been thinking about? What do you think of all this?"

"I've been thinking about, well, things... to keep me hard, sir. And I think all of this is intriguing, and it's making me extremely curious and a little bit nervous. Master Gregory is very friendly, and handsome."

"He's the devil in a suit," Tobias said with a grin. "And what things are you thinking about?"

Noah glanced in Tobias' direction and then looked straight ahead again. "Honestly, sir?"

"Of course," Tobias said, surprised. "Always."

"I've been thinking about the incredibly hot sounds you made when my tongue was in your ass."

Tobias was grateful he wasn't normally the type to blush. "I'm glad the utter meltdown of my nervous system is so pleasant for you," he said with a smile.

The door Gregory had vanished through opened, and he returned with a tall, broad man following him. "This is Andre," Gregory said. "A genius with leather and silk."

Tobias stood and nodded. "Andre. This is Noah. You know what I want?"

Andre nodded once.

"Good. Let me know if he softens or comes, other than that, he's in your hands."

Andre took a step back and held the door open. "This way, please," he said softly.

Noah glanced in Tobias' direction.

"Go on, pet," Tobias said reassuringly, giving Noah a pat on the shoulder.

With that, Noah stood silently and made his way across the room to Andre. He paused by the door, then stepped past the much larger man and disappeared into the hall beyond him.

Tobias looked at Gregory and the two of them began to laugh.

"Oh, the poor lad," Gregory finally managed. "He looked terrified."

"He'll be fine," Tobias said confidently. "He'll also come back down here over the moon and with another admirer."

Gregory tilted his head. "I don't know about that. Andre sees a lot of bodies."

"It's not his body," Tobias said, fully aware that he was sounding like a smitten old man. "It's just him."

Gregory beamed at him and gestured to another door.

"Ah. You're in love. Come. Let's go find a nice crop for you to use on your boy. Show him how much you care."

Tobias laughed and followed along as Gregory led him up narrow steps to a large open space. There was a whipping doll at one end of the room, and each wall was lined with racks and shelves and cases of floggers and other toys. "It's like... walking into a feast," Tobias said.

Gregory nodded. "We have some wonderful suppliers. The in-house work is on the right; you should be able to find something suitable."

Tobias didn't doubt it. He fingered the crops and swung a few experimentally, always looking for another.

"So how long have you had the boy?" Gregory asked curiously.

"About six months." Tobias swished another crop and set it down, moving to the canes for a moment. "We're renegotiating."

"Going well?"

"You want to take him off my hands?" Tobias teased, walking toward the dummy.

"I wouldn't dream of it. I have my hands full as it is, and I doubt your Noah would take to another easily."

"You're right." Tobias laid into the dummy with the cane and shook his head. "Ship this to me. I won't use it on him here." He moved back to the crops and picked up the three he liked best. "Negotiations are barely started, but I doubt there will be issues. Though... I've already told him I'm going to ask for a live-in arrangement."

"How did he react to that?" Gregory asked as Tobias tried the first of the crops on the dummy.

"I'm not really sure. Which bothers me. However, I have a secret weapon, so I'm not worried."

"And what's that?" Gregory asked, shaking his head. "Not that one. Try the short tail."

Tobias nodded and switched crops. "Real estate. I want more. I think he'd feel better about it if we were both moving, not just him into my space. My current flat is a little... uptown."

"And he's downtown?"

Tobias laughed. "Not what I meant. He works downtown." He swung the crop again. "This one, I think."

"Good choice. Will you bring it tonight?"

"We've been invited?"

"You're being invited now. That crop, your boy, those chaps. It'll be a grand time."

Tobias found himself smiling broadly as he nodded.

19

There was no mistaking the club for anything other than what it was.

At the door Tobias showed a card that Gregory had given him, and he and Noah were both looked over rather carefully before being admitted, but once inside they were swept into a world Tobias had rarely visited; he had his doubts if Noah had ever been a part of anything like it at all.

In a small room to the side of the entrance Noah was relieved of his long coat, the only article of clothing that had made him fit to leave the hotel room, and Tobias clipped a lead to his chest harness. Tobias himself wore a dark suit, his starched and pristine appearance in direct contrast to the way Noah was so blatantly on display.

"All right, pet," he said softly, palming Noah's rampant erection. "No talking at all. Not to me, not to anyone. If you need help, signal me some other way. Keep hard, keep your eyes down, and make me proud. Do as you're told, and everything will be fine. Understood?"

Noah nodded sharply and said nothing. He seemed to be a little nervous, but Tobias had expected as much. He knew Noah would settle once he got used to the atmosphere; he wouldn't have brought Noah here if he'd thought this was more than his boy could handle.

Tobias turned and led Noah from the foyer with Noah tight at his heel. At the large double doors they were met by two men who once more checked Tobias' card, and then the doors were opened to them. As they stepped in, the music and sounds flowed over them, and Tobias tugged slightly on Noah's leash.

It was a sex club. Where their own club at least pretended to be a gentleman's club and had the lower floor reserved for non-play, this one had no such pretensions. Tables were scattered about and there was a bar, but the whipping post at the far end of the room was in use, and a man standing at the bar was quite obviously finger fucking his sub.

Tobias grinned and moved slowly through the room, exchanging looks and nods with various people, none of whom he recognized. The Tops were sizing him up, taking a good look at Noah, and trying to place him. He was merely existing, letting his demeanor speak for him.

"Tobias!"

He turned to the right, searching for the owner of the voice and finally spotting Gregory sitting at a table near the back. He nodded and made his way over, Noah keeping to heel easily and smoothly.

"Hello, Gregory." Tobias laid his crop on the table and pulled out a chair. He sat and Noah sank to his knees beside him. "Nice crowd," he said, patting Noah's head.

"It's a bit quiet," Gregory said with a grin. "No one's actually fucking on the tables yet."

Tobias knew he wasn't exaggerating.

"Looks nice," Gregory said, looking at Noah. "Andre does good work, and he had... quite a bit to work with, didn't he?"

Tobias smirked. "He did fine." He pet Noah again and winked. "We had a lot of fun dressing him. Poor baby was a mess until I got him all tied up."

Gregory laughed. "I'm sure he hated every minute of it. Still, he's a pretty package."

"I like it," Tobias said with another quick grin. "You're here alone?"

"Heavens, no! Martin is fetching my drink; I expect he's having some trouble, as I've switched off my usual without telling the bar." He gave Tobias a wicked grin. "I have a new cat to try out."

Tobias glanced over to the bar and tried to pick out Gregory's boy. There was only one sub without a Master by his side, and he was pointing to a bottle on the wall. Even from where he sat Tobias could admire the bar layout, with all the non-alcoholic mixes on one side and the spirits on the other. Martin's shoulders suddenly sagged and the bartender picked out a white bottle.

"Coconut? God, tell me you're not going tropical on us?"

Gregory shrugged. "It was a cold winter."

Martin turned slightly and Tobias stared. "Is that a steel plug?"

"Ah, yes, something new we've just got in. You like?"

Tobias shrugged, one hand playing over Noah's shoulders. "I've got a fondness for glass, at the moment."

"Oh, nice," Gregory approved. "Here he comes."

Martin walked toward them, going to his knees and shuffling the last five feet, his eyes down and the glass carefully held up for his Master. Gregory took it without a word, but once he'd put it on the table he favored Martin with a deep kiss, one hand going to the boy's crotch to fondle him.

Tobias caught movement out of the corner of his eye as Noah reached forward and gave his cock a couple of quick hard tugs. Apparently Noah's nerves were making it difficult to maintain his erection with his thoughts alone. He seemed to settle quite a bit, however, as Martin joined them at the table; a lead to follow, another boy to take cues from, perhaps.

"Gregory." A tall man in black leather stopped alongside their table and offered his hand to Gregory. A Frenchman by the look of him -- something about the way he stood and the full day's shadow on his chin gave him away. He had a submissive with him, Tobias noted, following the lead he held loosely in his fingers to a boy on his hands and knees behind him. From his angle, the boy appeared to be completely naked apart from his thick collar, and he was sporting the marks of a recent flogging on his shoulders and ass.

"It is a pleasure to see you," the man added, speaking carefully and with a thick French accent as he shook Gregory's hand.

"And you," Gregory said with a smile. "Jean-Pierre, have you met Tobias? He's over from America and has kindly graced us. Please, sit!"

"Ah, no," Jean-Pierre turned to Tobias and shook his hand as well. "It is a pleasure. America, you say? How long will you be visiting?" He moved past Tobias and took a seat at the table. His boy crawled to Jean-Pierre's feet and lowered his head and elbows to the floor. This time Tobias got a good view of the wide black base of the plug in the boy's ass and the metal cage locked around his cock and balls.

It was beginning to look like Noah was decidedly under-decorated.

"Just the week," Tobias said to Jean-Pierre. "So we're doing as much as we can fit in." He leaned back in his chair and rested a hand on Noah's shoulder for a moment, squeezing it gently. "Mostly sightseeing and shopping so far, however. Oh, and enjoying a great deal of food, as well."

"This is good. There is much to see in the city." Jean-Pierre leaned over and removed his boy's lead. He ordered him to the bar in a curt manner and the boy crawled away, never standing all the way there. "This is Michel, he is, how do you say... punished, yes? Punished this evening. He is often more light, you see? But not tonight."

He looked down at Noah and tilted his head to the side, perusing Noah's body slowly with his eyes. "And your boy, he has nice cock, yes? He is good boy?"

Tobias smiled. "He's a good boy," he said easily. "Sometimes too good -- punishment is rare, and I usually flog him simply because I want to. Not that there's anything wrong with that," he added with a wry grin. He tugged on Noah's harness and said, "Show off for us, pet. Let the Master take a better look at you."

Noah stood, raising himself tall. His posture, as ever, was perfect -- head high, chin level and eyes low, and his forearms were clasped neatly at his lower back. He even arched slightly, which was a nice touch, showing off his erection and his muscular thighs.

Jean-Pierre was duly impressed, and Tobias felt his chest fill proudly. The man looked Noah over critically, standing to get the view from behind as well. "He is beautiful, yes. Very nice. Where do you find these two, Gregory? His trousers must be your work, yes?"

"Andre fit them, from my work," Gregory said. "Really, Tobias, let the boy kneel, he's far too tempting."

Tobias grinned and pointed to the floor, stroking Noah's hair when he was settled. "My apologies," he said, blatantly unapologetic.

Gregory snorted and looked at Jean-Pierre. "I found Tobias a decade ago in a bar somewhat like this," he began expansively.

Tobias laughed and picked up his crop. "Stop right there."

With a grin, Gregory sat back in his chair, his legs spreading as he tugged Martin to kneel between them. He didn't appear to pay any attention as Martin began to nuzzle his balls through his trousers. "We could talk about how Jean-Pierre found me."

"Oui, oui, I could do that." Jean-Pierre grinned at Gregory and then looked at Tobias. "I was looking for a designer for a leather, eh, hangs from ceiling..." The man waved his hand slightly over his head.

"Sling," Gregory said helpfully.

"Sling, yes," he repeated for Tobias, his voice as rich as his accent.

"Total deprivation suspension," Gregory clarified further.

"Yes, just so. Exactly. I was turned away from two different shops in the city because what I want was complicated, yes? Specific. But Gregory, he said no problem. It is a very nice piece. I insist on trying these things myself before I use them on the boy, and so when I went to pick it up, Gregory," he glanced at Gregory again. "He very kindly tied me up."

When he looked back at Tobias, he was still grinning, but he leaned over and spoke more quietly. "It was not the experience I expected it to be, you know? Gregory give me the full treatment, so to say, yes? He is lucky I did not kill him after."

Michel returned with Jean-Pierre's drink, crawling to his feet. Jean-Pierre took the glass and then pointed at the floor, and the boy sat on his heels, then folded forward with his forearms and forehead flat on the floor. Jean-Pierre leaned over and whispered something in French and then stroked a hand lightly from the boy's hair down to his rump where he gave the plug a twist and a push. Michel moaned.

Noah, for his part, seemed as if he were ignoring the conversation and the other boys completely.

Tobias grinned at Gregory and tugged at Noah's hair. "You're either very brave or foolish. Not that Jean-Pierre seems to mind, in hindsight." He bent over and stroked Noah's face. "Fetch me some water, pet."

Noah stood and gave Tobias a small nod, then made his way across the room to the bar. To his credit, he didn't rush, and he didn't look back at the heads that turned while he waited his turn.

"Ah, no. Gregory and I occasionally keep each other sharp, now." Jean-Pierre looked over at Gregory and grinned.

Tobias had his ears on Jean-Pierre but his eyes on Noah as his boy pointed to a bottle of spring water on a shelf behind the bar.

"No one will touch him," Gregory said, one hand lying flat on the table. The other he tangled in Martin's hair as the boy continued to tease him.

"I know," Tobias said with a nod. "But I like to watch him." He glanced at Jean-Pierre and shrugged one shoulder. "It's hard not to." He looked back and watched as the bartender gave Noah a glass full of ice and the bottle of water. "You two really play with each other?"

"Of course!" Gregory said happily. The hand on the table

flexed suddenly, and he moaned. "That's it, boy. A little more and I'll let you suck it."

Tobias rolled his eyes and watched Noah come back to him, his gaze going first to Noah's erection.

"He is lovely to watch, yes." Jean-Pierre was definitely watching, and Tobias noted that he kept his eyes on Noah while the boy set the glass down, filled it from the bottle and then knelt once again next to Tobias' chair. "Lovely." Jean-Pierre sipped his drink again.

"You have a collection of admirers, pet," Tobias said as he picked up his glass. "Well, one or two, anyway. I'm sure that when Martin is allowed to actually look at you he'll be added to the count."

Gregory laughed, the sound tight. His face was beginning to flush and his hand was flexing rhythmically. "Martin will adore him. Just not yet."

"Oh, don't let us interrupt. Happy to watch, aren't we, Jean-Pierre?"

Jean-Pierre laughed. "Just so, Martin has excellent skill, Gregory tells me." He finished his drink and sent Michel off for another. "You belong to club like this in America?"

The Frenchman turned his head at a deep grunting sound and Tobias followed his gaze. Not five feet away, a man had his sub bent over a table and was going at him hard. "Seems a bit early in the evening for that, no?"

Tobias made a show of looking at his watch. "It is, actually." He watched the pair for a moment, taking in the sub's obvious pleasure at being so used and turned back to Gregory. "I think I'd rather watch Gregory getting his cock sucked, though."

It wasn't so much the watching, or even the fact that Gregory was someone he knew and the other pair were strangers; the look in the submissive's eyes reminded him too much of how Noah had been when Tobias had taken him in the parking lot. It made his prick fill, made him want. So he watched Gregory instead.

Noah remained quiet but leaned his head into Tobias' fingers a bit more as Michel returned with his Master's drink.

"Indeed. Oui," Jean-Pierre nodded. He accepted his drink from Michel. "Do you want to watch them, boy?" he asked, but the boy hesitated before answering. "Tell me the truth, I will not punish you for the answer, my darling."

Michel looked uncertain but nodded his head yes.

"You have been good boy tonight. You kneel here, and you watch Martin, yes? Is good." He gave Michel a pat on the rump and then the boy knelt, raising his eyes to Martin but no farther.

"An audience, boy," Gregory said, the hand in Martin's hair tightening. "Just the way you like it."

Martin moaned, loud enough that Tobias could hear him over the noise of the bar. His head nodded, curls bobbing as he moved. Tobias could see that he'd managed to soak the front of Gregory's pants, the fabric clinging to a hard erection.

"Good little slut," Gregory said. "All right, then. Take it out and show them what you can do."

Martin moaned again, his own hips jerking. The light glinted off the steel plug in his ass, and Tobias shifted in his chair, his legs spreading a little more.

Gregory's pants were opened in haste, his cock springing free and into Martin's fingers. The boy made a happy sound and immediately began licking it, his head twisting and turning so everyone watching could get a good look at both Gregory's dick and the way Martin's tongue flicked over it.

Gregory grinned and looked down, watching as Martin took him into his mouth. "That's it," he murmured. "Suck it."

Tobias suddenly realized he was holding onto Noah's hair a little more firmly than was strictly necessary and looked down at his boy.

Noah wasn't watching, his eyes were studiously downcast. He wasn't touching himself either at the moment; there was no need. His erection stood rigidly out from his body and was a warm shade of red. It strained enthusiastically against the laces of his chaps.

Michel made a sound and pressed his palm against his caged cock. Jean-Pierre made no effort to stop him -- his eyes were on Gregory's cock and Martin's busy tongue. He, too, shifted a bit in his seat, leaning back a bit farther and uncrossing his legs.

"You've got them hard, little one," Gregory told Martin. He was a little breathless, his hand kneading the table top.

Martin moaned again, his own knees spreading as he really set to work, taking Gregory deeper into his mouth.

"God, yes," Gregory groaned, his hand finally going to Martin's head along with the other. "Such a mouth..."

Tobias doubted that Martin was as good as Noah, but Gregory was certainly enjoying it. The man was starting to push into his boy's mouth, his cock slick with Martin's spit, shiny and wet, the head a dusky color they could all see every time Martin pulled back to show it off.

Tobias adjusted his own erection, not in the least ashamed to be watching. He noted the way Martin licked at the beads of pre-come Gregory produced, the way the boy's body shuddered each time. If Martin wasn't careful, he'd be getting punished for shooting without permission.

Michel whimpered and Jean-Pierre frowned. "No, my darling," he said, reaching down to pull the boy's hand away from the cage that prevented him from getting hard. "You are being punished tonight, yes? Hands behind your back."

Michel clasped his hands behind his back, making him look a lot like Noah, who was in much the same position. Behind them, the man fucking his submissive came loudly to the applause of a small but admiring crowd.

Tobias slipped his hand across Noah's shoulders, suddenly feeling like there was far too little contact between them. He watched as Martin played with Gregory's balls and circled the swollen head of the now fiercely hard erection. Leaning over to whisper in Noah's ear, he said, "You're better, pet."

Noah leaned into Tobias' touch and turned his head just enough so that Tobias could see him smile. All of this sitting and focusing was good for him, Tobias decided, since he'd been a little scattered since they'd arrived in Paris. However the evening worked out for them, Noah would be relaxed and deep in his space for it, and he would feel more like himself by morning.

"God," Gregory whispered. Then he fisted his hand in Martin's hair and thrust hard into the boy's mouth.

Tobias felt himself tense along with Gregory, could almost feel the man's orgasm building. When Gregory gasped, Tobias sat straighter, his gaze locked on Martin's mouth.

"Yes!" Gregory said tightly, pulling out and coming all over Martin's face and chest, his hand suddenly working his cock hard.

Tobias sat back, breathing heavily. He was a little surprised by how turned on the display made him.

Jean-Pierre grinned and reached over to pat Gregory on the back. "Bravo!" he teased. "Martin has managed to make us all stiff, eh? Bravo."

Tobias caught Noah as he glanced up quickly, presumably at Martin, and then lowered his eyes again.

"Liked that, boy?" he whispered, watching Gregory put himself away and Martin smear come into his skin with a whimper.

Apparently Noah had seen more than Tobias realized because he nodded yes.

"Good." Tobias reached for his water glass and drank about half of it, enjoying his current level of arousal. He was hungry for more, but not quite ready to drag Noah off into a corner. He looked at Jean-Pierre and grinned. "So what else do you do for entertainment here?"

Jean-Pierre lit up a cigarette. "There is a whipping post there," he pointed, "to show your skills, and also rooms in the back set for, eh, scenes, yes? Tableaux." He took another drag. "They are not private, anyone may come and see, but there are many to choose from. There is also entertainment later in the evening; they usually have men perform."

"Will you be performing?" Tobias asked. He had half a mind to go see what the rooms were, but thought it might be nice if Noah was the obvious one of them. He did, however, finger his crop. Flogging he could do -- which was not to say that he wouldn't happily fuck Noah in front of a crowd... just not this early in the evening.

Jean-Pierre reached down to run his fingers through Michel's hair. While he was there, he pointed at the floor again and Michel bent over his knees once more. "Michel has the remainder of his punishment to accept, so... yes, I think I might show off my arm a bit at his expense." The man grinned at Tobias. "You? I see you have brought a sturdy crop, eh?"

"Why, so I have." Tobias grinned and picked up the crop.

"It's a very nice crop, too. And you, Gregory? When you get your wind back, will you be entertaining the room at large?"

Gregory gave Tobias a look that would have been a glare if he wasn't sex addled. "I have my wind back, old man."

"Ah, so that's a yes?" Tobias teased.

"No. I think I'll have a bottle of water, watch you and Jean-Pierre, and then drag my little one into a corner for some private correction." Gregory petted Martin, who leaned into the touch and moaned.

"You and me then," Tobias said with a smile. "Would you like to use this?"

"We can start with it," Jean-Pierre replied with a grin. He reached over to his hip. "And finish with this." He gave the bullwhip on his hip a tug and set it on the table. "It is well balanced; Gregory's work, of course. You will like it."

Noah glanced up at the table and then back into his lap.

Tobias smiled. "That will do nicely, I think." He took a breath and poured more water into his glass before handing it to Noah. "Very nicely, don't you think?"

Noah took the glass Tobias offered him. He opened his mouth as if to speak but shut it abruptly and nodded once instead. The water was gone in two long gulps.

"Your boy approves, Tobias. He is something special, no? I look forward to seeing what he is willing to take for you." Jean-Pierre took one last drag off his cigarette, considered Michel carefully for a moment, and then put it out in the ashtray on the table and stood. "We can bind them together at the post, yes? A lovely picture, I think."

Tobias nodded, taking Noah's leash in his hand. "Lovely," he agreed as he stood up. "I assume the patrons will grant us enough room?" They certainly seemed willing to, several people already pushing tables to the side as they spotted the whip and crop.

"Oh, yes." Jean-Pierre led Michel to the post. The boy crawled all the way but stood as soon as he reached it. He faced it and held his arms out to his sides, parallel to the floor. "Good boy," Jean-Pierre praised him and gestured for Tobias to bring Noah over to the other side.

"Come now, pet. You and Michel can stare into each other's eyes and judge how good we are." Tobias smiled and smoothed a hand over Noah's back as they stepped up to the post. "Kiss me first, boy."

Noah turned so quickly and pressed his lips to Tobias' so eagerly it seemed as if he'd been waiting all evening for that very request. He leaned into Tobias and opened his mouth for him, yielding softly to Tobias' tongue.

Jean-Pierre made an approving sound while he closed the cuffs on Michel's side of the post around his boy's delicate wrists.

With real regret Tobias pulled away. "Thank you," he whispered. "Such a good boy. Make me proud."

Noah nodded and turned to the post, his arms coming up so Tobias could secure him. The wrists were easy, and Tobias made sure Noah had sure footing. He stood behind Noah and reached around him to tease at his cock, his thumb brushing the head of it again and again. "Don't come," he ordered.

Noah shook his head no. No, of course he wouldn't come, even if he could, through the ring and all the laces binding his prick. He watched Noah test the bonds and shift his weight from foot to foot. When he settled, Tobias knew that he was comfortable and ready.

"You first, eh?" Jean-Pierre asked, stepping around to Noah's side of the post.

"If you prefer," Tobias said easily, running a hand down Noah's back and cupping his ass for a moment. Then he stepped back and rolled his shoulders, suddenly aware of the gathering audience. With a grin, he slapped his crop against one thigh and undid his suit jacket. "I'm a little overdressed," he said mildly. "However..." He brought the crop down on Noah with a healthy snap, the crop leaving a nice red stripe.

Noah hissed and shifted, but didn't make any more sound than that. The gasp Tobias heard wasn't his boy's, it was Michel.

Jean-Pierre nodded approvingly and admired the length and width of the stripe. "This is a nice tool, yes?"

"I like it," Tobias said with a nod. "It's a little lighter than my favorite, but it's got wonderful balance. Here." He handed the crop to Jean-Pierre and stepped back, taking off his jacket. Immediately, a club employee was at his side to take it from him.

"Thank you." Jean-Pierre circled the post slowly, admiring both boys while he tested the weight of the crop and measured its sting on his thigh. He leaned against Michel's back to whisper something in the boy's ear that Tobias couldn't hear and then stepped back and laid the crop to the boy's bare ass, marking him vertically and raising a welt. Michel whimpered pitifully but stood his ground. "Très bien," he said and stepped away again.

"Very nice," Tobias complimented him, studying the mark. "Good definition."

He walked around to Noah and felt the line he'd made moments before, then quickly raised its match, precisely an inch above it. "I like symmetry," he said, holding the crop out to Jean-Pierre.

"You mean you're a stickler for details," Gregory called out.

"That, too."

Noah winced and whimpered softly, but Tobias knew that two strokes of the crop were just enough to force him deep and not nearly enough to push him near his safeword. Tobias enjoyed the sound, and a glance at his boy's prick was evidence enough that Noah was enjoying the new crop as well.

"Mmm," Jean-Pierre hummed thoughtfully. "Is very nice." He took the crop from Tobias and circled the boys again, then studied Michel's ass. There were already several marks from earlier in the evening, so Tobias knew he wanted to make his choices carefully. He brandished the crop wide enough that Michel was probably able to catch the movement out of the corner of his eye, and then laid a stripe on the boy's other cheek to mirror the first.

Michel made a sobbing sound and squeezed his eyes shut. Tears rolled down his cheeks.

"Ah, my darling. It is beautiful, you wait until you see," Jean-Pierre told the boy soothingly. He held the crop out to Tobias.

"It doesn't seem fair," Tobias remarked as he took the crop. "Your boy's been warmed up." He hefted the crop for a moment and almost negligently added a third, perfect stripe to Noah's ass. "However, you do have a wonderful touch."

"Ah, oui. He has had a turn at the post already tonight. I will admire your technique for a bit until you feel your boy is ready for the whip, yes?" Jean-Pierre stepped back, leaving the crop in Tobias' fingers. "You are very skilled, I enjoy how your tool is mere extension of your arm. Is very graceful, you understand? I am sure everyone that watches agrees."

Tobias grinned and looked over at Gregory. "What do you think?"

"I think you've gotten better, and I think you're showing off," Gregory said with a smile. There were a few snickers and one friendly nod from the gathered audience. "But we like those who show off, so please -- continue."

Tobias laughed and ran a hand over Noah's ass, giving him a little squeeze once more. "This ass was made to show off on," he said softly. "Such a good boy, pet. You're doing just fine. Making me hard." He was, too; as relaxed as Gregory had suddenly become, Tobias' need had been building, and the front of his trousers was utterly distorted.

Noah turned his head and glanced down at Tobias' crotch, then looked up enough that he could see Noah's smile in response. As if inviting Tobias to continue, Noah licked his lips and spread his legs even wider.

Jean-Pierre laughed softly from the sidelines. "Your boy is without shame. Is good. He wants you, yes?"

"He wants me, yes." Tobias was fairly sure he didn't sound smug about it; it was simply a fact. Of course, there was the equally obvious fact that he wanted Noah, which was just fine with him. His boy.

He stepped back and considered Noah's ass for a moment and then raised the crop. An instant later a new welt appeared, creating a T out of the first stripe. "Hang on, pet," he murmured as he adjusted his aim and made the second line a T also.

"One more." The third line became his initial as well, and he had to adjust his cock, giving himself a firm stroke as he did it. "Beautiful," he said, stepping up to check how Noah was doing.

"Well done! Is good for him your name is not Maurice," Jean-Pierre teased, laughing.

Noah's eyes were closed, his body a bit tense, and he was breathing through the sting. It only took a couple more deep breaths for his shoulders to relax, and his fists uncurled just moments after that.

Noah's jaw worked as if he wanted to speak. It wasn't in character for him to keep silent during a session; he liked to talk, and Tobias, under other circumstances, would have liked to hear him. Instead of speaking, Noah moaned as Tobias drew nearer, low and soft, a sound meant only for his ears.

"All right, pet?" he asked softly. "You look amazing."

Noah nodded and adjusted his stance once more. He pushed back from the post a few inches, which was just far enough to reach Tobias' shoulder. He kissed it, smiled at the floor and then turned back to face Michel.

Behind him, Tobias heard the snap of Jean-Pierre's bullwhip. He was testing his arm away from his boy. "We move on?" he asked, grinning at Tobias. "Your boy is warm now, yes?"

"Scorched around the edges," Tobias said. He went to stand next to Gregory, one eye on Noah's cock, the other on Jean-Pierre's whip. When he saw Noah swell a little more as Jean-Pierre cracked the whip again, he smiled. "Ready when you are, friend."

"You sound very confident," Gregory said in his ear. "I hope you've had good instruction."

"I learned from the best, and I have someone who's taken the time recently to make sure I've brushed up. When I collared Noah I used it after a lovely display -- I'm sure I can do just as well tonight."

Gregory shrugged. "We'll enjoy watching you try, in any event."

Jean-Pierre turned to face his boy. He barked something in French as a warning to Michel and then let the whip fly, not once, but twice in a row, stinging the boy once on each shoulder.

Michel screamed, and his knees gave out so that he was

hanging by his wrists. Jean-Pierre was already in motion and caught the boy by his hips, helping him to stand again. He spoke to Michel softly until the boy could stand on his own, and then walked away, leaving him sobbing.

"You are a good boy." Jean-Pierre told Michel, redeeming him loudly enough for everyone to hear. "You have taken your punishment bravely, and it is over, my darling. Any more strokes will be reward, yes?"

Michel seemed inconsolable, sobbing and whimpering as he leaned against the post. Impulsively, Noah stretched forward and kissed the boy on the cheek. It earned him a tentative smile, and Michel seemed to quiet a bit.

Tobias walked to Jean-Pierre and took the whip from him. "Michel is a good boy," he said with a smile. "I hope he gets a nice reward."

Jean-Pierre smiled at Tobias and adjusted his erection. "He will."

Tobias chuckled. "Lucky boy, as well."

He coiled the whip a little tighter and moved to the open area, then snapped it out. As he coiled it again he noted its weight and made the necessary adjustments to his swing, the second strike feeling better than the first. He nodded to himself and walked back to Noah as he looped it again. "Two, pet. Take them for me."

Tobias waited, knowing Noah's ritual. His boy checked his footing again, took a deep breath and let it out slowly, and then nodded. Jean-Pierre, Tobias knew, was watching critically.

"Good boy." Tobias didn't make a promise of a reward -- Noah knew very well that he'd be taken care of. With one more pat to Noah's marked ass Tobias moved back.

The room seemed quieter than it had been a few moments before, and Tobias took a moment to catch

Gregory's eye and then Jean-Pierre's. They were both watching him intently, their bodies still. With a sharply drawn breath Tobias let fly, the whip sounding large in the room as it cracked on the floor before licking Noah's shoulder. Once and then again it sounded, two identical welts rising up on Noah's shoulder blades. The one on the right covered the scar that no one else had probably even noticed.

Noah roared, holding nothing back. He rose up on his toes and then down again, then arched his back and shrugged his shoulders, moving as if trying to escape the sting. After a moment or two, the welts grew to an angry red, and Noah whimpered softly through shallow panting as he settled down. He pressed his forehead to the post and closed his eyes.

The room, which had gone so silent only a moment before, erupted in applause and congratulatory shouts in several different languages. A couple of the men watching gave Tobias friendly taps on the shoulder and another handed him a bottle of water.

Apparently, Jean-Pierre knew when he was beat. "This is very nice work, and your boy is strong. How many can he manage, eh?"

Tobias shrugged and sipped the water. "As many as I ask for," he said with a grin. "Seriously? He could probably take two more now, three if I told him he could come."

He passed the water bottle back and went to Noah before Jean-Pierre could reply. "Good, pet," he praised Noah, turning his head with his hand and plunging his tongue into Noah's mouth. His cock throbbed at the familiar taste, and he pulled back. "Very, very good."

He began to undo the cuffs, smiling at Michel. "Both of you."

"Oui, très bien!" Jean-Pierre added, grinning as he freed Michel from his cuffs as well. Michel went right to his knees. "Mais, non! My darling, stand up now, you are not being punished any longer, you know?" The boy seemed to have forgotten and was grinning all over again as he stood. Jean-Pierre kissed him and clipped his lead back to his collar.

Noah rubbed at his wrists for a moment after they were freed and then leaned against Tobias, still seeming a bit unsteady on his feet.

"Easy," Tobias whispered, hands going to Noah's waist. He looked around and took yet another offered water bottle, smiling his thanks to the man giving it to them. "Here." He held the bottle to Noah's mouth and let the boy take several swallows before he lowered it. "Better?"

Noah nodded, and did seem better for the cool water. He reached down and slipped his fingers around the lead attached to his chest harness and pressed it into Tobias' hand. The crowd started to break up.

"It is a shame he goes back to America," Jean-Pierre said to Gregory as he sat down at the table again. He pulled Michel onto his lap and pulled the key to the boy's cock-cage out of his pocket.

"Please, we'd spend all our time trying to keep up," Gregory protested with a grin. "And where's the fun in that?"

Tobias shook his head and laughed as he sat back down. "I didn't even take off my tie," he pointed out. "And you know very well that it's the boy's strength, not mine, that matters." He petted Noah, urging him to kneel as close as he could, touching him as much as he could. He was half tempted to pull Noah into his lap, but he wanted to see how he was reacting to the marks before he did that. Still, though... if he was about to watch Jean-Pierre bring his boy off, something had to give before he ruined his trousers.

Noah took the cues well, kneeling with full contact along Tobias' leg and resting his head on Tobias' knees.

Michel moaned as the cage was removed and gasped when Jean-Pierre took his prick in his fingers. It grew hard almost the moment it was freed from the restraint, and Jean-Pierre praised the boy quietly as he started to stroke.

Tobias bit back a moan, more for his own sake than Michel's, although the boy was lovely. He stroked over Noah's hair again and down so one finger could trace the silver collar. His collar on his boy, his marks on his boy, his boy being absolutely, perfectly well behaved. Pride swelled him, the high settling over him as he glanced down at where Noah rested against him.

He heard the growl coming from his chest even before he'd realized he was making it, and then he bent over, urging Noah to come to him, to crawl up his body and feel him, to curl against him and be held.

"Oh, a double feature," Gregory murmured with a smile.

Noah slipped into Tobias' arms easily, pressing warm fingers against the bulge in his trousers. Noah was pliable and warm and entirely focused on Tobias as he kissed Tobias' jaw and offered his mouth.

In the background Tobias heard Michel gasp and sigh and Jean-Pierre's soft encouraging voice.

Tobias kissed Noah quickly, taking his mouth almost brutally as he pushed into Noah's hand. He moaned into the kiss and sucked Noah's tongue for a moment, then let him go. "Watch," he urged, turning Noah slightly. "Watch and wait. I'll take care of you."

He settled Noah in his lap and slipped his hand down, skimming Noah's erection and cupping his balls before sliding two fingers farther back, dancing over the entrance to Noah's body.

"Maybe you *should* stay," Gregory said hoarsely, and Tobias spared him a quick glance, unsurprised to see Martin once more between his Master's thighs.

Noah's gaze was on Michel's erection and on the hand that was working it smoothly, rhythmically, almost hypnotically. Jean-Pierre's boy whimpered and moaned and started to rock his hips not so much into his Master's fingers but back to ride his plug.

"Ah, good boy," Jean-Pierre encouraged. "You see? Noah watches you, he knows you are a good boy. Mon garçon. My darling. Is good?"

Michel nodded enthusiastically, and then his breath caught and he started to shudder. Noah gasped and reached back to push his hand against Tobias' bulge again.

Tobias moaned softly and pushed into Noah's touch, watching Michel flex and shake, chasing his orgasm. His eyes were starting to drift shut, the shaking increasing, and Tobias' cock throbbed under the heat of Noah's hand. He could hear the wet sounds of Martin sucking on Gregory and he could feel Noah's urgency build. His poor boy was likely in pain, having been hard for so very long.

He pushed his fingers against Noah's hole and arched slightly. "Touch me, pet," he whispered. "I want you."

Jean-Pierre pulled Michel tight against his chest as the boy's hips began to jerk through his grip. The next moment he shot, and Jean-Pierre pushed the boy's cock hard to his body so the spunk soaked Michel's belly, his chest, and all the way up to his chin.

Noah groaned and his fingers deftly tugged at Tobias' fly, pushed past the rich fabric, and tightened around Tobias' prick. He turned in Tobias' lap so his back was to Tobias' chest, spread his legs wide to straddle his lap, and started to stroke Tobias as if he were stroking himself.

Jean-Pierre grinned and made a comment to Gregory that Tobias saw around Noah but couldn't hear. Michel had disappeared between the man's thighs and was already mouthing the rigid length under Jean-Pierre's trousers.

With a gasp and a roll of his hips, Tobias quickly sucked on his fingers, watching both Michel and Martin as they serviced their Masters. Noah was stroking him the way he liked it best, paying attention to what Tobias needed, and Tobias felt himself swell even more.

He shifted enough that he could open Noah, pushing two wet fingers in deep.

"That's it," Gregory said, and Tobias didn't know if it was to Martin or him, or even Michel. He didn't really care.

Noah gasped and leaned forward a little to give Tobias' hand more room, bearing down on his fingers. His hand stuttered, just for a moment, and then continued stroking slowly.

Michel had Jean-Pierre's cock down his throat and was making more noise than his Master was. Jean-Pierre was sipping a drink with one hand and holding a cigarette with the other.

Tobias worked his fingers deeper into Noah, moving quickly. His boy was going to ache in the morning for more reasons than he could really count right then, but he didn't want to hurt him. He felt Noah ripple around his fingers and he bit down on the nearest piece of skin he could reach. "Good boy," he growled. "Open up for me, sweetheart. Want to fuck you."

Noah moaned and lifted his hips, pressing Tobias' erection backward toward his hole. "Please," he started to beg, but caught himself before saying anything more.

Tobias ignored the slip, his cock actually leaping at the sound of Noah's voice begging for him. He panted, trying not to groan as he lifted Noah's hips and began to push in, steadying his boy as he eased Noah down onto his prick.

"Oh, sweet," Gregory purred, and Tobias could see him moving out of the corner of his eye, leaning forward over Martin's head. "Boy, watch. No, I... yes, that's it. Stop, watch. Use your hand."

Tobias bit his lip, Noah sinking a little more, taking more of him with a low moan. Taking him mostly dry should have been hurting, but Noah appeared beyond caring.

Finally Noah's ass sat flush on Tobias thighs and he hissed, shifting once and then again before he fumbled for Tobias' hand and pressed it to his erection. "Oh, sir," he breathed and didn't seem to notice he'd said anything at all this time.

"God," Tobias whispered. He couldn't remember the last time Noah had felt so tight, so incredible. He fumbled with the ties around Noah's cock, his eyes closing as he concentrated. Suddenly there was another hand there, and his eyes flew open to see Martin on his knees before them, quick fingers sliding with his own.

His cock throbbed and he thrust up hard.

Noah grunted. He was already breathing unevenly. "Fuck, yes." He arched forward, trying to find some leverage of his own. The slight bend in his shoulders put the red welts from the bullwhip directly in Tobias' line of vision. "Martin...?" Noah's voice sounded surprised, but as Martin got the laces open, Noah groaned heavily, relieved. "Yes, yes... the ring? Sir? Ache, so hard, please, please."

Noah was somewhere else at the moment, somewhere that only he and his Master -- and apparently Martin, too -- could go. Tobias felt his boy's need as keenly as his own.

"Take it off," Tobias ground out, his hips rocking and his

cock sliding in and out of Noah in short thrusts. "Take it off him, now!"

Martin looked back at Gregory and Tobias pushed his palm over the slippery, wet head of Noah's erection. At Gregory's nod, Martin's fingers joined his, wrapping around Noah and tugging at the cock ring.

"Christ," Gregory breathed, stroking himself. "Tobias--"

Tobias ignored him, ignored everything but the way Noah felt around him, moved on him. He thrust again, spread Noah's pre-come around, and just took in the scent of him. He bent forward and licked nearest welt.

Noah hissed at the warm tongue on hot skin. "Oh, God! Off, off, please! " he growled, and in the end it wasn't Tobias or Martin that managed to get the ring free; Noah savagely yanked the snap loose himself and tossed it on the table. "Fuck... oh, God, yeah." He started to come almost instantly, tightening around Tobias' intrusion and gulping in air.

Tobias caught one sight of Noah's come falling on Martin's face, and then Noah tightened around him like a fist and his head fell back. "Ah, fuck!" Tobias grunted, slamming into Noah and riding his boy's orgasm as his own welled up impossibly fast. He pushed again and came, the world fracturing around him as his climax was almost torn from him.

He felt Noah collapse backward against him panting harshly. "Master, so good, love you. Oh, God..." Noah whispered softly in his ear.

As the rush in Tobias' ears quieted down it was Jean-Pierre's voice he heard next. "I don't think he hears us."

Tobias kissed Noah just above his ear and looked over at Jean-Pierre. "I'm sorry, you said something? I was a little busy."

"Indeed!" Jean-Pierre laughed loudly. "We only were

saying how beautiful the two of you are together and, eh, how you say, in tune, yes? How in tune you are with your boy. Michel, water for them both, please. Quickly."

Apparently Tobias had missed the climax of Michel's efforts as well, because Michel jumped to his feet and ran off to the bar.

Tobias blinked slowly, not quite back in his right mind. "We're good together," he said softly. He turned his head and kissed Noah again. "Beautiful, sweetheart," he whispered.

Carefully, he lifted Noah a little so his softening cock could slide out; the warm trickle of his come that slid down Noah's thigh made him growl, his natural possessiveness as satiated as he was.

"Everyone survive?" he asked as Michel came back with water. He pulled Noah tight against him, holding him close.

Jean-Pierre nodded. He looked completely unruffled. "Better than you, it seems. Cigarette?" He tapped the pack so one stuck out and held out the pack out to Tobias. Michel set the water on the table and knelt, upright this time, at Jean-Pierre's side.

"No, thank you," Tobias said, shaking his head. "Feel too good to smoke."

Noah shifted and sighed, pressing his forehead to the side of Tobias' neck. He was heavy and limp and, by the sound of his breathing, quite possibly dozing.

"You come to Paris often? What are your plans for the rest of the week, eh?" Jean-Pierre asked curiously. He opened a bottle of water and handed it to Tobias.

"This is the first time in ten years," Tobias said, taking the water. "Thank you."

"He abandoned us," Gregory said with a dramatic sigh.

"It was a vacation!" It was also an old argument.

"So you say."

Tobias rolled his eyes, smiling. He took a mouthful of water and swallowed happily, not sure when he'd become so parched. "We're here as a gift to the boy, and to talk over our new contract," he said to Jean-Pierre. "The rest of the week will be taken up with seeing more of Paris, talking a lot, and, I expect, handing out a few spankings."

Michel giggled softly at the mention of spankings, and Jean-Pierre swatted him affectionately on the head. "The boys get tired later at night, yes? Noah, he talk a lot in a club where he is not to be heard, but no one will frown on him after such a performance. Boys who know better, though..." Jean-Pierre frowned playfully down at Michel who looked contrite but couldn't contain his grin.

Tobias grinned. "They're good boys, and Noah did very well." He pet Noah carefully to avoid his welts. "However, he was... not silent." His smile grew. "I think he'll be pleased about that, actually -- he seems fond of my hand warming his ass."

"And your crop, too. You have changed my mind about Americans, Tobias, they are often more bravado than skill, but you are not so. I am impressed." Jean-Pierre looked over at Gregory. "I am going to send Michel to clean up; you want Martin to go also?"

"Goodness, yes. Not that I think your lad's come is nasty, Tobias, but it's all over my boy." He made a face and shooed Martin off with Michel before leaning over. "Is he asleep?"

"He seems to be," Tobias said, "but I can't swear to it. Why?"

"You fucked him bare, man. Is that normal for you?"

Tobias resisted the urge to laugh. "With Noah, yes."

"Gregory." Jean-Pierre slapped at the man's arm. "Be polite. His boy, his way, yeah? Surely they have an agreement." He looked at Tobias for confirmation.

"Of course." Tobias looked down at Noah, uncaring of the club, their opinions, of anything other than the fact that he loved Noah so much it made him ache. "We're... serious, though that's not really the word for it. Aside from contracts or agreements -- we go beyond that."

"It shows." Jean-Pierre nodded, giving Tobias a smile. "How long have you been together?"

"Six months." It sounded like such a short time. The only other time he'd felt this sure of anything had been with Phan, which was a sobering thought.

"So that was a provisional contract then? And you'll be renegotiating for long-term?"

Tobias nodded. "And live-in, as well as defining some new rules about play and boundaries."

"Uh?" Noah mumbled, still half-sleeping against Tobias.

"Good luck with it," Jean-Pierre said with a wink.

"Thanks," Tobias said dryly. "Shh, sweetheart. I've got you."

Noah sat up a bit and reached up to rub between his eyes with the heel of his hand. "I..." he shut his mouth quickly, suddenly remembering where he was. He turned to Tobias and his brow furrowed. He looked like he was trying to ask for something and was obviously frustrated with his inability to speak. He made a sort of hose gesture near his dick and sighed dramatically.

"Bathroom?" Jean-Pierre asked, and Noah turned in his direction and tapped a finger on his nose. Jean-Pierre just laughed.

Tobias laughed with him. "Off you go, then. The other two are cleaning up as well; see if you can't hurry them a bit, pet." As Noah climbed off him, Tobias made a show of putting himself back in his trousers. "And find me a damp cloth, please."

Noah nodded at him and wandered off stiffly, his path a little roundabout and his steps sleep addled. Tobias assumed his ass was working against him, too, and the way Noah had to clutch at his laces to keep his chaps up was adorable.

Grinning, he looked back at Jean-Pierre and Gregory. "Well?"

"You've got a fine lad," Gregory said with a smile. He lifted a water bottle and inclined it toward Tobias as a toast. "Here's to a new contract, a long time with him, and may you return to show off for us again."

Tobias lifted his own bottle, his grin growing wider. "I'll drink to that."

Tobias was more than hopeful that he'd get exactly what Gregory had wished for them; his confidence had grown to the point that he had every intention of moving them into negotiations as soon as they'd had some sleep. With that thought, he went to find his suit jacket; it was time to take Noah back to their bed for the night.

Noah returned just after Tobias did, laced up and looking more awake and less disheveled. The chaps didn't have quite the same effect in the front with his prick soft, but he looked pretty good anyway. He was flanked by Michel and Martin, who were both looking refreshed themselves.

Carefully, Noah knelt by Tobias' chair with the cloth that Tobias had requested.

"He looks stiff," Jean-Pierre told Gregory with a grin.

"He does, doesn't he?" Gregory replied, winking. "He'll be moving slow tomorrow."

Tobias nodded, dabbing at the assorted bits of mess on his trousers with the cloth. "And on that note, I think I'll take him home and put him to bed. Ridden hard and put away wet doesn't make for a healthy boy, does it, pet?" He tossed the cloth on the table and picked up Noah's lead. "Thank you for the entertainment," he said to Jean-Pierre.

Jean-Pierre stood, and so did his boy. "A pleasure meeting you, Tobias," he said with a smile and shook Tobias' hand. "We will meet again, I hope."

Michel gave Tobias a respectful bow.

Noah got to his feet slowly and followed Michel's lead with a shallow bow to both Jean-Pierre and Gregory, and then stood slightly behind Tobias' shoulder. He was looking sleepy again.

Tobias laughed and shook his head at Noah before exchanging a quick embrace and a kiss on each cheek with Gregory. It was one of the few ways Gregory had embraced European life, and Tobias had long suspected it was simply to gather more kisses from everyone. "Thank you, Gregory. I'll be in touch, and I suspect I'll have another order for you soon."

"Oh, I like the sound of that," Gregory said with a smile. "Take care of yourself, old man."

"I will. Goodnight."

The three men exchanged another fast round of well wishes, and Tobias led Noah to the doors, taking only a few moments to gather their overcoats. "Let's get you back to the hotel, sleepy boy," Tobias said fondly as they stepped out. There was a car waiting for them, which pleased him to no end; the club was very efficient.

Noah was asleep almost before the car pulled away, taking them back to the hotel.

20

They'd slept hard, and Tobias was unsurprised to find Noah still dead to the world when he woke the next morning. He got up and ordered breakfast, taking a quick shower before it was delivered. He signed for the meal still dressed in his bathrobe, and after pouring himself a cup of strong coffee he took the flowers from the cart and slipped back into bed.

"Noah," he said softly. "Time to wake up, sweetheart." He teased at his lover's cheek with a carnation, urging him to wake.

"Thought I smelled coffee..." Noah mumbled, his eyes still closed. He turned his nose right into the flower and inhaled deeply. "Mmm. That's not coffee." He smiled and opened his eyes, blinking the sleep away. "Good morning, sir."

Tobias clicked his tongue and waved the flower a moment to make his point, and then kissed Noah on the tip of his nose. "Good morning. How do you feel? Need a hot bath?"

"Right. Flowers." Noah smiled but then his brow

furrowed as he rolled over. "Oh, my, quite sore," he said with an embarrassed grin. "Mostly in the good way."

"But not entirely, I'll bet. All right, then, let me take a look at you." Tobias urged Noah to lie on his stomach and took a hard look at all the welts and red marks, finally deciding that he was fine, if achy. "Spread your legs, Noah," he said softly. "I want to make sure you didn't tear when I fucked you. Which, by the way, was a major highlight of the night. You were tighter than hell that way."

"I suppose you'll be disappointed if I tell you that most anything after the bullwhip was a blur? I mean I remember thinking that I was going to pass out if that ring didn't come off, and I remember you feeling incredibly huge, and the rest is kind of... ah." Noah hissed softly. "Ow. That's pretty damn sore. Bruised?"

Tobias nodded to himself. "Yeah, you're out of commission for a bit. Sorry, love. No tears, but you're pretty red." He stretched out next to Noah, mostly on top of him, and hugged Noah to his chest. "Sorry. And seeing as how you don't remember, you tore off the ring yourself and came all over poor Martin. He was just trying to help, and you made a mess of him." He tried very hard not to laugh.

"What? Oh, my God. Martin was helping? All I remember is you. What kind of a slut am I?" Noah laughed softly. "I should send the poor guy flowers." Noah tangled his fingers with the hand that was curled around his chest.

"It was beautiful," Tobias said softly. "You were beyond anything." He took a deep breath and snuggled Noah a little tighter to him. "So, up until you left your brain behind, you had a good time? It worked?"

"Well, I got over being nervous quickly enough, and then I rather liked the place. The music was good, and I felt very in my space, you know? And those chaps turned heads and everyone thought you were such a stud, and I was so... yours." Noah grinned. "It was good, except for the fact that I couldn't speak to you. I get not being allowed to talk to anyone else, or other subs or whatever, but I really didn't like not being able to answer you, or react to you in a way we both enjoy, you know? With words. It was frustrating, not being able to communicate the way we're used to."

Tobias nodded. "I agree with you, really. It's an old, old rule, though, and when in Paris... Oh, and you got over that after your brain landed in your cock, by the way. There will be a spanking at some point, when it occurs to me. I'm insanely proud of you, sweetheart." He rubbed a circle on Noah's belly and purred a little, utterly content.

"Oops." Noah grinned, but he didn't seem terribly contrite. "Well, if anyone asks, you can just tell them you have that effect on me. Did you have a good time? Your friends seemed like good guys."

"I had a wonderful time, thanks to you. And, yes, they're good people. They were very curious about us, you know. Gregory just about had a fit when he watched me take you bare, and Jean-Pierre seemed curious about our contract."

"Damn, I really did miss a lot, didn't I?" Noah shook his head at himself. "Well, I have two things to say to that. I'm incredibly smug that we trust each other enough to fuck bare, and I am also curious about our contract." Noah turned his head and looked Tobias in the eyes, Tobias' flowers relieving him of his submissive restraints for now. "Tell me more about this moving in together idea of yours."

"I want you to live with me," Tobias said simply. He tried very hard to sound calm and relaxed about it, but a frisson of hopeful tension settled at the base of his spine. "I want you there each night. If I could figure a way to work it, I'd move us to the farm, but we can't do that. What do you think? Generally, I mean."

Noah looked thoughtful, and maybe a little worried. Something was eating at him about it, but Tobias thought he knew what it was. He was just hoping he was right.

"Generally? Generally speaking, I really wish we could do it. I think we could live well together... but," Noah reached up and slid a finger over Tobias' jaw. "I'm concerned about what you're actually asking me. I can't be a 24/7 sub, Tobias. I have a career that's important to me. I have friends, and other commitments that I don't want to give up."

"I don't want you to," Tobias assured him. "And I don't think 24/7 would work for us, anyway. We'd have to discuss downtime, and what we do expect -- which is where I can see the negotiations getting complicated. For example, I want your weekends. Even if you agree to move in, I want them; I need that kind of dedicated time, the length and breadth of it."

"Weekends aren't the complicated part, Tobias," Noah reassured him. "That's our time regardless, unless I ask you for one here and there for a family thing or if I just need a rest. I wouldn't want that to change, I really need that time too. It's the rest of the week, with working and all, that might be the hard part to work out." Tobias noted that Noah was still speaking noncommittally. He was being very careful not to agree to anything yet. "What about Phan owning half of the condo? I mean, if I moved in... well, it's kind of uptown for me, but if I did, I don't think I'd want that."

Tobias nodded. "I've been thinking about that. I want him to have a safe place, someplace to go, you know? I can sign it over to him. I'm sure I can find something downtown... maybe a building." He tried very hard not to hold his breath at that as he let it sit there, between them.

Noah looked at him a little confused. "Downtown?"

"Well, yes. Downtown. Where you work," Tobias said slowly, not sure why he was explaining.

Noah smiled and Tobias felt his posture change as he relaxed a little. "You'd really move downtown? Wait, a building? Are you serious?"

Tobias blinked and let himself smile. "Yes. And yes."

"Oh. Well, that," Noah plucked the carnation out of Tobias' fingers and stuck it behind Tobias' ear. "That would... make this a much easier decision for me."

"Oh, really?" Tobias wasn't sure if he should tease or not, but couldn't resist. "I knew you liked real estate."

"Mmm... real estate. So hot," Noah's voice was deadpan, but he punched Tobias lightly in the arm. "So... since you seem to have given this a lot of thought, Dr. Vincent, which I have to tell you I appreciate, suppose we did move into a place downtown? What were you thinking for logistics? Any other bombshells I should mull over?"

Tobias shrugged. "About living together? Depends on the building, I suppose. Play area in town, you can have some space if you want it, whatever. If you want things to think about, we're going to have set out rules for playing with others, and we have to decide on the length of the contract." This time, he did hold his breath.

"I've been thinking about the length," Noah said, nodding. "I mean, not that I want to scare you off or anything, but I was thinking we've maybe moved beyond a term contract. That maybe we could call it open-ended and just put in a provision to either touch base at regular intervals, or build in some way to talk as things come up? Especially if I'm moving in, you know? That's a long-term decision in my mind, and I wouldn't agree to it if I didn't see us together in a year or two, or... a lot longer." He glanced up at Tobias and searched in his eyes. "Is that... am I completely off base with this?"

Tobias grinned, the last bit of tension leaving his body and making him as relaxed as Noah. "That's perfect," he said, his hand sliding over Noah's skin. "And exactly what Bradford suggested when I told him I didn't want to lock the time frame down."

Noah laughed. "Oh, I should have known you'd have discussed it with that old busybody," Noah joked. "He's a meddler, though. A sneaky meddler. I called him about it, too."

"You didn't!" Tobias stared at him and finally rolled onto his back, laughing. "That bastard. I bet he's got it all written up for us. So, what advice did he offer, aside from that? Don't tell me he didn't, because I won't believe you."

Noah was still laughing as he sat up and slid carefully out of bed. He made his way over to the breakfast tray and looked it over. "Well, the conversation started with me asking if he thought it was outrageous to suggest that we live together, and if he had any ideas on how it might work out. You know where that goes. You want some more coffee?"

Noah poured himself a cup, the sun coming in the window reflecting off his cock ring. "The next thing that he suggested was that I think about our personal relationship as a separate thing from our Dom/sub arrangement and find a way to be sure that it's protected now that I'm wearing your collar."

Tobias nodded. "And did you come up with anything? Because aside from making sure we have set, specific times when you're in your sub role, or some sort of signal for when one of us needs a scene, I'm not really sure where to take that. Your own space... downtime each evening after work..." He sat up and leaned back against the headboard. "I mean, we could make a huge long list of what we will or will not do, but that makes things rigid and inflexible. A relationship shouldn't feel like it needs a rule book."

"I definitely don't want a rule book," Noah said as he crossed around the bed to refill Tobias' cup. "And I'm not sure I'll need downtime every night after work. I mean, I can certainly see the merits of you having plans for me the minute I walk in the door." He grinned. "I like the idea of having my own space, and I think as far as downtime after work, if I've had a rough day and I think I need it, I would hope that a phone call to let you know on my way home would take care of that. I'm not concerned about being able to ask you for what I need, I know you'll hear me, and I know if you disagree with me that we'll discuss it. I think Bradford just wanted me to evaluate those things before we sat down at the table, you know?"

"That makes sense," Tobias said easily. He smiled his thanks for the coffee and shifted farther up on the bed, worried mostly about slopping coffee on the sheets. "I'm really not concerned about communication; I think we're pretty good about that. We should talk about play, though. We've been getting into some more intense things, spontaneously."

"Like the other night." Noah nodded and went back to the tray to put a plate together.

"Like the other night," Tobias agreed. He looked down at his coffee mug and gave it a quarter turn in his hand. "I almost hit you," he said finally. "I didn't -- hadn't -- intended things to get that intense when we started. I've never really cared for rape fantasies, it seemed like a cop-out. But that was..." He didn't know what it was, aside from stunningly hot.

"Hot," Noah finished his thought for him. "It was hot. So

apparently you get off on it more than you knew. I don't think it's a cop-out, I think it's more of a physical expression of an intellectual power-exchange, if that makes any sense. Does it bother you that you wanted to hit me?"

"I hit you all the time," Tobias pointed out with a slight smile. "No, it bothers me that I sank so deeply into the scene, that I wanted to overpower you, that I fed off your struggles that way. Every time you said no I got harder, and *that* bothers me."

"It was a scene. I mean, it wasn't one we'd discussed, but I knew what you wanted and I went with it. Are you afraid you wouldn't have stopped if I'd used a safe word? That would be something to worry about. Getting turned on by me saying 'no' when, in this particular case, you knew damn well I was enjoying myself? That's not something to lose sleep over."

Tobias sipped his coffee and thought honestly about that, trying to remember the event clearly. He knew he'd been lost in a fog of arousal, needing so much to get Noah off that it almost caused physical pain. He knew he'd been desperate for his own release. Could he have stopped, really?

Finally he put the coffee cup down and scrubbed at his face. "I would have stopped," he said. "But I really would have hit you, if it would have made you come." His palm itched and he rubbed at it, the urge to hit Noah while pounding into him a mocking memory. "If we're going to do it again you have to know that."

Noah brought a plate over and set it in Tobias' lap. "Thank you," he said leaning in farther to kiss him. "I'm not entirely sure what it says about me that it very well might have, but I'd like to do it again." He sat beside Tobias with a plate of his own.

Tobias nodded, trying to look noncommittal. Something like that either took a lot of planning, like the scene in the parking lot, or happened spontaneously. He picked up a strawberry and bit into it, thinking about the other things they had to .work out. "Phantom," he finally said. "Or Martin, or whatever. We should talk about playing with others. You have standing orders about Phan, and Martin wasn't playing so much as an accident, but we should talk about thirds anyway."

"Would it be terribly transparent of me to request that we talk about each instance as it comes up? Or at least as we see it has the potential for something to come up? For me it really does depend not just on who it is, but the circumstances around each scene." Noah looked over at Tobias and then back at his plate. "That is transparent, isn't it?" He sighed. "Okay, so I like Phan, and there will be times when I might be really into a scene involving him, but I know there will be times when it just doesn't feel right to me. I'm not even sure I can tell you what those times might be, it's just... a reservation that I have."

"That's fair," Tobias said. "Not really easy to navigate, but fair. It's my job to be in tune with what's going on, Noah, so I'll do my best. You always have your words, and I'll never take them away -- and you can always refuse. You know that." He leaned over and brushed his lips over Noah's cheek. "Would it be a huge shock to know that I like you and Phan together?" he asked with a smile.

"Hardly," Noah said, chuckling. "And don't get me wrong, I like Phan and me together, too. Honestly, I'd say most of the time I'll be up for it. You know I'm attracted to him, but I just don't know that I can agree to a hard and fast rule there. If you want to set one, if you want something in writing, then I need an out written in for me as well."

Tobias snorted. "I'm hardly going to make a rule that you have to have sex with Phan whenever I want you to." He grinned. "For one, Phan would have to sign off on it, too."

"Oh, please, Tobias, can you imagine Phan ever saying no?"

"Ego!" Tobias laughed and kissed Noah again. "He'd be an idiot to say no."

"Well, perhaps." Noah laughed, too. "But I meant that he's such a sensual person and I don't see him turning down an opportunity to play in your stables." Noah took a bite of Danish. "Oh, this is really yummy." He held it out for Tobias to take a taste. "So what else, besides third parties and living arrangements, is on your mind?"

Tobias bit into the Danish and shrugged. "Nothing, really. Oh, that is good, thank you. I'm wondering about limits -- we've gotten through your cage, where should we go next? What would you like to try? More suspension? Sensory work?"

"Best birthday present ever," Noah said with a huge smile. "Seriously, that was a priceless gift. Can I say thank you again?"

"You can always say thank you. I like your thank yous. A lot. Stop avoiding the sensory questions." Tobias grinned and took another bite of Noah's Danish.

Noah glanced at Tobias. "Excuse me, I think you've had enough of my yummy Danish." He winked and took a bite.

"You offered!" Tobias tried to look highly insulted, but couldn't really keep back his grin. "That's not part of the thank you, then? And don't think you're getting away with avoiding this, Noah."

"I'm not avoiding it, I'm procrastinating."

"Ah, I see. So it's our next project then. That could be fun." Tobias raised an eyebrow at him.

Noah snorted. "For you."

"Well, yes." Tobias nudged him with his elbow and began to eat another strawberry. "Tell me about it. Is it something you want to get past, or do you want to leave it? Be honest with yourself."

Noah sighed. "You know I don't like obstacles. Part of the point for me is to get past them. I want to be broader, gain more experience, so yeah, I guess it's the next project." He ate the rest of his Danish in one bite.

"Okay. We can do that. Anything else you want to do? Try? I'd like to play out of our comfort zone once in a while. Step up the fantasy play."

Noah looked at Tobias sidelong, grinning. "I love the fantasy stuff. Do you?"

Tobias grinned and nodded. "Oh, yeah. I have some ideas..."

"Yeah? Want to share or surprise me?" Noah stole one of Tobias' berries.

Tobias just grinned and picked up the last berry.

Noah laughed. "Tease. Okay, so out of our comfort zone... what do you mean by that exactly?"

"I mean not the stables, and not our home. Possibly not even the club." He considered the berry for a moment and finally took a bite. "I'm not saying public sex, but maybe going to other clubs. Play acting -- I could pick you up somewhere, or something. A discreet tour of the underground clubs. Just... getting out."

Noah almost wiggled. Actually, he did wiggle. "I love it."

"I thought you might," Tobias said with a pleased smile. Always ready to play, his boy. "And you? Anything you want to try? Hell, any rules you want made? It's your negotiation, too. Tell me. Am I too hard on you, not hard enough? What do you need, baby?"

"More deep days," Noah said easily. It seemed that he'd given this some thought. "I need to work a little harder once in a while. Even fail occasionally, you know? You're indulgent, maybe too indulgent sometimes." He looked at Tobias squarely. "I have loved every minute of getting to know each other, Tobias, it's been quite possibly the best six months in my memory. So don't get me wrong, I want to keep some of what we have now. A lot of it. But I need to keep working. I'm a good sub, I'm confident in that, but everyone can grow. I need you to be tougher with me sometimes. Maybe a weekend a month, or something? I'm sure it would benefit you, too."

"Okay," Tobias said slowly. "Harder how? More restrictions? More overt expectations, like kneeling, serving, chores? Or deeper scenes? Flogged longer and harder?"

"More serving, yes. More of a critical eye? Longer scenes, maybe test my concentration a bit more? It's hard for me to explain it well; I was kind of hoping you might see it better than I do. More... intensity, I guess. More demanding of me." He sighed. "I'm not saying you're not demanding or tough on me, you know that, right? I mean I'm not criticizing you, I just need you to... push me. Amp it up a bit now and then."

"No, no, I understand that," Tobias assured him. "And I think I know what you mean. If you want a hard-ass once a month, you got it. No bitching though." He grinned. "I can be a real bastard."

"Good. Prove it." Noah grinned, looking relieved. It was true that the way Noah served him now, Noah made it seem as natural as breathing. And maybe it was.

"I will," he promised. He leaned over and kissed Noah's mouth. "This is going rather well."

"I knew it would." Noah got out of bed again and went back to the food table. "Want anything? Oh, man, if we move in together you can come to police functions as my spouse." He chuckled.

"I will, you know," Tobias said softly. "If you want me to."

Noah looked at him. "Well, at least you're good looking; it'll be harder to make fun of us." He came back over to the bed with another plate. "I'm out, but it's not... popular to be gay. The guys are happier if they don't have to see it. I'm used to it."

"I know." Tobias looked at him, studied him. "But I'll do what ever you need, Noah. I love you, and I'd be proud to let anyone know that I'm your spouse."

Noah looked at him for a long moment before smiling shyly. "You're sweet, you know that? You're a tiger with a kitten inside."

"It's Paris. It makes me mushy," Tobias deadpanned. "I could spank you, if you'd prefer. Or take you to brunch -- although we seem to be eating already."

Noah leaned on him. "I'm not hungry," he said, munching on a piece of fruit off his plate anyway. "Do we need to hammer out the living together details now? Or was this more of a pre-negotiation negotiation?"

"Hmm. Just a general statement of intent, I think. We have three more days here; how about you think about what you'd like, and we can talk about it later?"

"Fair enough." Noah set his plate aside. "So what were your plans for today before I ruined them by letting you fuck me dry last night?" He shifted so he could kiss Tobias' chest. "And what should we do now?"

"You didn't let me, I took you," Tobias growled, his hand stroking over Noah's hair. "And I'd actually planned some walking, so perhaps we'll skip that. Theater tonight. Maybe you'd like to have an early dinner somewhere? And until then we can... oh, I don't know. Nap? Read? I'm sure we can find something entertaining to watch somewhere."

"Oh, yes, I brought along several engrossing novels." Noah snorted. "It's Paris! I'm not spending the day reading and napping. Doesn't this place have a spa?"

Tobias laughed. He'd actually brought a novel, but he'd be damned if he'd tell Noah that now. "Yes. There's a pool, a sauna, a hot tub, full gym.... I'd be pleased if you didn't opt for some stranger massaging you, though. Your marks are sort of distinctive."

"The one time you don't want to show them off," Noah winked. "How about a soak? Maybe the hot tub is private, hmm? Could be nice."

"Sure." Tobias stood up and gave Noah a long look. "Hot water would probably be a good idea for you, and I'm not about to turn down the chance to get you wet and mostly naked. If it's private, then naked is a sure bet." He winked and headed to the closet. "Better put something on to get there, though."

"I thought naked was vogue in Paris?" Noah slid out of bed, still wincing a bit, and disappeared into the bathroom. He emerged moments later smelling of toothpaste and wearing a thick hotel robe. "Better?"

"Not really, but at least we're fit to be seen in the elevator." Tobias took the keycard and put it in his own robe's pocket. "Shall we?"

Noah slipped out of the room ahead of Tobias and perused the map of the hotel that was next to the elevator doors. "Tenth floor," he said. "And I won't maul you in the elevator this time, I promise."

"Damn," Tobias said under his breath, grinning widely. The elevator came, empty, and they stepped in, Tobias' hand sliding over Noah's ass. "Can I maul you?"

"Well, that would be your prerogative, of course," Noah said as the doors closed.

Tobias laughed and crowded Noah into the corner, careful of his shoulders. He pressed a kiss to Noah's mouth and then another before the elevator dinged at them. "Better hit the floor button, I guess," he said, stepping back to do so.

"Hmm?" Noah mumbled, tugging Tobias back over as soon as he had.

Laughing, Tobias kissed him again. "There are security cameras, you know," he pointed out. He waved and grinned at the camera and then kissed Noah again. "Now behave until we're in the water, will you?"

"Oh, very well." Noah settled for tangling fingers with Tobias for the remainder of the elevator ride.

The spa was warm and had that soothing smell that most did, a combination of aromatherapy and massage oils. As it turned out, naked wasn't an option -- it was a requirement in their hotel hot tub. They were first sent for a quick shower, then wrapped in thick towels and bustled off to the tub. It was big enough for four but it was indeed private, and they were brought a pitcher of fruit juice and a bucket of ice and then left to their own devices.

Tobias dropped his towel as soon as the door was closed and eased himself into the water with a sigh. "Oh, this is nice. Hurry up, sweetheart, you need this." He slid down a little more, the hot water relaxing him almost immediately, soothing muscles he didn't even know were sore.

Noah added his towel to Tobias' and slid into the tub with him. He winced as the hot water hit sore skin, but by the time he was chest deep he'd adjusted. "Oh, yeah," he breathed, leaning his head back against the edge of the tub. "I don't think I've ever been in a hot tub before. If I have I don't recall."

"You've been missing out," Tobias said, sounding utterly contented to even his own ears. "A hot tub is a luxury of the finest degree. Maybe we should have one in our new place."

"Oh, I think that's an excellent idea." He slid closer to Tobias and leaned into the crook of his arm. "This trip has been incredible so far. Paris is beautiful and kinky and more than I expected."

Tobias opened his eyes and smiled, looking into Noah's eyes. "I'm glad you like it," he said sincerely. "I really wasn't sure if you would or not -- Spain was probably a safer bet, but Paris is... Paris. Oh, we have to shop for presents tomorrow. Deidre wants anything not perfume, lace, or too girly."

"Chocolate. Godiva."

"That works." He kissed Noah slowly and pulled away just enough to smile. "Okay, bright boy. How about Bradford?"

"Hmm." Noah pulled back another inch and mulled that over a moment. "Bradford. Well, cologne for sure. And maybe something from your friend Gregory's boutique? The silk flogger, maybe? It was pretty." He slid a finger along Tobias' hairline and over his ear.

"It was nice, yes. But maybe a cane; Nikki would like that." Tobias smiled and ran a hand over Noah's leg, the water making every touch smooth. "How about Phan? Not that the brat needs any more toys, but we should get him something fun."

"I don't guess you know his measurements?" Noah grinned mischievously.

Tobias made a show of biting his tongue. "I know his measurements. Maybe you're the brat who won't get presents?" he teased. Of course he knew Phan's measurements. All of them. They were more or less seared into his head after years of dressing Phan in all sorts of things.

Noah pouted, but pouts never suited him, and he seemed to know it because it was followed by laughter. "Okay, fine. So we can bring him a Frenchman. He'd like Jean-Pierre, I think."

Tobias laughed, his head tipping back into the water. "Jean-Pierre would be at a loss with our Phan. And Phan would be over the moon. However. I don't think we can do that." He smiled at Noah and tugged him closer. "How about a T-shirt that says 'I'm the boy' in French?"

"'Je suis le garçon!' Suitably tacky," Noah said, still chuckling, and kissed under Tobias' chin. "He'll love it. God, this hot water feels good."

"You feel good," Tobias said without thinking. He followed it up with another kiss, his tongue sliding along Noah's as he pulled Noah into his arms. "I love you," he whispered, his hands petting wet and warm skin wherever he could.

"I love you. So much," Noah answered him and deepened the kiss. His fingers slid through Tobias' hair and then down across the tops of his shoulders. "Sometimes I can't believe this has really happened to me. Finally."

"I know," Tobias agreed. "But we've earned it." He chased Noah's chin for a moment, scattering more kisses as he went and tugging at Noah's nipple ring with his fingers. "More than earned it."

Noah hissed at the tug. "Mmm. You should get a piercing so I have something to tug on," he teased biting his lip as Tobias continued to play with his ring.

"Yeah? Where, do you think?" He tugged Noah's nipple again.

"Well, I'd say your nipple because they're so sensitive,

but you're going to tell me you don't want it visible, right? So what about," Noah slid his fingers underwater, lower and lower, past Tobias' cock and behind his balls. "Right here." He grinned. "No one would know it was there but me." He stroked the sensitive skin there with one finger.

Tobias shuddered, his hips pushing into the touch. "Naughty. I like it. Tell you what, I'll think about it." A great deal, he figured.

"Do that." Noah grinned and as Tobias' hips pushed forward, he slid his finger farther back, gliding and stroking over Tobias' hole. "I think it would be pretty hot."

Tobias made a noise that was mostly moan. "Tease," he said, his cock going stiff just like that. His chest felt tight, like he had to fight to breathe normally, so he didn't, settling for quick and light. "God, Noah." His fingers fumbled over Noah's nipple, slipping and sliding.

"Not necessarily. You're hard already." Noah stretched out and lowered his mouth to one of Tobias' nipples, which was just below the waterline. He lapped at it through the warm water and pushed the tip of his finger into him, toying with the tight ring of muscle inside.

Tobias gasped, his hips pushing down without him telling them to. "Noah," he whispered, one wet hand holding onto Noah's head and petting his hair.

Noah's tongue made a splashing sound in return, and he pushed his finger deeper, just one, stretching him gently. He hoped the heat of the tub and the noise of the jets covered his moan as Noah pressed his body closer, his own hard prick poking Tobias in the hip.

"Please," he said into Noah's ear. "God, yes." His legs spread and he moved to the very edge of the seat. He let go of Noah's head for fear of drowning him and gasped again as Noah dragged his teeth over one swollen nipple.

"I love it when you're like this," Noah encouraged, taking advantage of the better angle and slowly adding a second finger. "I didn't think I would, the concept made me uncomfortable; but to look at you now, you're so hot. Fucking irresistible. I'll do anything you want." Noah's breathing was uneven now as well, and he kissed Tobias hard until they were both nearly breathless.

"Anything I want?" Tobias whispered. "I want you in me. I want to feel you moving with me, making love to me, Noah."

He'd known Noah wasn't crazy about the idea, and when he was acting the Dom to Noah's sub he'd never ask for it. But with Noah's fingers in his ass and Noah's mouth moving over his, he had to. He had to feel it, he felt like he'd go crazy without it, and he was more than prepared to beg.

"Jesus." Noah moaned, low and deep in his chest. "Want you, too. Right here in the tub?" Noah asked. He didn't sound like the idea bothered him in the least.

"Right here," Tobias growled. "How? Want me like this? Over? God, just move, sweetheart. Need more!" His hips twitched and thrust and it was all he could do to keep his hands off his cock, so he stroked Noah's instead.

"Oh, God, I want you." Noah knelt on the bottom of the tub and considered it. "Over," he said finally, and it was probably a good choice given how much shorter he was than Tobias and the unforgiving hard plastic of the hot tub seating. "I have lube in my robe." He pointed to the robe as Tobias maneuvered, just inches from Tobias' fingers.

Tobias reached for the robe and froze, his fingers holding the fabric. "You planned this!" he said over his shoulder. "Minx." He lunged for the lube, wiggling his ass with a laugh.

"Would I do such a thing?" Noah asked impishly. He pinched Tobias' wiggling ass soundly.

"You would and hey!" Tobias laughed again and waved the lube. "Want it?"

"Only if you do," Noah teased and held his hand out.

"Want it," Tobias confirmed, passing the tube back. "Now." He spread his legs, his cock straining in the hot water. "God, please."

And he got it. He saw the tube of lube bounce up on the ledge near the robe again and then Noah knelt behind him and pushed at him, his cock hard as it stubbornly but slowly filled him. "Ah, fuck, tight," Noah said, a strain in his voice as their hips finally brushed together. "You okay? Jesus."

"Slow," he gasped, trying to relax as his own hips pushed back. From the waist down his body was overeager. "Oh, God, Noah!" he cried out as Noah pushed deep. "Move. Stay. Anything! Just please--" Words gave out on him and he shuddered, squeezing hard around Noah's cock and resisting the urge to thrash and ride.

Noah gripped his hips and tried to pull back. He grunted against the hold Tobias had on him. "Breathe. Breathe, baby." He gasped, trying again with more success. He pulled back slowly and then dove in again, keeping it gentle at first, but giving Tobias the movement and the pressure he wanted. His fingers dug into Tobias' hips as he started to thrust in and out, in and out until Tobias grew more pliable and Noah's need was more evident. "Oh, God, so good." Noah shivered and started to fuck Tobias in earnest, deeper and faster, punching Tobias' prostate over and over.

Tobias clung to the edge of the hot tub, his arms locked. His legs began to shake and he lifted one knee to the ledge just below the water line, opening himself up further and making sure he wouldn't fall over. "Oh, God!" he yelled as

Noah plunged into him again. "There! More, please, more. Fuck me!"

One of Noah's hands came up and gripped Tobias' shoulder, and his thrusts became harder. The water splashed around them and their hips slapped together as Noah drove into him again and again, panting heavily and grunting each time he sunk deep. "Jesus, baby," he managed between harsh breaths. "Fucking sweet ass."

It always went so fast, part of Tobias noted. By the time he got Noah to the point where they could do this, Tobias was so turned on -- both by Noah and the sheer idea of being fucked -- that everything sped up and was over before he could really, truly enjoy it. His erection was so hard it was going to hurt before long, and his ass felt stretched wider than ever before. His orgasm was already creeping up and down his spine, and all he could do was push back, trying to get Noah farther into him.

"Love you," Noah grunted, leaning over his back and gripping the edge of the tub for yet more leverage. He plunged deep, taking what he needed, and giving, Tobias knew, every ounce of energy he had. Noah committed fully to everything they did together, and this experience was no exception. "Love you."

His hips jerked erratically once, and then again, but Noah got his control back, groaning with the effort. "Tell me you're close, baby," he almost begged. "I'm so ready to go."

Tobias nodded, panting. He let go of the tub with one hand and wrapped it around his cock and tugged once. "Oh, God!" he cried out, coming hard and jerking on Noah's shaft. "Love you," he whispered, his body tight and aching as he spilled, cock pounding in his hand.

"Yes!" Noah's fingers went back to grip Tobias' hips and held their bodies flush together as he came, spilling every last drop into Tobias with a tight groan. "Oh, oh, God, yes. Tobias." He hung there for a long moment until they'd both gone still and the room was filled with the sounds of their breathing. "Jesus." His grip relaxed and he dropped his forehead onto Tobias' back.

"Uh-huh." For Tobias that was as lucid as he could be right then. He thought it would be about half an hour or a lifetime before he could think clearly again; he could still feel Noah's dick twitching inside him. "Oh, God," he moaned. "So good to me."

Noah didn't say anything. Warm lips pressed kisses across his shoulders and back, and warm fingers slid over his thighs, his sides, and finally wrapped around his chest as Noah hugged him close.

Tobias purred, the sound rumbling in his chest. He felt limp and relaxed, utterly content to stay like that forever. Noah holding him, in him, loving him. "You're amazing," he whispered. "Give me whatever I need, like it's just there for me to take."

"It is." Noah rubbed his forehead between Tobias' shoulder blades and kissed him there. Still securely tucked inside Tobias and keeping his body close, Noah started to rock his hips gently. "I'm yours, I want you to have every part of me."

Tobias moaned, Noah's cock rubbing inside him just right. "Sweetheart." It seemed like the only thing to say. He held onto Noah's arm, keeping himself wrapped up in Noah.

Noah moaned back and Tobias felt him filling inside him, if he'd ever actually gone soft to begin with. "Just want to hold you, feels so good."

"Are you... oh, Jesus." Tobias rocked back, gliding slowly as Noah stroked in and out. "Feel so good." Tobias had no idea if he would be able to get hard again, or come, or anything like it... and he didn't care. He just wanted to feel, to float on the intensity of being loved this way. Slowly, he let Noah move in him, let Noah take him again.

They rocked together for a long while and Noah showered his back with nibbles and kisses. Noah wasn't in any hurry at all. Every thrust, every movement was easy and free of tension. He was tasting Tobias, feeling, experimenting. "I love your body," he told Tobias. "I love savoring it. I love that you asked me this time, told me you wanted me and asked me to make love to you. I know it's hard for you to do, but it sounds so good."

Tobias shuddered, turning his head far enough for a kiss. "I love you. I love being in you, and I can't even describe what this feels like. Thank you for doing it, for giving me this." He rocked back a little more and the angle changed just a bit. "Oh!" he gasped, his ass spasming. "You might just get this old man up again."

"I'm feeling very patient," Noah said and then kissed him as he took advantage of the new position they'd achieved.

"Oh, good. I used up all my superstud last night." Tobias' tone was teasing, but he was feeling the tingles of heat in his body, his erection starting to fill as Noah moved in and out of him. This is what he wanted, what he craved. "I need this," he whispered. "Not all the time... just. Now. I need it now, love."

"Me, too." Noah reached up and caught his chin, turning his head so they could kiss again. "Me, too, baby."

It was hard to know how long they simply enjoyed each other after the talking stopped. The air was rich with soft moans and heavy breathing, accompanied by the constant swoosh and gurgle of the hot tub.

Noah's fingers found Tobias' and tangled with them, while one hand remained perched on his hip. His thrusts were measured and slow, and even as Tobias felt Noah's need build, his pace didn't.

Tobias found himself pushing back with more eagerness. The desperation wasn't there, just arousal and love; passion heating like the water they played in. He sighed and rocked back, moaning every time Noah's cock slid over his gland. He felt hyperaware of every thrust, every movement, every kiss. "Sweetheart," he said softly. "God, you feel so good. Make me hungry."

"You make me want you, lover. Your heat, your body. This is so good, you feel a part of me like this." Noah's breath was thinner, coming quicker, and his hips were starting to grow tense. He licked up the length of Tobias' spine. "Taste so good."

"Oh, God." Tobias gasped, his back arching. "Touch me?" He was suddenly right there, right on the edge of orgasm, and he had no idea how it had snuck up on him so quickly.

Noah's hand slipped from his and found Tobias' cock. Fingers gripped him firmly and started to stroke in time with Noah's thrusts. "You feel so good, so good." Noah's teeth grazed Tobias' shoulder, and he caught the muscle there and held it between his teeth. His thrusts were heavier now, but not rushed; deeper, but not urgent.

"Oh, God, oh, God, oh, God!" Tobias chanted, his orgasm starting to roll over him in waves. It wasn't exactly languid, but it went on for ages, starting at his toes and pushing right through him. "Noah! God, yes, sweetheart! Oh, *God!*"

"Ah!" Noah cried out, letting go of Tobias shoulder. His body shuddered as he followed Tobias over into release. Tobias heard soft sobs and long moans in his ear. "Baby, Tobias, baby," Noah panted at him, as his orgasm washing through him. The earth didn't move, Noah didn't scream or slam him; he didn't claw at the tub or any of the things he'd done earlier. This time it was quiet, and obviously intense. "Love you."

"Love you," Tobias whispered back, still shaking. He had to move, had to turn and sit and hold his lover; the need to do so was almost as deep as his need to come had been. He waited only a moment, long enough to make sure Noah had finished coming, before shifting and easing away. He moaned as Noah slipped out of him, hating the loss, but knowing it had to happen or he'd fall. Turning, he gathered Noah to him, thankful for the water around them to hide what he was sure were tears. "I love you so much," he said softly, his arms wrapping tight around Noah.

Noah pressed his face into Tobias' neck. His own tears didn't seem to bother him so much, and his shoulders shook slightly while Tobias held him. "That was incredible. So good. So intense, my God." He pulled away just enough to kiss Tobias soundly.

"It was amazing," Tobias said simply. "You are amazing. You know that? You do things for me no one ever has; making love to me is such a small part of that."

"I can say exactly the same thing about you. Exactly." Noah smiled and wiped at his eyes with the back of his hand, laughing softly. "God, I'm such a sap when I'm well laid."

"You're in good company," Tobias admitted, smiling. "Want some juice? Just to sweeten us up some more. We're not quite saccharine enough."

Noah laughed harder. "Yes. Yes, please."

Tobias grinned and looked at the pitcher and the glasses. "Oh, oh. Trouble."

"Trouble...?" Noah look perplexed.

"In order to pour, one of us will have to let go. And I'm

not ready." Tobias blinked innocently. "I think I just hit saccharine."

"Oh, God, it's making my teeth hurt," Noah groaned. "Tell you what. I'll get it, and you can watch my ass, it's the next best thing." Noah physically moved Tobias' hands and slid over to the tray.

Tobias watched Noah's ass. It was a nice ass, nicer than most, and he had very fond memories of being in it, of spanking it, of marking it. It had his initials on it. "Mine," he growled before he could stop himself.

Noah poured them each a glass. "Tobias, you're so possessive. Do you have any idea what a turn-on that is?" He moved back, hands full of juice, and seated himself on Tobias' knees. "Thirsty?"

"Thank you. And thank you." Tobias slid one hand over Noah's thighs. "I'm glad you like possessive -- I can't seem to turn it off."

Noah sipped his drink. "I love it. There's nothing better for the ego than knowing you're wanted, trust me."

"I want you," Tobias said in a low voice. "All of you. All the time. Trust that."

"Oh, I do. I definitely do." Noah kissed him again. "Wow, I feel much more limber. Think it's the tub or the sex?" He grinned.

"What's the right answer here?" Tobias asked with a wink.

"'Yes.' The right answer would be 'yes.'" Noah chuckled and slid off Tobias' lap to the seat beside him where he could soak.

"Yes," Tobias said dutifully. He laced their fingers together and smiled, relaxing back. "So. Want to move in with me? Sign on for another go round, lasting until we say so?"

"Yes. Yes, I do." Noah smiled and finished his juice, setting it aside.

Tobias smiled at him and took another kiss. "Good. I love you."

"I love you too... sir." Noah winked at him and returned the kiss.

21

Tobias had asked at the hotel, being very explicit about what he wanted, and the concierge had come through for him very nicely. The bistro was perfect. The food was lovely, the coffee was incredible, and there was even live music. He and Noah were seated along the side, looking out a huge window, and the waiters were not the sort to hover around them. They had privacy and could see and hear whatever they wanted.

On the table between them was the folder with their old contract, the suggested new one, blank paper and pens.

"Where do you want to start?" Tobias asked, handing Noah a copy of the new draft. "Residence or new rules? Time frame?"

"You certainly come prepared." Noah looked over the contract. "Hmm. Well, let's do the easy stuff first. Time frame."

"Open with built-in checks set for every... six months?" Tobias suggested. "Or would you prefer to have it at a year with a contracted statement that if you or I feel the need we can request a renegotiation before that at our discretion?"

"Actually," Noah set his coffee down and leaned forward. "Don't take this the wrong way, but... I was thinking, since we'll both be getting used to new living arrangements, that our first one should be after three months. I'm willing to agree to a year with the option to renegotiate after that."

"That makes sense," Tobias said easily. He wasn't in the slightest worried about Noah backing out after they'd moved in together, and tweaking could very well be needed. "All right then." He made a note of it on the contract, quickly figuring the date they were to talk again. "Late July. Anything else about the time frame?"

"Nope, open-ended is great."

Tobias smiled. "Residence. I'm going to sign the condo over to Phantom, but as that's between him and me, I won't put it in here. In here, I've stated that within the next month I'll make a clear effort to locate a suitable residence for us. Which we have to define." He grinned wryly. "How much space do you want, sweetheart?"

Noah snorted. "I'm going to be honest, Tobias. I have some money stashed away, but not enough for a down payment on a place in the city. You're welcome to what I've got, but beyond that, what you buy, and how big, and all that? That's really up to you, I'll just be happy if it's downtown near-ish to where I am now."

Tobias shrugged. "It's for us both. I want to make sure you like it, that there's something you need. Do you want a room to yourself, two? I'll take care of main living, playroom, the cars... all that sort of thing. But you're going to live there, too, as my submissive and as my partner. You have a say."

Noah studied Tobias carefully. "One room is plenty. Something with a view of the street. And in a perfect world, since I'm doing most of the cooking, the kitchen is important." He licked his lips and picked up his coffee.

"Right. So, nice kitchen, room with a view." Tobias wrote it down and looked up. "Anything else?" Really, it was like pulling teeth to get Noah to ask for anything for himself.

Noah shrugged. "A garage might be nice. I could have a bike..."

That made Tobias stare. "A bike?" he said faintly. "You'll need leather."

"Oh, I have leather." Noah grinned.

"I'll get you more," Tobias promised. "Garage." He looked over the contract and made another note. "Guest room. Security. I really am looking for a small converted warehouse, aren't I? Or a floor of a larger one. Oh... soundproofing..."

Noah snorted. "Or a brownstone. There are a lot of those around. I'm leaving the rest of the logistics to you."

Tobias grinned. "All right then. I'll take care of it. Now... rules. Do you want contracted duties for around the house, or is the current service agreement good enough?"

"That depends on whether I'll be expected to do more than I have been." Noah winked. "If the chores are going to remain more or less the same, then I don't see a need to change the agreement. But if you want me vacuuming naked every evening, we're going to have to talk."

Tobias snorted. "Once a month?" He leaned forward a bit and picked up his coffee cup. "Seriously, though. You wanted harder. I won't make you do anything unreasonable, and I won't make you a slave -- I have a cleaning service at the condo and will happily continue that, but if you'd prefer to have everything laid out rather than at my whim, say so now. It's your ass."

"I think I'll be happier in service to you than to a contract," Noah said easily.

Tobias nodded and let it go, making a note. "You'll keep

your safe words and right to refuse anything; I keep my obligations and duties toward your health. Play with others as situations arise? I take responsibility for the sexual health of any other partners."

Noah nodded. "Thank you. And so what about money?"

"What about it?" Tobias asked, confused.

Noah raised an eyebrow. "Well, I'll be pulling a paycheck. You want it? You want part of it? Should I pay half the mortgage and utilities or just pay you?"

"I don't want your money," Tobias said evenly. "Save it. Put it in an account somewhere. Buy your bike. Buy a horse."

Noah looked like he'd swallowed a lemon. "I'm not a kept toy, Tobias, I'm a submissive."

Tobias stared. "A kept... Jesus. I know full well you're not a toy, kept or anything else. But you're my submissive, and it's my job to protect you. To care for you. To--"

"Not to pay for me, Tobias," Noah interrupted. "Not to pay for. You don't pay my rent for me now, and you're not going to pay my way when we move in together, either. Protecting me has nothing to do with money."

"You won't be able to afford half," Tobias said bluntly as he put down his pen.

Noah chewed his lip. His jaw worked and he stared at the table but said nothing. When he finally looked up, Tobias saw the hurt and anger in his eyes. "I know. What exactly is the point of telling me that?"

"The point is that there's no point in offering. I can do this for us. You're fully aware that I have a lot of money. It hasn't been an issue before, and I don't see why it is now. I know you're not after it -- that's why I can give it."

Noah pushed back from the table. "Excuse me a minute? I'm just going to hit the men's room." He didn't wait for an answer, just disappeared toward the back of the restaurant.

Tobias watched him go for all of three seconds before following. He moved carefully, not wanting to attract attention, but he still managed to get there at the same time as Noah. "What's wrong?" he asked as they walked in together. "Noah--"

Noah stopped and looked at him. "I have to pee, Tobias."

"Right. Well, I'll just wait and see if that stick gets out of your ass while you're at it, and then you can tell me what the hell is wrong here. Because until you do, I'm just going to be in the dark and making it worse."

"Stick in my ass? What about the fucking steel rod up yours?"

Tobias growled. "Once more. What the hell is wrong here? What's wrong with me paying the rent? It's not like I'm renting *you*."

"No, it's worse. It's like you're buying me." Noah sighed and stepped farther into the men's room. "I really do have to pee," he said, pulling down his fly.

Tobias' jaw dropped and he stared for far longer than normal. "I am not!" he protested loudly, drawing a strange look from a man washing his hands. "Noah. That's not what I'm doing, and you know it." He took a deep breath and pushed his hand through his hair. "Don't you?" Doubt crept into his voice.

"Look, I know that's not your intention. You don't think that way, I know that. You think that you're taking care of me, that it's all part of your responsibility toward me. But, Tobias, it's not." Noah peed, put his dick away, and went over to the sinks. "Nowhere in that contract does it state that you have to pay for everything." He sighed as he washed his hands. "I'm sure that to you whatever I can pay you will be insignificant pennies, but to me, it's hard-earned money. It's important to me that I contribute. Otherwise, I become indebted to you; I'm no longer self-sufficient. I don't want to move in with you. I want to move in together. If you pay for everything, then it will always be your home that I live in. It will never be ours." Noah grabbed a towel and dried his hands. "Can we go sit down now, please?"

"Fine," Tobias said faintly. He stood where he was until Noah walked past him, trying to understand what Noah was saying. He finally followed Noah back to their table, noting the irony of following and not leading for once.

"Look," he said as he sat down. "I'm not trying to take anything away from you. I simply have no idea what on earth I'll do with your money. I don't need it, is all I was trying to say, but you obviously don't see any kindness in me paying for your housing. So give me what you're paying for rent now and I'll... do something with it." He had no idea what, exactly, he'd do with it, but there was always a bank account waiting to be opened. It was the best offer he could manage under the circumstances.

Bradford hadn't said anything about money. Phantom hadn't had any, and then he was a slave -- even if he'd had money, it would have gone to Tobias. Noah was nobody's slave.

Noah reached across the table and took Tobias' hands in his. "I do see kindness in you wanting to take care of the rent, the bills, of me. I do. I see plenty of kindness in everything you want to do for me. I'm sorry that I can't make you understand what this means to me. I'm obviously not explaining it well enough. You're usually so intuitive when it comes to me, I suppose I just assumed you'd see this, too."

He pulled one of Tobias' hands up to his lips and kissed his fingers. "I'm sorry I got upset with you. If I can figure out a better way to explain it to you I will, but for now I'd appreciate it if you could just accept that I need to do this. I don't care what you do with the money; it's yours once I give it to you."

He could do this. A nice little investment portfolio, some stock somewhere... Noah would have a retirement plan, if nothing else. He nodded, his gaze not leaving Noah's eyes. "I'm sorry I don't understand. But if this the way you want it, that's fine."

"It's what I need. Thank you." He let go of Tobias' hands and picked up his coffee. He exhaled heavily, puffing out his cheeks. "So... Okay. What's next on the list?"

Tobias shook his head, feeling more than a little foggy. He picked his pen up and looked over the contract and his notes. "Play. Scenes. Others." He looked up and shrugged. "Tell me your thoughts."

"We already discussed this, didn't we? I'd prefer to discuss other partners as they come up. We both like the fantasy stuff. And we discussed that we'd like more scenes, um... 'outside our comfort zone' I think is how you put it." Noah was speaking slowly. "Right? Was there more to it than that?" He hesitated, watching Tobias and fiddling with his cup. "I really threw you with that money discussion, didn't I? I'm really sorry."

"You have nothing to apologize for," Tobias said immediately. "I just never thought about it, and certainly not from your point of view. It's my error, and for me to apologize. I do. I'm sorry I made assumptions and didn't think it through. The last thing I want to do is... is... restrict you in ways we haven't agreed to. Thank you for speaking up."

He rolled his eyes at himself and put the pen down again. "I'm really sorry, Noah," he said sincerely. "And you're right, all that stuff is in there. Look it over, see if there's anything else you want to add in -- I'll just drink my coffee and try to find my dignity."

Noah looked down at the table and put his hand on the contract. He ran his fingers over it and glanced up at Tobias a couple of times before picking it up and turning pages.

"If it helps, I don't really think you have a rod up your ass." Noah gave him a hint of a grin over the top of the contract.

Tobias snorted. "Might help if I did, but I don't suspect I'll get the hot tub treat anytime soon." He raised an eyebrow and tried not to smile. "Special occasions only, yes?"

"Well, hmm." Noah pretended to study the contract critically. "I don't see anything about restricting it to special occasions in here." He glanced back at Tobias and winked.

"Oh, did I forget to put that in?" Tobias said lightly. He shook his head and leaned forward to pick up his coffee cup. "Thank you," he said softly. "Does it look okay to you?"

"It looks fine; we just haven't talked much about the logistics of me working. I know you'll respect what I think I need in terms of time before work and such." Noah sighed. "Since I'm not even sure what those things will be yet... well, what do you think about just adding something about how you'll respect my needs with regard to work and leave it at that?"

Tobias nodded, not really needing to think about that. "Sounds fine to me. We can talk about that again at the three month mark, as well, see if we need adjusting."

Noah put the contract down. "Then I guess I'm yours. Indefinitely." He grinned. "Maybe you should take me back to the hotel and tie me up to celebrate."

Tobias thought he should be used to the way his body continually betrayed him, but he wasn't. He shifted in his chair and pushed the pen at Noah. "Sign it. I'll tie you down and flog you until you beg."

Noah picked up Tobias' copy with all the handwritten notes about what was to be added and signed it. He set the pen down and stood, moving to Tobias. As shamelessly as he did everything else, and with no apparent concerns about who might be looking on, Noah knelt on the floor beside Tobias' chair.

Tobias was almost winded by the gesture, his left hand going to stroke his boy's hair, the right reaching for the pen. With a flourish he signed his name and then slipped a finger under Noah's collar and tugged gently. "Mine," he whispered. "Come, pet. I believe there are some very expensive silk ties waiting for us at the hotel."

22

Noah was asleep, or should have been. Tobias had ruined at least one tie on him, broken in the new crop rather well, and nearly rendered Noah back into the state he'd been in after the dry fuck.

They both should have been asleep, really.

Instead, Tobias was in the sitting room, wrapped in a thick robe and looking over their contract one more time. Almost absently he noted the time and made the adjustment to home, then picked up the phone. After the switchboard had given him an outside line to the international operator, he dialed Bradford's home number, hoping the man wasn't yet in bed.

"Hello?" Bradford sounded a little tired, but he didn't sound like he'd been pulled from sleep by the phone.

"Bonjour," Tobias said with a grin. "I hope I didn't wake you."

"Oh, it's the Frenchman!" Bradford sounded pleased. "What the hell time is it over there? Four A.M.? Why are you calling me? Uh-oh. Is everything all right?"

Tobias laughed. "Everything is fine. I just didn't fall

asleep after. No, just wanted to touch base, see how things are... let you know you've a new contract to put in your collection..."

"Oh, congratulations!" Bradford sounded honestly pleased. "That's excellent news, glad to hear it. So will you be living together? You must be; you sound too sated and happy not to have gotten everything you wanted. Excellent."

"Not quite everything -- there was a minor sticking point, but we got past it." Tobias grimaced at himself and quickly went on. "Yes, we'll be living together, but we're both moving downtown. I have some house hunting to do."

"I'm glad you managed to work it out, whatever it was. And house hunting sounds like fun." Tobias heard the sound of a closing door. "You'll be returning soon? A couple of days, right?"

"Yes, day after tomorrow. Miss us?" he teased

"Yes. I was hoping you might have an evening free for dinner this week. I need to talk to you about, well, about Phantom."

Tobias closed his eyes and sighed. A feeling not unlike dread knotted in his gut. "What's wrong?" he asked after a moment. "Is he having nightmares again?"

"He's all right." Bradford said quickly. "I know he'll be thrilled to hear about your new contract. I'd rather not worry you needlessly while you're away, I just wanted to get on your radar for next week. When are you available?"

"You're sure he's okay?" Tobias asked, suddenly struck by the knowledge that if he had to, he'd drag Noah out of the bed and head to the airport. "Ah, shit," he whispered to himself, sinking into the couch. "Um. I'll have to check with Dee. If nothing else, we can have dinner on Wednesday; Noah's busy both then and Thursday."

"He's not at his best, but he doesn't need you this minute,

either. Don't you dare drag your boy away from his vacation early; I am taking good care of Phan, I promise." Bradford clucked his tongue. "Why don't we say Wednesday; that will be fine."

Tobias stared at the far wall. "You'd tell me if he did need me, right?"

"Of course I would." There was a momentary halt in their conversation. "Tobias, I would."

"Yeah, okay." Tobias conceded the point, pushing his worry away. "All right, then. Wednesday, dinner. At the club, or do you want to go somewhere?"

"My place. Then you can see him for yourself, too."

"Do I need to?" Tobias shook his head. "That's not what I mean. I want to see him; I miss him, aside from the fact that I have to talk to him about the condo. Does he *need* to see me?"

"Didn't we already have this discussion?" Bradford sighed. "Let it go. See you Wednesday. Go back to your boy."

Tobias rolled his eyes. "You brought it up," he bitched. "But, yes. I will go back to my boy, in the nice warm bed, and get some sleep. You go... flog Nikki or something."

"I meant that I knew you would want to see him, you grump," Bradford teased. "And Nikki is due for his evening punishment, isn't he? Great idea. Goodnight. Have a safe flight home."

"Thanks, and I'm not a grump. Goodnight, Bradford; give Nikki an extra stroke for me, if he's good." He hung up the phone to the sound of Bradford laughing at him, and sat awhile, waiting for thoughts of Phan to fade a little before he went in to Noah.

23

B y the time the plane had reached cruising altitude, Tobias was feeling mostly human again. "Tell me why it was a good idea to stay out that late last night?" he asked Noah, trying not to moan pitifully as his ears popped.

"Because, sir, it was our last night in Paris?" Noah suggested, bringing him a bottle of water now that they could move around freely. "Because that club was one of the classiest places we've ever been? Because you wanted to see Gregory and Jean-Pierre again before you left town in case it was another ten years before you take me back to Paris? Because we could sleep on the plane? I'm sure we had a good reason."

"Oh. Right." He took the water bottle and drank about half of it in one shot. "Thanks, pet." He forced himself to sit like a human who had been raised properly, and gave Noah a grin. "I doubt we can get away with not going back sooner than that. Hell, Jean-Pierre was ready to follow you home."

He had been, too. Noah had been allowed to speak at the

second club, and he'd whimpered and begged so prettily. He knew how to use his voice, that was for sure.

"Mmm. Jean-Pierre is a fine looking man, isn't he? And Gregory's boy, Martin, was... energetic. He's someone I could stand to get to know better." Noah winked and flopped next to Tobias, resting his head on Tobias' shoulder. He chuckled. "We really have to go back to the real world, huh? I was so enjoying being a kept boy in Paris."

Tobias snorted. "Don't start, brat."

"Thank you," Noah said turning his head in Tobias' direction. "For the trip. It was amazing. Incredible. I loved every minute of it. I hope my pictures come out."

"You took pictures?" Tobias asked, startled for a moment. "Oh! The tower, right." He hoped to hell he wasn't blushing. "I need sleep. And you're welcome."

Noah laughed. "Don't worry, you had your clothes on. And seriously, I'm going to be talking about this for a long time. Why don't you lie down? The couch should be big enough for you."

Tobias nodded and swung his legs up. "Come here, pet," he invited, holding one arm out. If they curled up tight they could snuggle without hurting each other. "It was a good trip."

Sometimes Tobias was amazed by his own understatements. He amended it to add, "Last night was almost as amazing as the first evening with Gregory and company. But nowhere near as nice as the hot tub."

"I'm glad you have your priorities straight," Noah grinned, snuggling into Tobias on the couch. It was a tight fit, but not uncomfortable. "Mmm. Hot tub. I love hot tubs." Noah laughed softly. "Let's have a hot tub."

"Okay." Tobias wasn't about to argue that one. He ran a

hand over Noah's side, soaking up his body heat. "When do you have to go back to work?"

"Monday, bright and early. But I left my uniform and gear at your place, since we're coming home on the weekend. You?"

"Rounds Monday morning, but I have to call Deidre as soon as I can manage it. We're coming up on a birth cycle, so I have to touch base and see what needs doing. I think I should have bought her more chocolate."

Noah winced melodramatically. "Uh-oh. Sounds like you're in for a long week. Isn't the birthing cycle thing when you end up being called at two A.M. to go deliver a cow?"

"Or a horse or a lamb... Once, I had a horse foaling in one stall, a bitch having a litter of puppies in the next, threat of a cow going into labor in the next barn, and Dee about to have kittens. It was insane." He laughed softly. "The easiest was the pup. She didn't need me at all and was just happy to have clean straw."

"And the toughest was Dee?" Noah was giggling. "Sounds like we're in for some interrupted evenings. Fairly warned. Just promise me you'll shower before coming back to bed."

"Hell, I'll shower before coming home. Do you have any idea how messy births can be?" Tobias shuddered and rubbed a slow circle on Noah's stomach. "It may be quiet, we never know. Some animals have a harder time than others, that's all." He kissed the top of Noah's head. "Oh, and I have dinner with Bradford on Wednesday this week, did I mention?"

"I'll have you know I delivered a baby in the backseat of my squad car two years ago," Noah said proudly. "I don't need to see that much of a woman ever again, thank you. And, no; special occasion? Or just to catch up with him after Paris?"

"You did?" Tobias was impressed. "Good for you, I'd always thought those sorts of things were urban legends. And he's worried about Phan. Or something. I don't know, he wouldn't tell me."

Noah turned his head and looked at Tobias. "He's worried about Phan and he wouldn't tell you why? That doesn't sound right."

"Well, he wants to talk to me about Phan," Tobias said. "He said Phan was fine and not to worry... but I do." Rather a lot, he was willing to admit to himself. He itched to get home; he wouldn't be surprised if he called Bradford and pestered him before Wednesday.

"Hmm." Noah tucked his head into Tobias' arm and didn't make any further comment than that.

Tobias tried to put Phan out of his head, but couldn't, quite. "Will you see him on Tuesday?" he asked.

"Oh. I hadn't thought about it. I suppose I will, yes, we didn't talk about canceling it."

"You don't have to," Tobias said, trying to sound neutral. "You can tell him you have jet lag -- likely, it will be true."

Noah's brow furrowed and he turned his head to look at Tobias again. "You want me to cancel it?"

"No, I just don't want you to do anything you don't want to," Tobias explained. "Honestly, I really want you to see him. I want to know how he is, and he'll likely tell you the truth."

"He usually does, or tells me enough that I can guess it." Noah nodded. "Why wouldn't I want to see him? You're worried that Bradford's holding something back, aren't you?"

"I don't know," Tobias said. "He wouldn't out and out lie to me, but he's concerned about something. And I didn't mean to suggest that you wouldn't want to see him; just that you don't have to." He sighed. "Okay, maybe I thought you wouldn't want to see him. I don't know why."

"Because you're still worried that I don't trust you when it comes to him. Except that I do. Phan, I'm still a little shaky on, but that's not really his fault." Noah leaned up and kissed Tobias under his chin. "I'll see him. And I suppose you want a full report? I feel like a spy."

Tobias smiled, feeling a little more at ease. "He knows you're reporting back. Unless you want to be a spy. Oh, we could do that, I'm sure. 007, a nice tux..."

"Ooh. And gadgets!" Noah grinned and Tobias knew he'd set himself up for something. "Hmm. I want a pen that really writes but has a secret and unending supply of lube in the cap, and I want a gun that shoots bullets and rubbers. Oh! And you have to promise that I always have hot men chasing after me like Pierce Brosnan's Bond girls."

"Hey! I'll be Bond," Tobias laughed. "You can be Doctor No. Only you're more a Doctor 'Oh, yeah, sir'. Or maybe Golddick."

"Pfft." Noah sniffed at him. "You'd like that wouldn't you? No, if I'm the spy then I am 007. You can be one of my Bond men... one that secretly indulges me in my fantasies of being tied up and fucked."

"I see," Tobias said evenly. "You do know that I'm a double agent and I'll leave you tied to the bed after stealing all your secrets, right?"

"As long as you steal them well, I won't argue much." Noah winked.

Tobias snorted. "You won't argue at all. You're kind of easy that way, you know."

"I am not!" Noah protested. "Well, all right. For you, maybe I am. Sometimes. Occasionally."

"Pretty much every time." Tobias grinned and rubbed another circle on Noah's belly. "I like it, though."

"Good, because I can't help it." Noah chuckled softly. "You have a way of turning me into babbling jelly."

"Oh, what a lovely description!" Tobias said with a laugh. "So we're agreed that you're easy, my boy, and that you'll spy for me. Am I correct?"

Noah snorted. "I suppose so, sir," he agreed with a tone of playful sarcasm. "Weren't you going to nap or something?"

"Or something. Talking about playing spy was more fun, but sleep could be good. Oh, and we can nap on the way home, too -- nice thing about having a driver."

Noah settled down again. "Would be cool if we could arrange to put the hot tub in the safe room, don't you think?" he asked, totally out of the blue. "Oh, and what will be in your playroom in our new place?"

"Oh, good idea!" Tobias got an immediate mental image of their new safe room, all white with large windows and lots of plants, a nice sofa and the hot tub in the corner. "Hmm, playroom. Let's see. A cross and a whipping post, manacles on the wall, a sling..."

"Mmm. A couple of trunks with your gear, funky lighting, a big comfy chair like the one you have at the farm..."

"A closet for costumes, some pillows, a huge mirror..."

"Ooh, a mirror. Kinky. Spanking bench? Sound system?"

Tobias shrugged. "Probably. The frills we can work out later. Did it get warm in here, or is that just me?" he asked with a grin.

Noah laughed. "You're a dirty old man, sir."

"Ah, I believe you may be right," Tobias said, pulling Noah a little closer. "Now hush, and try to sleep. Or I'll be forced to take matters into my own hands -- again -- and you won't be able to walk off the plane." He grinned and winked. "Though, at the moment, it feels a little beyond me to be honest. The old man part is sneaking up on me, I think."

"Right. Sleep now, fuck me later." Noah tangled his fingers with Tobias' and snuggled in tight. "I think we're going to land a couple of hours before we took off." Noah yawned. "That'll be weird."

"We'll forever be younger than we were yesterday," Tobias pointed out. "Or something." He closed his eyes and tried to figure out what he meant, the thought getting lost as he listened to the engines and finally fell asleep.

Book Four: Bondage

Tobias and Noah's journey continues.

In this final installment of the full Deviations series, Noah and Tobias come back from Paris with a renewed contract and a deeper personal bond, but find that things don't go as smoothly at home.

They face a crisis that could threaten their brand new contract, as well as their personal intimacy. This has a ripple effect, but with careful and deliberate communication, Tobias and Noah finally learn that they can evolve with it, instead of collapsing.

They experiment with scene after scene, making them longer and deeper, which allows them to explore more than they've ever dared. They even move in together. When Noah is forced to face the dangers of his job, he begins to question why he became a cop in the first place.

Tobias is also questioning his commitment to his own work, and soon enough, their external life is changing enough that they're forced to lean on each other to get through. How will they achieve a comfortable balance between their outside lives, their scenes, and their deep, love and devotion to one another?

A NOTE FROM THE AUTHORS

Hey there!

We just wanted to take a minute to say thank you for taking the time to read Discipline. We hope you enjoyed it. We know everyone is busy and our TBR (to be read) lists are out of control, so it means a lot to us that we ended up at the top of your pile this time.

If you have a moment, please consider dropping by the site where you purchased this book and leaving a review. All honest reviews are much appreciated.

If you're looking for more of Jodi's work, why not join her newsletter? Just go here: http://bit.ly/whatsupjodi.

And you can find Chris Owen at http://www.chrisowen.net/.

Thank you for reading!

Jodi & Chris

Soft Limits: A Deviations Novel
by Jodi Payne
This standalone can be read at any point in the series.

F
ans of the iconic Deviations Series will fondly recall Bradford as the beloved owner and Master of the exclusive, male-only, BDSM club that anchors the series, and also as the wise man who introduced Tobias and Noah.

Dominant Bradford's story is one defined by sudden opportunity, unimaginable heartbreak, and new-found purpose. His calling is to provide a safe and supportive environment for men in the lifestyle. Bringing Doms and subs together is his superpower, yet ironically, he feels fated to be alone himself.

In this prequel to the series, you'll discover how Bradford is first drawn to Nikki, a hungry young man living on the streets, and the unexpected ways Bradford grows and changes while helping Nikki understand a world of strange, new desires.

Deviations readers already know how Bradford and Nikki find their happy ever after. Soft Limits is a deep-dive into Bradford's story, into what makes the Dom tick, and how he ended up with ownership of the club. It also introduces Nikki, the sub that tests Bradford's patience, steals his heart, and soothes his soul.

———

Interested in learning more about Jodi's books? Want free fiction, release news, anecdotes, coffee and drink recipes...?
Join Jodi's newsletter!
What's Up with Jodi?
http://bit.ly/whatsupjodi

ABOUT JODI PAYNE

You're gonna love this guy...

JODI takes herself way too seriously and has been known to randomly break out in song. Her men are imperfect but genuine, stubborn but likable, often kinky, and frequently their own worst enemies. They are characters you can't help but fall in love with while they stumble along the path to their happily ever after. For those looking to get on her good side, Jodi's addictions include nonfat lattes, Malbec and tequila any way you pour it.

Website: jodipayne.net
Newsletter: http://bit.ly/whatsupjodi
All Jodi's Social Links: linktr.ee/jodipayne

ABOUT CHRIS OWEN

Chris lives and writes in eastern Canada. She's inspired by the day to day minutia of life, shiny things, and overheard bits of other people's conversations. Chris is a lover of cheese, curling, dogs, words, and craft beer. Her stories are usually built around totally normal people doing normal things, until everything goes sideways—that's when the fun starts. Chosen family plays a huge role in the stories Chris tells, and there is always a happy ending. Chris always has a Dio in her bag or pocket, along with a hankie. Just in case.

Website: chrisowen.net

Facebook: https://www.facebook.com/profile.php?id=100015072407034

Twitter: https://twitter.com/chris_owen

Enjoy the Deviations Books? Try a new series.

Breaking the Rules
The Triskelion Series, Book One
By Jodi Payne and BA Tortuga

https://jodipayne.net/books/breaking-the-rules/

Saul Reynolds manages a busy bicycle shop in downtown Boulder, Colorado. A recent CU graduate, he's also a Dom, and has many friends his age in the scene. Saul's an old soul, and even at twenty-five, he's had enough experience to understand his own desires. He's had plenty of lovers and he's played the role of part-time Dom, but he's never found the perfect combination of lover and sub in one man.

Troy Finch lost his lover in a rodeo accident twenty years ago, moved to Boulder, and has worked as a line cook in his friend Carter's diner ever since. He's attended many parties at Carter's home with couples in the BDSM lifestyle and feels comfortable in a submissive role, but without a Dom of his own, Troy hasn't explored what that really means to him. He has needs he doesn't entirely understand and finds his only outlet at the hands of Carter's husband, Geoff, a tattoo artist who has used Troy's skin as a canvas for as long as they've known each other, covering Troy in colorful, intricate triskelia.

Troy doesn't know what he was thinking accepting a dinner invitation from a kid half his age, but everything feels right about their evening together, including Saul's Dominant side. The rules for a twenty-five year old gay cowboy from years ago, though, are totally different than for a twenty-five year old college grad in Boulder now, and despite Saul's confidence, Troy isn't sure whether they can make it work.

Saul and Troy manage to bend a good many rules in the name of caring and compromise, but in the name of love, there are some rules they're just going to have to break.

This is a "true series" and should be read in order.

————

Interested in learning more about Jodi's books? Want free fiction, release news, anecdotes, coffee and drink recipes...?
Join Jodi's newsletter!
What's Up with Jodi?
http://bit.ly/whatsupjodi

Readers of this series may enjoy
Used and Rare, Collected

Used and Rare, Collected
By Chris Owen
https://books2read.com/b/3IrywD

Dave and Archie are happy. They work in construction together, they share a couch, pizzas, beer, and usually a bed. Desmond and Wyatt are happy. They share a home, a love of books, and a lifestyle that's heavy on power exchange. When Archie sends Dave to build book shelves for his old friend Desmond, Dave is happy to oblige and doesn't even mind the initial misunderstanding about his relationship with Archie—he's even amused by it. But when things get twisty between the four of them can Dave keep it from getting kinky and still keep everyone else happy? It's difficult being the only vanilla cookie in the jar.

———

Interested in learning more about Chris's books?
Check out her website:
chrisowen.net

ALSO BY JODI PAYNE

MM and Gay Romance

A Whole Latke Love

Soft Limits: A Deviations Novel

Stable Hill

Creative Process

Linchpin

Whence He Came

With BA Tortuga

Heart of a Redneck

Land of Enchantment

Wrecked

Window Dressing

Flying Blind

Special Delivery, A Wrecked Novel - *Coming November 2020!*

The Cowboy and the Dom Trilogy

First Rodeo, Book One

Razor's Edge, Book Two

No Ghosts, Book Three

The Soldier and the Angel

The Collaborations Series

Refraction

Syncopation

ALSO BY CHRIS OWEN

MM and Gay Romance

An Agreement Among Gentlemen

Bareback

Natural Disaster

Running Away to Home

911

Cheek to Cheek

Turn the Other Cheek

Shady Ridge and the Neon Sky

Pyke's Peak

Carbon and Ash

Converge

Merge

Prove It

Used and Rare, Collected

With Jodi Payne

The Deviations Series

Submission

Domination

Discipline

Bondage

Safe Words: A Deviations Novel

Printed in Great Britain
by Amazon